NO ONE
WILL SEE ME CRY

a novel by

CRISTINA RIVERA-GARZA

translated from the Spanish by

ANDREW HURLEY

CURBSTONE PRESS

Printed in Canada on acid-free paper by Transcontinental /
Best Book
Cover design: Susan Shapiro
Front cover painting: *Mi Mujer* by Manuel Gonzalez Serrano;
courtesy of Christies Images Inc. 1988.

This book was published with the support
of the Lannan Foundation, the National
Endowment for the Arts, and donations from
many individuals. We are very grateful for
this support.

NATIONAL
ENDOWMENT
FOR THE ARTS

Library of Congress Cataloging-in-Publication Data

Rivera Garza, Cristina, 1964-
  [Nadie me vera llorar. English]
  No one will see me cry / by Cristina Rivera-Garza ; translated
from the Spanish by Andrew Hurley.— 1st U.S. ed.
     p. cm.
  ISBN 1-880684-91-8 (pbk. : alk. paper)
  I. Hurley, Andrew. II. Title.
  PQ7298.28.I8982 N3313 2003
  863'.64—dc21

                                    2002152755

published by
CURBSTONE PRESS 321 Jackson St. Willimantic, CT 06226
    phone: 860-423-5110   e-mail: info@curbstone.org
                http://www.curbstone.org

The author wishes to especially thank Rodrigo Navarro for his excellent editorial help.

The translator wishes to express his thanks to Cristina Rivera-Garza for her generous help in answering questions and catching errors and oversights in the translation, and to Jonathan J. Dillow and Matthew Ferrari for their help with silver-mining terminology.

To lrg

*For Hilda Garza Bermea
and Antonio Rivera Peña*

Patient demonstrates good conduct. Likes to work; is dedicated and good-humored. Talks a great deal; that is the symptom of patient's excitation.

"Psychopathological study
of patient Matilda Burgos,
non-violent ward, first section."
Professor Magdalena O. viuda de Alvarez
Department of Serapes and Rebozos
Mixcoac, D.F., General Insane Asylum
June 30, 1935

Beware of those who say we are the beautiful losers.

—*Diane di Prima*, Pieces of a Song

1

_~_

Glints, gleams, gradations of light, images

We see by something that illuminates us,
by something that we do not see.

Antonio Porchia

"How does one come to be a photographer of crazy people?"

Inside Joaquín Buitrago's head there is a buzzing that will not let him sleep or rest in peace. _Matilda._ A word, a fluttering of wings. Wide awake, muscles tense and eyes open, he strikes a match. The orange light reveals his nicotine-stained fingers and the face of a pocket watch whose two gold hands, one atop the other, seem to have stopped forever at exactly twelve o'clock. With the same flame, he lights the oil lamp, the left burner of the stove, and a Monarch cigarette. On his face there is a shadow, almost violet, that threatens to become a smile, although it freezes into a grimace on his lips. Even without seeing it, that expression disturbs him, embarrasses him, but there is nothing he can do to wipe it off. He is happy. But he doesn't know what to do with his happiness.

Shirtless, Joaquín passes his handkerchief from time to time across his forehead, around his neck, to wipe up the sweat. At the same time, he runs water into a blue enamelware pot. He is preparing the infusion of sweet almonds, morphine chlorhydrate, and orange-blossom syrup that no longer relieves his chronic insomnia but whose smell at least makes him dream, even with eyes open and muscles tense. He has tried everything—tincture of calumba, tincture of bitterwood, tincture of gentian, and cinchona bitters, thirty milliliters of each, mixed with ten centigrams of morphine. Three spoonfuls a day. Twenty. Whole glassfuls. He has also tried opium in ricewater; potassium bromide, perfect for those suffering from spiritual cares, depressive afflictions and excessive intellectual effort; sodium bromide, recommended in cases of constant irritation; paraldehyde in infusions of bay-leaf or linden. No remedy has been able to conquer his sleeplessness. Finally, only this almond emulsion is able to relieve it, as he awaits the light of dawn on the horizon. Then, between six and eight in the morning, he falls asleep on his cot, just as everyone else is waking up and the city once again begins to tie itself into its knot of noise and speed.

Light distracts him. He cannot help it. The moment a hint of amber light crosses that shifting boundary between darkness and the absence of darkness, his pupils turn toward the color as though by instinct. He has spent many years now pursuing light the way others stalk an animal. Years of hiding his face and body behind lenses, Gaumont Stereo Spido Metalliques bought in Paris and Eastmans or Graflexes shipped directly from Rochester. Many futile years, unrolled like a canvas of black muslin pierced from time to time, a very few times, by ephemeral, luminous punctures of light. Fireflies like women, and vice versa. Motionless, shackled once more by this phototropic automatism, Joaquín examines the four walls of his room. He takes a drag on the cigarette, hooks strands of greasy hair behind his ears, crosses his arms across his naked chest, and looks. There is nothing else that he does or remembers with more pleasure. Joaquín is a tense man, a man who feels comfortable only on the margins of days, behind mirrors. In the wan light of the oil lamp, the peeling layers of paint create shadowy landscapes on the adobe walls of the room. There is an autumnal woodland spreading without order or direction. In the background, aquamarine mountains and skies mantled with purple. Here and there, dogs' muzzles, open mouths, red with ire and melancholy, and in the background, in what was perhaps the first layer of original paint, curls of white snow, forced to fall by onslaughts of salt air and the humidity of the rainy seasons. Snow. The snow of time—gentle, white, lasting. For a moment, the desire to feel snowflakes is so fierce that Joaquín has to close his eyes. Then, sheltered within the shadows of his head, he remembers how much he dislikes the color white.

"Matilda," he mutters as he shakes his head and pours a little of the emulsion into a small clay cup. The liquid leaves a bitter, burning sensation on the tip of his tongue. Once in his stomach, though, the almonds and orange blossoms create a cool evening on his lips.

"How does one come to be a photographer of crazy people?" she had asked him. Joaquín, unaccustomed to hearing the voices of the subjects he was photographing, thought it was the whispering of his own conscience. There before him, sitting on the bench where the mad men and women were brought for him to photograph, wearing a blue uniform, the woman who was supposed to be sitting motionless, scared, with her eyes blank and a little thread of drool hanging from the corner of her mouth, was actually behaving with the irony and haughtiness of a young woman of the old nobility posing for her first *carte de visite*. He knew; he had done so many of them—hundreds. Before his arrival at the prisons and, after that, madhouses, he had been a professional photographer. A young man in a frock coat and shined shoes, a man to whom the most diverse women opened like doors. All it took was a phrase, a certain suggestive tone of voice, to bring out the most refined coquetry, the frankest female exhibitionism. What he sought was the slight flinch, the moment of bewilderment, the cracking of their modesty, the very marrow at their center. That was before. Nothing like it for years and years. Not until he ran into Matilda again. Instead of cowering back against the wall and staring silently into the void, she had leaned into the camera, arranged her long, mahogany-colored hair with suggestive gestures, and asked the only question that made him think of death. His death.

The photographer could have answered with the words he always spoke to himself: damned morphine. Or those he never spoke to himself but that today, July 26, at 3:30 in the afternoon, came suddenly into his head: Rome, the impossibility of the Roman light. For a few moments, still unable to believe that a madwoman had asked him that question, he was tempted to tell her of the miracle of his three years in Italy. 1897. The all-consuming practice of photography. Rome fixed forever on albumin-coated papers, gelatin-silver plates. Rome, wounding his twenty-six-year-old retinas. Three long Italian summers. A landscape of hills, clouds, rivers. A woman: Alberta. Rome, which had split his life in two: before and after. Before, Alberta; after, morphine.

"What's your name?" The sound of his own voice surprised him.

"Matilda. Matilda Burgos."

He repeated the name a couple of times, trying to focus the woman's attention on the lens. Then, the third time, the fourth, he began to taste it, savor it, chew it, squeeze it. She yielded. Her smile first, and then her eyes. The woman was now posing. At that instant, the July light was transformed and the water of the Tiber was up to her knees. Alberta was shouting his name and waving her hands as though he were on the other bank.

"Here I am," he told her.

"No, you are here," murmured the woman, bringing his hand toward her legs. Joaquín didn't know what to do. She pulled him toward her, mussed his hair, mocked his clumsiness.

"So, how does one come to be a photographer of crazy people?" Matilda's question jerked him rudely out of the waters of the Tiber and brought him back to Mixcoac.

In a very soft voice, almost inaudible, Joaquín said to himself, "Every failure begins with light, with the desire to capture light forever." Then upset, reacting with his customary hostility, he said something aloud:

"Why don't you tell me how a woman goes crazy?" And Matilda's only answer was a shrug of her shoulders and a wink of her left eye.

"You really want me to tell you?"

Joaquín Buitrago, who had forgotten how to laugh, was amazed to feel on his lips the loud burst of a guffaw. The sound echoed through the asylum, and since it had nowhere else to go, it entered him through his ears. The sound continued to echo in his head all day and all night. It was not the monotonous buzzing of a bee, but rather the quick, sharp crack of a glass shattering in his blood. Like always at six o'clock in the morning, he collapsed—exhausted, woebegone, and still tense—onto his rickety cot.

At eight o'clock on the morning of July 27, 1920, Joaquín recalled with absolute certainty where he had seen Matilda Burgos before. He instantly got up and went over to the brass trunk, which with the cot, the chair, and wooden table, made up the room's only furnishings, and his entire belongings. He anxiously opened it. Then, with extreme care, he removed his most treasured possession: the collection of stereoscopic photographs, mounted on pasteboard, that he had taken just after his return from Italy. Each card held the image of a naked woman, a woman exposed yet covered with desire. Looking through the viewer's two eyepieces, he viewed the photographs, one by one. An expression of satisfaction came across his face. As he shuffled through the cards, his unsociable, skeptical demeanor changed, and he seemed possessed by vertigo. He remembered himself at twenty-eight. His thick, still black eyebrows shadowed his sunken eyes with the playfulness of youth, and his aquiline nose regained the angle of his determined will. He once again believed in the possibility of fixing the uniqueness of a body, a gesture. The possibility of stopping time. There they were once again, imperishable, the unmistakable poses of the women of the bordellos. *My women.* In rooms filled with bric-a-brac, surrounded by figurines and mirrors, wearing transparent robes from the distant Orient or sometimes totally nude, the women were posing as though entering a pact. He remembered neither their names nor the names of the places. He hardly noticed the dates. He rarely took notes. The only thing that Joaquín was able to remember was stored in glints, gleams, gradations of light, images. Under this spell, everything was real and everything was possible. Outside it, all that existed was whiteness, the saturation of color that he associated with death and the beyond. What color might limbo be?

Card number seventeen was of Matilda Burgos, and Joaquín, without taking his eyes off the eyepieces, smiled. He didn't even realize he was doing it. Matilda had chosen the marble table and the fake bearskin; she reclined on them. Then, naked, she had leaned back on her right arm and without another word or gesture ordered him to begin the session.

"After all, you're the one who wants the photographs, not me."

Joaquín, amused, instantly obeyed.

Like all the other women whose portraits he had made in that particular bordello, Matilda chose the scene and the poses. Some of the women preferred to remain in their own rooms, lying on the same mattresses they worked on. Others, though, suggested a visit to a nearby brook. Some removed their clothes without the slightest hesitation, while others chose exotic Chinese regalia, and a few decided to face the camera in their customary dishabille. They had all no doubt seen the erotic postcards then in vogue on the market, and although Joaquín explained that their photographs had no commercial value whatsoever, most of them went through efforts partly ludicrous, partly sincere to imitate the languid or provocative poses of divas such as Adela Eisenhower or Eduwiges Chateau. Then, as the session went on and

Joaquín's unthreatening attitude managed to create a tenuous confidence, some of the models, never many, would begin to "flow," as he called it. When that happened, it would be slow, almost subterranean, and might even pass unnoticed. At those times, Joaquín always thought about the movements of a sunflower. Sometimes it was just a gesture of amazement, a flicker of shyness or disgust and tiredness, the interrogation barely visible on the face: "What the hell am I doing here?" And then the women would turn inward once more, to the place where they saw themselves as they wished to see themselves. And that was the exact place that the photographer yearned to know, yearned to halt forever. The place where a woman accepted herself. There, seductiveness did not turn outward, nor was it one-way; there, in a gesture indivisible and unique, seductiveness was not a hook but a map. Joaquín was convinced that it was possible to reach that place. Joaquín Buitrago had still believed in the impossible that day when Matilda removed her clothes with no embarrassment whatever and, reclining on the marble table as she sought his eyes behind the lens, she asked him:

"How does one come to be a photographer of whores?"

He thought about Alberta; there was no help for it, although he preserved his calm. The only sign that he had been disconcerted was the slight tremor of his fingers as they adjusted the Gaumont. *Will you dare answer this time, Joaquín?* It was the question he had always refused to answer, no matter who asked it—much less if he asked it himself. Sometimes, on those rare occasions when he was sitting in a bar with acquaintances from San Carlos Academy, he would try cynicism. "We're all men, no? Do I really have to explain it?" And yet to find precisely the right tone of irony, he had to be drunk or distracted, his mind on something else. Had to be not himself. On other days, days sober and tense, the adrenaline would steer him directly toward vagueness. Rather than answering with complete sentences, he would utter words like *beauty, spirit, eternity*—which he would pronounce with the feigned lightness of a scholar. In time, as he attempted to ward off the curiosity of his acquaintances at all costs, Joaquín became expert at fabricating evasions, and eventually, tired of word games, he came even to avoid the acquaintances themselves. A man can seldom admit that he takes photographs of women in order to return to the place of a single woman. Alberta. In those cases, he preferred solitude. Preferred to retain the memory of Alberta whirling around, telling him, "All things are possible, Joaquín, except peace. Had you not noticed that?"

Joaquín finished the session with Matilda in the most absolute silence. The image of Alberta, leaving him, beaching him forever on the bank of a river, dogged his steps all the way back home. The blue dog of memory nipping constantly at his heels.

To develop the plates he used silver bromide; taking great care in the developing, he was able to achieve clear bright tones. Afterward, covered with sweat, the exhaustion of several days without sleep, and the shock produced in him by the images, he looked at them again before putting them away once more in his brass trunk. He sat on it. Suddenly, the fragility of the stereoscopic photographs brought on an attack of anxiety. Would eternity, too, wind up shattering? Was there nothing inside him that could be kept safe, unharmed by Alberta's distance? Unable to answer, always unable to answer, Joaquín lit another Monarch and, flicking the ashes on the wood floor of his family home, patiently awaited the light of dawn so that he might rest. Without peace.

He dreamed of Alberta. Of the miraculous opening that had been Alberta. Within her sex, there had been light; within her mouth the light had been born; within her eyes, the light had died. As sometimes happened in Rome, in the dream Alberta set her own luminosity upon Joaquín's hands.

"Do whatever you want," she told him. The smile on her

face was horrendous. It utterly shook him. He accepted her gift without hesitation, without gauging the consequences.

"What if I want to die?" he asked naively.

"You can do that, too."

A certainty like a shooting pain woke him. It was eight o'clock in the morning and the May sun was already breaking through the curtains. The pain prevented him from breathing. The pain pierced him, like a rusty pin under his fingernails. The pain would not allow him to see anything else. He could not move. *How does one come to be a photographer of whores?* Because of this, this thing that cannot be expressed. This thing that is pronounced Alberta and means impossibility.

A little after noon, a messenger knocked at the door. A dark-skinned, ragged child asked for don Joaquín Buitrago and then handed him a lavender-colored envelope. Inside, on a card of the same color, he found the following sentence: *All those with sick minds, no taste, and a complete lack of understanding of art consider nudes to be immoral.* It was signed "Matilda Burgos." Joaquín threw out the envelope but he kept the card inside his right vest pocket for several days. Weeks later, when he decided to pay another visit to the bordello, up in Salto del Agua, where Matilda worked, a madam with masculine hands, her nakedness barely covered by a Chinese-inspired red silk robe, informed him that her boarder had disappeared with a man purporting to be an engineer from the United States.

"I don't know what these Indian girls have got that makes the gringos go crazy for 'em," she exclaimed in sincere bewilderment. "You want another one of the girls?"

Joaquín declined, saying no more. The news was not particularly surprising, he thought. And anyway, he wasn't entirely certain that he really wanted to see Matilda again. The piano music and noise of the place befuddled him. He wanted to strip off his shirt and run half-naked down the halls of the house; he wanted to slap the fat cheeks of the bureaucrats, soldiers, and clerks that swarmed through the place with their "sick minds, no taste, and complete lack of understanding of art"; he wanted to kneel before the women's laps, which perhaps contained all the light in the world. Instead, Joaquín looked at his pocket watch, turned, and walked in the direction of the nearest cantina. It was not yet eleven p.m.

In the Temple of Love, at one of the back tables, some members of the photographers' guild were already half drunk. They were deep in a discussion of something or other as they downed their snifters of brandy or their Moctezuma beers and took long drags on pipes and cigarettes. When Joaquín walked through the door, one of them, Abraham Lupercio, stepped away from the argument and shouted to him.

"What do you say, my lean and hungry Buitrago? Are we photographers or graphic journalists?" When he heard the second term, Joaquín could not conceal his distaste. Nor could he free himself from Lupercio, who had his arm around Joaquín's neck. All he could do was feel the humiliation of the moment.

"Behold. Another pure man has entered," Lupercio announced to the congregation. Agustín Casasola, Jerónimo Hernández, and even Luis Santamarina turned to greet him. Of them all, only Jerónimo knew what Joaquín's work was like. It was after a drunken binge. Jerónimo had declared that women no longer had any mystery, that they had to be invented anew. Joaquín tried to argue the contrary but, lacking words and arguments, he opted to take out the stereopticon and show Jerónimo his cards.

"You see? You see what I mean?" he asked him several times, anxiously awaiting the reply. For Joaquín, the miracle of the women on the other side of the lens was not just obvious but also irreversible. One needed to change nothing; all one needed to do was learn to see. They were all there, the women, suspended within themselves, so contained that their power threatened to destroy the eye that spied upon them.

"You see?" he asked again. But Jerónimo's only reply was silence; he did not take his eyes from the eyepieces, from the images. Then, turning to look straight at Joaquín, he muttered:

"This is what you went all the way to Rome to learn, *flaco*? This is very minor work." Joaquín's discouragement came not so much from the criticism of his work as from the impossibility of communicating his vision. Would no one ever see?

"Well, although I continue to maintain that the pure are destined for failure," Víctor León raised his beer bottle in the Temple of Love, "I drink to them."

Uncomfortable, with a glass of whiskey in his hand, Joaquín took enormous delight in the idea of failure: it was lavender-colored and smelled of silence. While the others self-confidently ticked off the names of their best equipment—Graflex, Eastman, Dehel, Proritor II—Joaquín greeted failure and motioned it to take a seat beside him. Against all expectations, he felt, relaxed, at peace, sitting beside it. For the first time, Joaquín believed that he might be able to rest, believed that in failure he might finally, perhaps, be able to find peace, silence, be able to go against the current of progress, of time itself, and believed that he, like the whole country, needed nothing more. When Joaquín left the Temple of Love, he did so to take his leave, once and for all, of history. Outside, the first light of day was striking the city, beating it, bludgeoning it to death. Few people remembered his name. In time, when someone would ask about him, they would ask about the "fellow who did the photographs of whores." The answers varied down through the years. For a while, and intermittently, he had a position taking photographs of prisoners in the Belén prison, and then, when no one was interested in them, he agreed to do portraits of the mad men and women for the files of La Castañeda

Insane Asylum. The madhouse. After that, no one asked about him anymore.

"How does one come to be a photographer of crazy people? All it takes is knowing how to use a camera and living in this country after having seen Alberta's light. That's all it takes, Matilda."

The following days are filled with rain.

As he walks through the downtown streets, Joaquín observes the light of his own figure in the shop windows. He does this hesitantly, turning his head to the right slightly and then back to the left, as though he were afraid that some passerby might make fun of him. But he is curious. His hair is too long for the time; the wide lapels of his jacket are out of fashion now and his gaunt face makes one think of sleeplessness, illness. If it were not for the whiteness of his skin and a certain fineness of his features, people would surely give him wide berth on the sidewalks. But despite all, (even if he wanted to) Joaquín could never hide his aristocratic bearing and the appearance of owning property, possessing wealth. That appearance and a contemptuous hostility were what finally protected him from unwanted harassment by the police or doctors. The trained eye of the police officer was unable to associate his appearance with that of the vice-ridden or the homicidal, despite the similarities; they always arrived at the conclusion that Joaquín was another of those nostalgic Porfiristas gone to seed. His manners are so delicate they are almost absurd. No one in the city walks in the drizzle without an umbrella anymore, or without apparent destination, the way Joaquín does. The slowness of his movements has very little to do with the speed and urgency of 1920.

"Sr. Canalejas is expecting me." The measured, quiet tone of his voice commands not respect but confusion. When she hears it, the maid who has opened the door hesitates between inviting him in and leaving him waiting outside, but when she realizes that the rain is now coming down in sheets, she leads him, still hesitantly, into the library. While Joaquín waits in the leather armchair, he rests his hands on the wooden box lying in his lap, the box containing half of the series of nudes. Joaquín breathes with relief when he observes the small pre-Hispanic clay figures the collector exhibits and jealously protects behind glass doors. He harbors the hope that in years to come, when everything has passed, his photographs will occupy a similar place. Perhaps someone will see them after all. Perhaps someone will look at the women's bodies and, taken somewhat aback, smile uncertainly. Perhaps someone will learn to see. He is saying goodbye to all of them. He is telling them goodbye even as he observes their motionless, tense hands. The absence of calluses or scars, or of dirt under their fingernails, suddenly stuns him.

"So you finally decided to sell me your photographs, Buitrago?"

Joaquín nods, and in the same movement places the box on the desk.

"They are all yours."

"And may I ask what I have to thank for this change of heart?"

"No, Sr. Canalejas, you may not."

Matilda Burgos. The name descends to the tip of his tongue. It is salty. With the money in his pocket, Joaquín walks to Sebastián Blanco's jewelry store and, without giving it much thought, buys a silver identity bracelet and has her name engraved on it. *Matilda Burgos.* Then he goes to a stationery shop and purchases a pencil and a notebook with a dark, heavy pasteboard cover.

"You promised to tell me how a woman goes crazy, remember?"

"It's a long story," the woman replies as she clasps the bracelet on her left wrist without the courtesy of a thank you, or even so much as a glance at Joaquín.

"Don't worry, we have all the time in the world."

They are in a room in the asylum, beside a window, shielded from the sunlight by the branches of flowering chestnut trees. Neither of them notices that it is raining. July rain.

The first thing that Joaquín notices is that Matilda has the habit of cracking her knuckles. She does it without even realizing. Matilda is distracted. Her mind seems to be somewhere else. Later, as he begins to observe her more closely, he sees the little scars on her knees, hands, forearms. Matilda also tends to bump into windows, chairs, and other furniture. She seems to have difficulty fixing her attention on the objects of the world, but wherever she goes, she carries all the light of the asylum. A crown. It is on that that Joaquín Buitrago fixes his gaze.

August passes in silence. Matilda speaks to the doctors and nurses, but rarely to him. She complains about the quality of the food, the dirtiness of the wards, the lack of privacy. She complains about the country. She is in the habit of using the word *shit*. "Shit nuthouse." "Shit world." "This is all just shit." Most of the time, however, all she asks is to be left in peace. As she makes her way to the sewing workshop, where she spends most of the day making serapes, Matilda sometimes notices Joaquín's lank figure, spying on her from a distance. Sometimes he sits at the entrance to the dining room, pretending to read a book. Other times, he hides behind the rough trunks of the trees. She can't imagine what the photographer might be looking for, but she knows that whatever it is, she has it. She likes to think that—think that she, now possessing nothing, still has, down inside, somewhere within her, the magnet that always winds up attracting the iron.

"Have you ever seen men fly like birds, Joaquín?" she asks him one day. The photographer imagines for a second that Matilda is referring to his well-known addiction to morphine. He fears that she, the madwoman, is mocking him to his face, as so many others have done. He is about to react with rage, defensively, but then he hears the echo of his name. Matilda has used his Christian name. That's enough for today. Joaquín.

Their few conversations make no sense. Matilda runs off halfway through the conversation and then mingles, irretrievable, among the other inmates. Sometimes she smiles at him from a distance, holds up a hand and waves at him as though she were running into him at the entrance of a motion picture theater. She gives the impression of not knowing where she is. Matilda may really be off somewhere else. Where? The doctors talk about her, and when they do they invariably wind up smiling, sometimes sarcastically, sometimes in irritation. That Matilda, beyond help. She talks too much. Tells outlandish stories. Writes letters. Diplomatic dispatches. "Shit world." She is keeping a diary. All her papers go into file number 6353, and there they remain, at the margins of days and language, like Joaquín, like the madhouse itself.

Another day in August, Joaquín sees Matilda out on the lawn, near the fence, and he approaches her. She shouldn't be there; neither of them should be. The inmates need special permission to walk through the hospital grounds, and photographers have no excuse whatsoever for approaching them. Yet it happens: the encounter. He has never seen a woman so alone, so hermetic, so separate. Her eyes give no sign at all of homesickness or of a desire to escape when they look out toward the avenue. It would be easy to do if she wanted to. Matilda, despite the complaints and the screaming, has made no effort to run away. She is there. When he comes up to her, the asylum's incessant screaming and shouting grow as distant as a murmur and then, when Matilda turns her face to him and greets him with a broad smile, the sounds disappear completely. Silence. Matilda will always create silence around her.

"Poor Guadalupe," she says. "She thinks praying the Magnificat will scare the devil out of her cell."

"And it won't, eh?"

"No. Praying doesn't work for anything, Joaquín. You know that yourself."

The photographer does not know what he is seeking in Matilda Burgos' head crowned with light. There must be something more in the silence of his life. It is coming closer and closer. He is convinced. He can feel it in the air and in the sweet voices of the morphine. This time he is not afraid of dying. It doesn't matter. This time he will not let her go. His objective is getting to the files and rummaging through the information on Matilda. Joaquín has to know about her life. There are at least two ways of doing that. The first is going directly to the records office and simply asking the shift clerk for the file. Although simple and possible, this path has one insurmountable problem: gossip, people talking. After thinking it over, Joaquín opts for a route that is longer but more discreet, more in keeping with his temperament and his routines. He has to stop his infantile spying and focus all his attention on the doctors. One especially, Dr. Oligochea. Eduardo Oligochea, the medical resident who admitted Matilda to La Castañeda one July 26th. The process is slow, and if one is not paying attention it can go as unnoticed as the movement of a sunflower. Joaquín begins by saying hello to the doctor very respectfully that morning. Good morning, doctor. And he then continues with a few comments on a subject hit upon on the spur of the moment: the Lumière brothers.

"I didn't know you were interested in moving pictures, Buitrago."

"Very little, really, doctor. My real passion is photography." Joaquín can hardly conceal the embarrassment, the shame of uttering the phrase "my real passion is photography" as though taking photographs of madmen in a room forgotten by the world were really devoting oneself to *photography*. As though he were not actually the only photographer of his generation who had not taken photographs of generals, revolutionaries and their camp followers, presidents, and massacres. As though that night in 1908 when he walked out of the Temple of Love he had not stepped forever off the stage of history.

"But you know how it is," he adds, "one has to make a living."

The doctor smiles patronizingly, but then, in an instant of true compassion, he allows his eyes the gleam of incipient complicity. What else might Joaquín have appealed to but their shared situation as professionals come down in the world? Despite all the pomp and circumstance with which don Porfirio Díaz had inaugurated the institution, everyone knew that ten years of neglect and the passage of a revolution had transformed La Castañeda into the waste can of the modern age and all the ages to come. This was the place where the future ended; both men were conscious of that fact.

"You're right, Buitrago, one has to make a living."

At first they spoke little, and hesitantly, in their rare conversations. Although they began to play chess from time to time and have coffee together in the afternoons, Dr. Oligochea lost no opportunity to show Joaquín the mistrust and measured rejection of a man who had no desire to befriend a loser. Like the entire country, he foresaw a brilliant future for himself. La Castañeda was simply a hurdle he had to clear in order to reach better hospitals, the experience he needed in order to have a chance outside, in the United States or another Latin American country, to become a real psychiatrist, a professional of true prestige. He did not want to be Joaquín's friend; he did not want to put down roots inside the walls of the madhouse that he walked through and cursed every morning. But the photographer was unyielding. He persevered. Matilda's file, tucked away in one of the filing cabinets in the records office, awaited him. To overcome Eduardo Oligochea's reticence, Joaquín would have to transform his own failure into something else. A seduction, perhaps, a stubborn fascination.

In his insomnia, the ceiling of Joaquín's room became his private atlas of the world. The white of the empire gave way, little by little, to the sinuous courses of rivers, the shadow of leafy trees, some mountains, and here and there a building. Later, much later, the faces appeared. Even more than the days, Joaquín anxiously awaited the nights of summer. When his mother ordered the lights off and the servants retired to their rooms off the rear patio, all he had to do was wait for his father to finish reading his books or reviewing prescriptions in the library and the house would become an unexplored universe. Barefoot, Joaquín would roam the hallways of the upper floor and then, carefully, trying not to make a sound, descend the wooden stairway. On nights when the moon was full, objects in the kitchen would sparkle and gleam with glints of moonlight. The glow of the pewter, aluminum, and blue-glazed tiles would color the white walls and tile floors with hues of silver and mercury. Joaquín could stare at those lights for hours, never feeling the slightest weariness, never thinking a thought. Later, empty, he would return to his room to watch the rain. The living room, dining room, and library with their Persian rugs and cut-crystal chandeliers never interested him. Nor did he pay the slightest attention to the facade that gave the house the look of a Swiss chalet.

Summer rain. Through the window he would watch it fall, sometimes gently, sometimes with the violence of storms. Before the rain began, when thunder and lightning would split the sky in the distance, Joaquín would strip completely naked and sit on the wood floor with his legs crossed, awaiting the blessing of the rain. The pleasure of the world made wet, illuminated only by flashes and gleams of lightning, would keep him awake. He would not think of anything, really; he would wish for nothing, want nothing. Those summer nights were the culmination of some long-awaited thing that germinated in his mind. The images of those nights would seldom emerge during the day. In the light of the sun, any eye at all might draw out the secret logic of things and their shadows. At night, though, everything changed. The other eyes would close and his, ready to discover something beyond, would open.

The cracks in the ceiling would come to have names, exotic sounds that Joaquín would savor like candy. He would pronounce them softly, under his breath almost, until they no longer had any meaning. Just above his pillow was the River of Passion, bordered by almond-covered corozo palms, acacias with tiny leaves, and campeche trees with trunks as black as mourning. Beside it, a starving flock of seagulls flew above the dark waters of the Tagus, which generously nourished the roots of a grove of olive trees. In the right corner, cobwebs outlined the mazy windings of the Amazon.

In the streets of Santa María la Ribera he would find rats, opossums, crippled dogs, leery cats that allowed no one to approach them, and lethargic, sleepy pigeons. All of them scurried away in fear when they heard his footsteps on the sidewalk. The moths, on the other hand, stood guard around the turpentine lamps. The watchmen at first suspected he was a murderer or some common thief, but after taking note of his measured, metronomic rounds, they reached the conclusion that he was not dangerous. Alone, greeting them with a Good evening and a polite nod and turning his eyes toward the darkness as though it were a woman, Joaquín appeared to be a young man with no concrete objective.

In the darkness, Joaquín discovered pain. It was not a

word, not even a sensation; it was an image: the face of a woman in rigor mortis. He came upon her lying in the street just moments before the police arrived with their lanterns and their loud voices. He knelt beside her and, without thinking, passed his hands over her hair wet with rain and blood. Then he sat down beside her, on the asphalt. He stared at her. Her lips were bruised and bloody from a beating and her arms and legs were bent at tortured angles. He tried to pray but no prayer came to his mind. The world was, as he had imagined, a merciless place, without reprieve. The woman's face imprinted itself on his memory. This was his first photograph.

Pain obsessed him. Camera in hand now, Joaquín frequented the morgue. It was not something that everyone did, but it was not unheard-of, either. Both medical students and the simply curious, these latter often also *poètes manqués,* had found a way to sate their morbid curiosity, their fear of death or life, in the abandoned bodies of men and women. In the common grave, no one had a name, an age, or a history, and all lay there lifeless, inert, and open, freed perhaps, relaxed before the eyes of the living. With its brightly-varnished box and metal tripod, Joaquín's camera focused on the details. He never took photographs of entire bodies, or panoramas of the complete scene. Instead, his attention would focus on the blue fingernails of the man who had ended his life with cyanide, on the scar on a woman's right inner thigh, on the reddish marks left by the rope around the neck of a young woman who had been strangled, on the hair still clutched by the fingers of a woman who had resisted her killer. Taken at close range and from unusual angles, the photographs did not so much reveal as conceal the images of death, protect them. The observer had to pause at every picture, look at it with great attention so that suddenly, without warning, death would emerge whole, as sharp and piercing as a needle. The astonishment of the sight would then inevitably be accompanied by the nausea brought about by pain. So that's how we all were? So this is how it all ends? Yes. *Here you are, then...after the pitiless struggle in which you broke, at last, out of the prison to which pain had sentenced you.* That was all, perhaps. Joaquín sought to capture the pain at the instant it turned into its own absence, turned into nothing, nothingness. That was the only possibility he envisioned: everything was pain, and the rest was the brutal rest, the brutal peace of death. Photography was a way, his way, of stopping the wheel of the world's pain, spinning ever faster under the lights, on narrow metal tracks. It was the year 1900 in Mexico City, and for Joaquín the new century, far from causing him curiosity, brought him only the bleak smile of the condemned man. Meanwhile, his collection of photographs, like his summer nights, continued to be private.

"What about you, doctor? What do you think of pain?"

The thin figure of Joaquín Buitrago is becoming less disagreeable. As he talks, as he reveals himself to Eduardo Oligochea, many of his gestures take on meaning, significance, *raison d'etre.* His slowness, for example. The way he leans over things. The gravity of his voice. The photographer is no longer a simple mortal of his times, he has become a morphine addict. Joaquín has managed to arouse not only the doctor's curiosity but his scientific interest as well. A neurotic? A case of incurable melancholy? A manifestation of schizophrenia? The doctor wants to know more, one can see it in his eyes, in the way he draws out their afternoon meeting for coffee with complex questions— questions for which Joaquín rarely has immediate or linear answers. Talking, for Joaquín, is digressing. He confuses verb tenses and pronouns. He omits dates. "He," he says, referring to himself, as though describing another man. He refers to the past in the third person also. Eduardo Oligochea listens in silence, trying to organize the morass of his words, tie together the loose ends of his stories. He takes notes. There has to be a beginning, a conflict, and, at last, a solution, or at least a moral. Soon, however, he realizes that it is futile; Joaquín might as well be speaking to the air.

The medical resident does not interrupt him. "I'm all ears." Inside, lined up in rigorous order, his own emotions are safe and sound. Mute. He doesn't want to wake them. He is not interested in sharing them. If there is one thing he has learned from the manuals of anatomy, beside the filthy beds of hospitals, seeing the pus and poison of death, it is to keep well hidden, under one's skin, the pronoun *I*. His meetings with Joaquín are pleasant because they take place in the third person.

Him.

While general opinion applauded the speed of trams, the grace of bicycles, and the benefits of public lighting, Joaquín devoted himself to criticizing urban policies, which he invariably called futile. In an effort to demonstrate how mistaken this line of thought was, his classmates at the San Carlos Academy would take him for walks under the ash trees on the Paseo de las Cadenas and in the Plaza Mayor. Under the blue afternoon sky, they would point out to him the proportion in the design of fountains and gardens, their harmony with the metal kiosk where tram tickets were sold, the contrast with the populous marketplaces to the south and west where one could find every sort of merchandise one could desire. Then, walking quickly, they would pass along in front of such new iron-and-cement buildings as the Centro Mercantil and the Palacio de Hierro, and at the Boker house they would entertain themselves by riding the new elevators. On the Alameda Central they would pause to admire the Moorish Pavilion, standing just across the way from the

Iglesia de Corpus Christi. Piled together into a carriage, they would ride past the Reform Club, which was the Englishmen's country club. And as though all that were not enough, when the sun began to set and dusk to fall, and weariness needed a bit of alcohol, they would make stops in the bars that encircled the center of the city, especially the San Cosme, where, amidst beer and cigarettes, they would continue an argument that Joaquín always lost.

"This city is fated never to perish, *flaco,* and you may as well resign yourself to that," they would say. Joaquín was famed for being not just stubborn but embittered.

On the few occasions when Joaquín tried to justify his ideas with counter-arguing tours of the city, he showed his friends his own geography. He would take them to the Morelos Hospital, where the prostitutes who spent their nights in the brothels and whorehouses cluttered with chinoiserie bric-a-brac and monumental mirrors brooded alone, on beds without sheets and in rooms filled with moans and vomit, upon the effect of syphilis and gonorrhea. There, the men's noses would be assailed with the smell of the slow decomposition of bodies. They would then walk past the public flophouses where for three or four cents, Indians and the unemployed might unroll a straw mat on the floor. Sometimes, if his companions dared, they would approach the borders of a slum known as La Bolsa, in whose narrow streets, dusty in the dry season and muddy throughout the rainy months, thugs and bandidos would sneer at them contemptuously. "What're you afraid of, you little dandies?" In the Plaza de las Vizcaínas, he would point out to them the filthy little "cup and saucer" houses made of two pieces, one laid atop the other, connected inside by a wooden stairway. Everything was gray. The air was pestilent. When they had the opportunity, they would go to San Lázaro to see the drainage project, which consisted of a canal, a tunnel, and a discharge hole. With amazement they would observe the shafts sunk from the natural surface of the ground to the level of the work below, sometimes as many as three hundred feet down, through which the material excavated would be brought up and the little air that kept the hundreds of workers alive would go down. Moving like ants in the darkness, wet with sweat and urine, those faceless men dug the trench through which the city expelled its excrement, first through the Tequixquiac cut and then through the Tula River to come at last, black and stinking, to the Gulf of Mexico. Toward the end of the evening, when the night weighed heavy on them all, Joaquín would take them to the neighborhood pulquerías or the La Joya Café in Peralvillo so they could rub elbows with the thugs and lowlifes and easy women of the "people."

"I think you're turning into an anarchist, *flaco*," they would say, and Joaquín would reply that he did have contempt for politics. Then, looking at them with the same amazement with which they had gazed upon the poor city in ruins, he would say that the only thing he truly desired was to understand other people's conversation. Their lapidary phrases. "This city is fated not to perish." "Woman must be reinvented." "The future is an infinite staircase."

"And you, doctor—what do you think of the future?"

When Eduardo Oligochea's interest is piqued by something, two vertical creases appear between his eyebrows, the index finger of his right hand pushes his spectacles higher on the bridge of his nose, and, without his noticing, his fingers toy with a pencil. The hours he spends sitting before the photographer leave a bittersweet taste in his mouth. Sometimes, smoking cigarettes in Joaquín's company, he wonders about the taste of morphine. Sometimes, while he attentively listens to Joaquín's involved way of linking phrases and picking apart words, the doctor even comes to question his own mistrust of the medical uses of hypnosis and free association. Sometimes, sitting with Joaquín, he

24

feels almost comfortable in the bare room he self-importantly calls his office in La Castañeda. The photographer's presence forces him to pay attention to the six-o'clock light on the white walls. The August rain. Sometimes, hearing the stories of Joaquín's ramblings through the entrails of night in the city, he cannot help thinking about José Asunción Silva: *And my shadow by the moonlight thrown walked alone walked alone walked alone across the solitary steppes.* Then he laughs. And then he pulls up short, his mouth agape. Joaquín's coherence surprises him. It reminds him of someone else. The person's name is on the tip of his tongue. A woman... He controls himself. No matter. For one instant, Eduardo Oligochea feels as relaxed as a man who has no need to prosper. Within that lightness, without a second thought, he invites Joaquín to step outdoors for a stroll, invites him to leave the office with him. He wants to walk. The clock on the Central facade of the institution's main building indicates that it is six-thirty in the evening.

The Insane Asylum has twenty-five buildings scattered across thirty-five acres. Inside the grounds, protected by high walls and iron bars, the mad men and women and the chestnut trees throw their shadows across a space cut off from time. The asylum is a city in miniature. It has watchtowers, streets, infirmaries, jails, housing. There is bustle, there are arguments and rows and sometimes even brawls, there is traffic in cigarettes and narcotic substances, there are suicide attempts. There are workshops in which the men manufacture caskets without hammering nails through their hands and rugs without slashing their wrists. They receive no wages. The women wash the blue uniforms until the clothing is faded almost white and, in the sewing shops, make rebozos and serapes, mend shirts, stitch up ripped sheets. There are poets writing letters to God; there are mechanics, pharmacists, police officers, thieves, anarchists who have renounced violence. Love stories take place. Muted melancholy. Social classes. Desperation expressed in wails and screams. There is no end to pain.

"It cost almost two million pesos, did you know that, Buitrago?"

They have stopped in front of the general services wing, directly at the foot of the steps, looking up at the six equidistant second-floor windows as though they were expecting suddenly to see the profile of salvation peeking out from behind the curtains. The monumentality of the building makes them feel small, mortal.

"Did you know that the Zapatistas took the hospital five years ago?" The doctor has a new smile. "One would think they hadn't left yet, no? Imagine, this place so remote from history yet so filled with it."

Without looking at him, Joaquín thinks for the first time about his history—the doctor's. He knows nothing about it. He knows nothing about what is inside the man, the years of study in medical school, the growing fascination with the body's imperfections and, later, the mind's. And he cannot comprehend him. The destiny that the doctor dreams for himself, the destiny he invents with every morning curse, stops at the entrance to these buildings. Eduardo Oligochea has hardly told him anything about his past or his future. Silence, however, does not disturb Joaquín. The only thing he can think about when he is with Eduardo, one afternoon after another, one confession after another, is Case 6353 and the path that must be followed in order to arrive at the history of Matilda.

As they return to the infirmary they pass by the buildings for men and women, their sections divided into wards for paying and charity cases, non-violent cases and dangerous cases, epileptic cases and contagious cases. There are inmates whose condition is indescribable. Some bodies move nervously, bumping into walls; others sit motionless on wooden benches, gazing inward on the purple plains of melancholy. Their eyes speak with ghosts buried in the walls, with the diaphanous voices of the air. Psychiatrists are still poets, men in thrall to the unknown profundities of the soul, men who, in their free time, write plays and metaphysical disquisitions. In their diagnoses, the adjectives are as important as the scientific terms. *Intense* logorrhea. *Strange* prolonged attitudes. *Frightful* hallucinations. *Countless* bouts of delirium. Eduardo Oligochea is different. Amidst the words and the pain, he seeks uniformity, exactitude. A scientific method. A way of explaining the life of the mind, the behavior of men and women which is based on experiments carried out with devices in good working order. If he were to choose between the somatic and systematizing approaches of the German specialist Emil Kraepelin and the psychological treatments derived from advances in neurology and incipient psychoanalysis, Eduardo Oligochea would incline toward the former. There is something in the abysses of language discovered by Freud that both seduces and infuriates him. He is still not exactly certain why, but isolated, random, disconnected words have always given him a kind of vertigo, never confidence or trust. What he wants is to compile painstaking clinical observations and, at the same time, analyze parts of the brain and nerve cells under a microscope, in order to reach new, unexpected, and innovative conclusions. What he desires above all else is to have a laboratory for psychological experimentation equipped with chemographs, ergographs, and Hipp chronographs that measure the tiniest fractions of time. Nothing like that exists in his "office" in La Castañeda. Here, within the four bare walls where he spends several hours each afternoon chatting with Joaquín, there is only cold, the distant echo of screams and shouts, and the files piled in a disorderly stack on his desk. Nothing more. At twenty-four years of age, Eduardo Oligochea is what he wants to be: a professional without poetry. But he betrays himself. He cannot help it. The slovenly figure of Matilda is approaching from the vegetable gardens. She is smiling as she walks toward him, stretching her left arm toward him as though they were in a wedding in the country, a family outing.

"Have you seen her before, Buitrago?"

"Who?"

"Her. Matilda Burgos."

"Yes," Joaquín says, he has.

Him.

His first woman. Her name was Diamantina. Diamantina Vicario. Her figure was diamantine as well. Even without being able to see her legs beneath the dark merino wool skirt, her arms beneath the long sleeves of her silk blouse, Joaquín imagined that her skin had the heat and glow of the sun. When she played zarzuelas or Chopin on the piano, the contact between her fingertips and the ivory of the keys made crackles of electricity in the air. A bit "modern." Her presence stirred him, moved him. The lightness of her perfect manners. Her pince-nez, and behind them alert coffee-colored eyes. The way she arched her eyebrows at an especially difficult passage. Her concentration. Her conviction. Joaquín was not expecting her. She appeared without warning and without warning disappeared. The nights of summer and then of winter were filled with her absence. Inside him, in a jungle theretofore unknown and unexplored, nostalgia burgeoned.

Before he saw her, Joaquín had only a vague idea of what a woman was. The only ones he had been close to were his mother, the maid with the long braids, and one or another chubby, ugly cousin. But these were not so much women as family members: asexual beings to whom he was linked by coincidence or fate.

He met her at one of the few family gatherings he grudgingly attended. The same people as always. Some of his aunts and uncles, asking him what he planned to do now that he had finished his studies at the preparatory school.

Some doctor friends of his father with their wives and children. Some attorneys describing their wagers at the Jockey Club while planning, at the same time, the future of the country. Several investors drinking lemonade. In the midst of all these people, with her back to them, Diamantina was playing the piano as though she were alone. She was not quite a guest. Joaquín's mother, following the advice of a close friend whose daughter took private piano lessons from her, had hired her to liven up the gathering and, while she was about it, salve her conscience with a good deed. The chords of the last piece had barely faded when Joaquín approached her, but realizing at the last moment that he had nothing to say, he stopped. It was too late. He was standing right beside her. His shadow covered her completely.

"How long have you been here?" The woman's voice did not disappoint him.

"My whole life."

"The next time we see each other, call me Diamantina."

He did. When he saw her again he called her Diamantina as though he had known her his entire life. Before knocking at the door of her house at number 35, Calle de Mesones, Joaquín explored the area for several days. He wanted to have a concrete image of what lay around her. In order to come to her, he needed a context. One by one, he examined the black and white tiles before her house. He stepped into the homeopathic pharmacy next door and examined the uniform bottles on the shelves. The pharmacy-clerk took him by surprise, and he had to buy a remedy for imaginary headaches. Out of the corner of his eye, he watched the men sitting on the red bench in front of the barber shop. The fragrance of brilliantine and steaming water made him nauseated. He wandered about under the arcades of the marketplace, where several merchants had set up shop: he observed all the things he imagined might be of interest to the eyes of Diamantina. The puppets and rag dolls, the saddles and bridles for equitation and for charros, the post cards and the purple ink made with German fuchsine, the peanut nougat and the amaranth seeds, the blotting paper, and the suitcases and other bags of genuine leather. Joaquín loved the city in those days. For the first time, he felt its incessant palpitations, its constant throbbing. He was inside it, in its very marrow. The speed that had always given him vertigo now was a source of amazement, lightheadedness. Its colors and its angles, its mechanical and human noises, its buildings of stone and of volcanic tezontle suddenly took on meaning: It was all there to adorn the existence of a woman in round-framed spectacles.

Diamantina opened the door. She was wearing a loose cotton dress and over it, an apron with smears of paint—green and yellow. The hair he had previously seen in a neat chignon now fell free over her shoulders. The black curls set off her angular features, the delicacy of her nose, the whiteness of her teeth. She was carrying a book.

"You want to hear something terrible, Joaquín?" Her eyes behind the gold pince-nez were full of irony. Still standing in the entry hall, not waiting for his reply, Diamantina read him some lines from Gutiérrez Nájera in an exaggeratedly grave voice:

Oh marble! Oh snow! Oh unsullied whiteness
by thy chaste beauty sown abroad!
Oh timid virgin, vestal chaste!
Thou art upon eternal beauty's statue,
and from thy white tunic purity was born.
To angels you give wings, and winding-shrouds to mortals!

When she finished, they both burst out laughing—fresh, youthful laughter. It was his first laugh in months. She looked straight into his eyes; she stripped him bare.

"Poor man. What kind of women must he know? 'Timid virgin,' for heaven's sake!" It was at that moment that Joaquín realized that Diamantina would never belong to him.

The big house was not just old and humid but also neglected, unkempt. The plants in the central garden grew without rhyme or reason, and with no harmony. Of them all, he could make out only the fragrance of mint, the sharp-pointed leaves of the tea plant, the *epazote,* and the wilted and battered-looking petals of some red and white geraniums. The little parlor into which she led him had only a few rickety armchairs on which were scattered books opened and turned face-down, half-darned socks, and a pair of gray cats. The only object of value was a grand piano in the center of the room. On the high walls, covered with the white scale of lime leeched from the plaster, hung five enormous oil paintings framed in rich wood. The images of women wearing velvet and silk gowns, rose-hued hats with ostrich plumes, and coordinated sets of earrings, bracelets, and rings had little to do with the disorderly and somber room they overlooked.

"They're the wives and daughters of politicians. It's the way my father makes a living," she said when she saw the intrigued expression on Joaquín's face. There was no one else; no chaperone, nurse, or maid was watching over them. Her mother had died when she was seven and her father was in his studio, where he spent more than fourteen hours a day. Still standing, separated from Diamantina by a little more than six feet, Joaquín imagined her hands removing her spectacles just before dawn. Diamantina had to be a nocturnal creature and that, surely, was the last thing she would do before slipping under the bedcovers. He imagined the moonlight on the gold. He heard her slow breathing. Diamantina was smaller than he had imagined, and older.

"You never thought it was going to be this way," she stated, not asked, while her gaze swept the four white walls without resting on any single thing. "The rich, Joaquín, lack imagination. You should do something about that. The sooner the better." There was no sarcasm in her voice.

"I think their world—*your* world—is about to end at any moment," she added.

"So do I."

Diamantina took him by the hand and led him across the central patio into the kitchen. She offered him coffee. Joaquín accepted. There was a map of the Republic of Mexico nailed to the adobe wall and, scattered across the map, push-pins of various colors. Red in the center of Veracruz state and the northern part of Sonora, white in Puebla. The charcoal stove with its three burners occupied almost all the space on the back wall, and on two equidistant racks on the right wall hung clay pitchers and bowls, enameled pewter pots, and iron frying pans. Between them, on a stone promontory, was one board for cutting vegetables and another for draining the washed pots and dishes. Diamantina dipped water out of the clay water-jug and poured it in a teakettle to heat. The two of them sat down at the rectangular table, a full yard of distance between their knees.

"What are you going to do with your life?" On her lips the question was open, the reply might go in any direction.

"I don't know," he said. "I detest medicine."

He had never said that before. Joaquín had not yet been able to tell his father that his profession frightened him, disgusted him, exasperated him. The insides of bodies left him unmoved. He fell silent when his father proudly showed him his scalpels and stethoscopes or when he went on for hours about the benefits of study at European universities. His own sincerity before a virtual stranger disgusted him, embarrassed him. He held himself back. Yet it had never occurred to him to ask the same question. Diamantina looked at his face; she liked it. The doubt in his eyes. The extreme narrowness of his pale lips. The angular tip of his nose. That desire to be anywhere else but there, next to her, and immediately the opposite desire. They drank their coffee in silence, quickly. Joaquín promised to come back.

He did. That same night. The sound of the piano drifted to the corner of the block, and there it turned and rode the tram tracks. The parlor window where he had stood a few hours earlier was still lighted. He rapped on it with his knuckles.

"I don't generally allow anyone to interrupt me, Joaquín." Her smile indicated that this interruption would be allowed. Under his jacket he was carrying the score of Chopin's *Minute Waltz*. He gave it to her.

"I can't offer you anything in return, you know?" she said instead of thanking him.

"I know." He put two of his fingers across the woman's lips and motioned her to go on practicing. Sitting on the floor cross-legged, Joaquín watched her for hours. As before he had lost himself in the ceiling of his room, he lost himself now in her face. *Your face, Diamantina. Your face which is my face, Diamantina.* The nightly ritual was repeated several times, punctually between eleven and four in the morning. Without telling her, on one of those nights Joaquín brought his Eastman and while she was concentrating on her fingers he took several photographs. Years later, when he came across them again in his brass trunk, Diamantina's absolute concentration on the keyboard astonished him anew. Her seriousness inspired compassion, pity. She was destined to live an entire life accompanied by herself alone. She knew that, and he should have known too, or at least imagined. His blindness had been so absolute that with the passing of time it only inspired the mute laughter of those things that are beyond help or remedy.

Don Luis Vicario, Diamantina's father, tried to warn him. One afternoon he unexpectedly led him upstairs to the tiny windowless room that contained his daughter's scattered books and papers. His wrinkled hands, covered with spots and smears of paint, flitted from cover to cover of the volumes as though they were flowers. The room smelled moldy. He also let Joaquín see the pencil portraits of her that he had done. Diamantina was at her piano in all of them. Don Luis's smile was filled with melancholy.

"It has taken many years to bring her to this, Joaquín. Only a cataclysm could change her."

He spoke to the young man of her stubbornness. Of the many strategies she employed in order to have her own way. He spoke to him of his daughter's fleeting marriage. Two years it had lasted. An unexpected death. Early widowhood. Despite these apparently negative comments, the older man's voice showed approval, almost admiration of his daughter. Joaquín felt a sudden desire to be old, so that he might speak with the same tenderness, the same discretion, about Diamantina. He imagined their life together, without children. He imagined himself a woman's second husband.

Joaquín enrolled in the San Carlos Academy. For the first time in his life, he was seduced by the idea of triumph. While he spent mornings mixing colors and doing studies in perspective, Diamantina was occupied in preparing lunch, feeding the cats, and going out to teach voice and singing lessons at the hospice run by the Welfare System. Then, in the afternoons, she would go to Reforma, to the big houses in the Colonia Juárez, to give two piano lessons. When she was done and on her way back home, she would sometimes stop in at the Saldívar bookshop, on Calle Bolívar, to see the new books that had come in and ask the owner if she could borrow one or two. The owner was a friend of her father's, and he never refused her. On Thursdays she attended dinner meetings in closed rooms behind the Palacio Nacional, where the diners spoke of nothing but politics. She rarely thought about Joaquín. When he came to her house at night and knocked at the door she was always surprised. An apparition. She grew accustomed to the miracle. The miracle of first forgetting him and then greeting him as though he had never left. Later came the miracle of their bodies. Joaquín could finally take off her spectacles and put them on the night table as they lay down in their bed.

Her naturalness was astonishing to him. Her silence; the lines under her eyes, the moles on her shoulders, the fine amber down on her calves. When he touched the vertebrae that ran down her back, their fragility made him tremble. With his lips on her half-parted lips he would try to drink in the air that rhythmically moved her chest. He felt alive and on the verge of death, and he liked both feelings. He wished he could photograph her that way, with her eyes closed and her head sunk into the pillow. He kissed her fingernails, inhaled the fragrance of her hair; with his fingers on the inside of her left wrist he counted her heartbeats. He put on her pince-nez and with his vision distorted by the lenses, looked out at the world. Nothing had limits: the objects of the world were in constant expansion. The woman, his first woman, was sleeping.

One morning he woke up between the threadbare sheets and the first thing he saw through the open closet door was the wool skirt she had been wearing when he met her. It was her only change of clothes. She had but one pair of shoes and one overcoat, both black. There was not a single decoration on the high, yellowing walls of the room. Besides the night table and the bed, the room was empty. A room without furniture: that was Diamantina. The rich, she would say, substitute things for a lack of imagination. And things, she would add, always wind up being an obstacle to imagination. Among her many fantasies, one of the most recurrent was setting fire to a bank. The Bank of London and Mexico City. Or to a jail, Belén. She wanted to be the cause of a monumental fire that would raze everything to the ground, so that after the holocaust the world could begin again. That was the first thing she mentioned when she woke up. The fire. They both smiled.

"Violence generates only terror, Diamantina," Joaquín muttered as he kissed the back of her hands.

"Then this is terror, Joaquín. Then we are living in the midst of a terror that has been going on for many years. Have you not seen its face?" The passion of her eyes frightened him. Was this the cataclysm that don Luis had told him about?

Justice. Diamantina went on and on about justice until the noon sun closed her eyes. Later, it was only on rare occasions that they ever spoke of the subject again.

Her body was a refuge for him. Inside her, the balance of light and shadow was perfect. Sometimes, looking at her as she spoke against greed, idleness, the wastefulness of the rich, the corruption of power, Joaquín thought he was with another person. The concentration was similar, but unlike what happened when she played the piano, her words exuded a rage as deep as a river. When she spoke, her hands, precise and graceful at the keyboard, would flutter nervously in space, adding exclamation marks, accents, periods to a reality she fiercely opposed. On those occasions, witnessing her gestures in silence, he was sure that what had led Diamantina to his body was not romantic passion but another force: the passion for salvation. His salvation. She, who was all unreality, had wanted to make him turn toward the world, pose him very delicately against the hardness of the days and the possibility of the future. And at least for a time, she managed to do that. She made him live with his feet on the ground, in the city.

Happiness disoriented him. During that time he never quite knew what to do, how to behave. His concentration on Diamantina was total. Sometimes, sitting at the table between don Luis and his daughter, the animosity of their conversations filled him with anguish. Between these two members of the Vicario family, every number, every name, every smallest piece of information had to pass through the sieve of analysis, every opinion had to be buttressed by evidence. They were both implacable. The headlines of *El Imparcial,* the newspaper under the orders of General Díaz, were the butts of their mockery, their incredulity. The rudimentary flyers for strikes to come filled them with new questions. Joaquín, accustomed to the laconic remarks of his parents at the dinner table, wriggled nervously in his chair at the Vicarios', expecting blows or shouts, and when things ended with the image of Diamantina serving coffee in the clay demitasses, leaving an absentminded caress upon her father's thin hair, the relief brought Joaquín even greater discomfort. Was this happiness? That same contradiction of sensations was present in every stroll, every walk they took together through the city. The lack of air, and then the denseness of the air, left him dizzy. Through her eyes, as she walked beside him, the life of the streets took on the bright, luminous, grotesque colors of a circus: The smiles of women selling flowers broadened, like half-moons of watermelons; the faded overalls of laborers resembled Impressionist paintings in constant movement; the candles hanging from wooden dowels in the hands of candle-vendors became the petals of a gigantic wax flower; the prostitutes at the doors of the churches smiled with the gentle kindness of Renaissance virgins; cart-drivers and beggars tended to look at things out of the corner of their eyes. In the market, Diamantina would haggle over the price of beans and mangos with all the skill and cunning of small-town matrons. Diamantina even nodded slightly to a piano student in the distance as though she, too, were the daughter of an attorney. Diamantina lighting candles and making the sign of the cross over her face before the image of the black Christ. Diamantina holding his hand in the crowd of people on the church portal, encouraging him to walk on even without knowing quite what was to come. Sometimes, watching her movements among the men and women that came to the Thursday meetings, he would lose the thread of the conversation as he disentangled the sudden angles of her body when she stood up to greet some newcomer. A hug. A quick kiss on each cheek. A couple of pats on the shoulder. Then, instead of listening to the speeches, Joaquín would lose himself in the imperceptible movement of Diamantina's fingers around the lobe of her right ear, the wrinkles that radiated from her lips when they moved in the death-rattle of laughter, the swish of her cotton skirt as it passed beside him. *Fat bourgeoisie. Down with dictatorship. Onward to life.* At any hour, anywhere at all, he would avidly observe her, with the urgency and resignation of a man sensing the approaching end of a spell.

"This is important, Joaquín. Stop looking at me like that," she would whisper in his ear in the middle of a meeting, visibly embarrassed. And then, so as not to distress her, he would stare at the flames of the candles, the bodies' trembling shadows cast on the walls, the black-and-white flags that served as decorations on the walls and curtains over the windows. There were long-haired women who, despite having bathed just minutes, perhaps, earlier, left in the air around them the fragrance of the tobacco they skillfully rolled into cigars in the cigar-factories during the day; men in discreet dark suits and fedoras who moved, however, with the rhythm of laborers. The youngest of them smoked cigarettes, and while they attentively followed the discussion that had begun at the main table they would stick their hands in their overall pockets. Children would run in and out among the chairs, under the tables, paying no mind whatever to the scolding of their elders. More than clandestine political meetings, these gatherings always had, since the very beginning, the tension and hurry of a fiesta. There, among them, Joaquín saw her play the guitar for the first time. And there, on a wobbly dais spruced up to look like a theater stage, he heard her sing patriotic songs and battle hymns interspersed with country melodies. Diamantina always introduced him as a friend of the family. Someone very dear to them. And so Joaquín was.

The first woman. Her name was Diamantina Vicario. He could not keep her even though he wished, with all his heart sometimes, that he could. It was not out of the curiosity of youth, out of the hope that the world held more and better surprises in the future, out of the ineptitude of his tender age, or because of those common lovers' quarrels. When they said goodbye on the platform of the central train station, they were good friends. She was going to Veracruz. She was carrying a rectangular suitcase filled with notes and pamphlets, and in the glints off her eyeglasses, the conviction that Joaquín's world was about to come to an end at any moment, once and for all. The woman's confidence was exactly the same size as his loneliness.

"Cultivate the imagination," she told him. She kissed him. Joaquín held onto that kiss for years and years. And with that kiss on his lips, while he used them to seduce other women, he dedicated himself to waiting for the second woman, who is always the real one, the definitive one. Later, when he chanced to read Diamantina's articles in *Vesper* or *El Hijo del Ahuizote,* it was that same kiss that he set upon the pages of the newspaper, and so it disappeared forever. Diamantina, who with absentminded patience had prepared him for his fall into reality, had never prepared him, however, for the appearance of Alberta.

"And you, doctor, what is your opinion of love stories?"

On fall afternoons, Matilda's face in the shadow of the chestnut trees makes him see visions. It is six forty-five, and the light flickers in the wind with sudden golden undulations. Sometimes, at that hour, Matilda's face might be anyone's. All it required was a bit of imagination. Dr. Oligochea takes his wallet out of his back pants pocket. He opens it without looking at Joaquín and, stretching his arm across the desk, lays a photograph in his hands. The bravery of this gesture is new in him.

"Look, Buitrago. Cecilia Villalpando. My fiancée." The pride in his voice is unfeigned.

"Pleased to meet you," murmurs Joaquín, his eyes staring into hers. They must be blue. On the little marble table on which she rests her right elbow there is a crystal vase filled with white lilies. The lace sewn on her dress disguises the lack of breasts, the almost sickly thinness of her torso.

Everything about her speaks of weakness, delicacy, pampering, piano lessons. Cecilia is the type of woman that awakens only pity, compassion, in Joaquín's imagination. The type of woman that makes him automatically, almost without thinking, exclaim the phrase "poor thing!"

"She suffers from asthma," the doctor says softly as he futilely seeks his friend's eyes, trying to explain. "Her father is a silk merchant."

When Joaquín lifts his gaze, the need for approval in the eyes of his friend upsets him. Suddenly he looks to Joaquín like a lapdog or a stripling of no more than seventeen, both with their mouths open, their tongues hanging out as though waiting to be patted on the head or given a tidbit to chew on. And now he expects a story in exchange for his own. Words of flesh and bone, traces of light, clumps of sand and blood able to make him close his eyes. Pearls just harvested from the bottom of the sea, fragrant daisy petals pressed between the yellowing leaves of a half-read book, a handkerchief embroidered with the initials of two names. He was expecting a story, but as often happens at bank-tellers' windows, Joaquín feels cheated. He had wagered too much. He had given much, far too much, for Case File 6353. Would he ever see it? The disillusionment leaves him mute, with no desire to make the slightest effort to erase the grimace of discomfort, shame, embarrassment, on Eduardo's face. Then, with no sign of compassion, he lays the portrait of Cecilia Villalpando face down on the desk. He says nothing. He observes Eduardo. The man sitting before him, who until now had acted with the quiet superiority of his rank, is no longer Dr. Oligochea; he is just Eduardo.

"As you say, Buitrago, Cecilia is the second woman." The nervousness of his own voice discomfits him almost as much as the contemptuous face—impenetrable now—of the man who has spent months opening up to him, layer by layer, as though he had nothing else to do.

"Come now, Eduardo. Don't be such an idiot. This isn't

even a woman. Cecilia is your ticket into the salons of the Colonia Roma." He had never challenged him before. This was the first time he had used the informal *tu*. A stripling lad. A puppy with an open mouth. A man who cannot tell a single love story with a real woman.

"All love stories don't have to end in tragedy. Or in morphine, Joaquín. Did you know that? Some men are fortunate enough that the second woman, the definitive one, actually loves them."

Joaquín smiles at him from his chair while Eduardo stands and, indecisively, glides from one side of his desk to the other. Leaning back against the rigid wooden seatback, and with exquisite slowness, the photographer lights a cigarette. Suddenly, for no reason whatever, what had been anger turns to commiseration. He has no desire to fight. No desire to convince anyone. The stripling lad has not the slightest idea of what he's saying.

"If you had been loved, Eduardo, you would know that it is never fortunate to be loved by a woman." Joaquín watches him fall into the soft seat of his chair and raise his eyes to the ceiling as though hoping to encounter the streambed of his night rivers. Without returning Joaquín's gaze, turning his chair to the left a bit to avoid having to look at him, Eduardo takes another photograph out of his wallet. Before laying it on the desk, he looks at it as though it were hard to relinquish possession of it even for a moment.

"Her name is Mercedes Flores. From Jalapa. A medical student like me. A girl who, after making love for the first time, had the brazenness to say 'I'm your man.' Just like that, in English."

Joaquín had had before his lens the faces of women as they wanted to see themselves. In the prison at Belén he had photographed the devastated eyes of the murderer who, after confessing his guilt, refused to show remorse. On the sidewalk in front of the Forget Me Not pulquería he had managed to capture the *delirium tremens* of a drunkard before he cursed life for the last time. In the darkroom at La Castañeda he had captured the Gioconda smile on the lips of Matilda. As though it were all inescapable, he has stood unmoved at each revelation, each unveiling. Click. When Eduardo slowly turns his face toward Joaquín, he does so without realizing it, looking out at a reality somewhere beyond. His expression shows no trace of pride or need for consolation. For a moment Eduardo is standing once more before Mercedes, playing again the intimate game of her words. *"I'm your woman." "Yes indeed, Eduardo, you are my woman."* They laugh then, the way men marked forever by a bad joke laugh. Then, at that moment, fascinated by the almost imperceptible movement of the sunflower, the only thing the photographer regrets is not having a camera in his hands so that he might once more fix the unique, unrepeatable instant when a man tells a story of love. For the first time.

"If loving is for madmen, allowing yourself to be loved is worse, isn't it?" Neither spoke. There was no need to agree or disagree.

"Mercedes wanted to be the Florence Nightingale of the Red Liberal Party. Write riddles in English. Return to Edinburgh and live there forever in a castle tower. Be the first Mexican woman to run, and win, the hundred meters in the Olympics. Retrace Rimbaud's adventures in North Africa. Chew tobacco. Ride a bicycle along the Great Wall of China. Have children. And all the while be called Mercedes Flores de Oligochea. She said the name had a nice ring to it."

The photograph is dog-eared at the corners. The years it has spent tucked away in Eduardo's wallet have left a whitish cast on the image. Sometimes, looked at out of the corner of Joaquín's eye, Mercedes' face and generous body seem to be hidden by a veil or to be sheltered within a curtain of transparent white silk. It is not a studio portrait. The photograph gives the impression of having been taken hurriedly, by the inexpert and trembling hands of an amateur.

Mercedes is not posing. There is excitement in her dark face, in the curly hair gathered into an unruly ponytail, in the broad cheeks of what might pass for a mulatto woman of the docks. One of her hands is raised up to the sky as though waving goodbye to a ghost or shooing away mosquitoes, while the other holds a fishing pole from the end of which dangles, perhaps wriggles, a trout. Her thick lips are frozen in the rounded syllables of a name. *Look, Eduardo.* Behind her, behind it all, stretches the peaceful water of a river. Mercedes looks full of energy. Despite time, her body still gives the impression that it may spring up out of the picture at any moment, without warning. The energy seems to make her not so much beautiful as mad. Fear. Mercedes is the kind of woman fated to destroy the professional reputation of any psychiatrist. Of any man.

"Mercedes Flores de Oligochea," mutters Joaquín. The name has a certain melody to it, all right. The song of an accordion.

In Mixcoac, in his office, Eduardo has stopped thinking of success, stopped thinking of the future. His face is contracted by the pleasure inspired in him by the smell of salt air, the horrid light of a distant noon. He is smiling. Then, suddenly, a muted involuntary groan emerges from his lips. A puff of time, like a burp of years issuing from his infested organism.

"How does one manage to forget a woman, Buitrago?" His voice, once again, is the voice of a stripling of seventeen.

"I fear, Dr. Oligochea, that you know better than I."

Neither speaks. As the light of the day grows weaker and the sliver of waning moon shyly ventures into the sky, the halls of the asylum are filled with the howls of the melancholics, the futile banging of the violent. What Eduardo recalls are Mercedes' onsets of indiscriminate high spirits followed by days of equally uncontrollable weeping. "I don't know what to do with this sadness, Eduardo," she would say. Her trembling voice, about to break, still filled him with impotence. "It's me, Mercedes—Eduardo. Everything will be all right." He is still undone by the dark circles around her eyes, the way she stares into nothingness, or places that no one else sees or imagines. Still. In his arms, trembling with cold, Mercedes still struggles to remember her own name— her maiden name and her married name. Her life.

"The first woman, you're right, Buitrago, is only given us so that we may not have her. Pity the man who gets to keep one." As soon as he picks up the photograph and puts it away in his wallet without looking at it, his face is once more the face that Joaquín knows. The face of the man who, before deciding to ring the bell at the door, looks with disguised covetousness upon the iron palings before the residence in Colonia Roma. The face of the man who, after his fingertips have brushed the cheek of Cecilia Villalpando, sets himself to acting like the professional with brilliant future and charming conversation with whom the silk merchant feels so at ease that he offers him a glass of whiskey in the library, away from the chatter of the ladies, before going in to dinner. The face of the man who, with discipline and no apparent effort, employs the silverware and wineglass in perfect observance of the rules of social etiquette. It is a masculine, measured sort of face that inspires respect. When he sees it now again, Joaquín feels that the possibility of obtaining Matilda's case file has slipped forever from his grasp. A man with that face would never agree to compromise his professional status by discussing with a poor devil such as he the case of one of the inmates. Joaquín has to do something more. He has to turn back time, force Dr. Oligochea to become once more the youngster he had been a few minutes before.

"When did you realize that she was the first woman?"

"A long time afterward, Buitrago. When I realized that no woman like her would ever appear again." He stops, hesitates, concentrates on the cracks in the ceiling, is about to smile. "No, it was even after that. Not long ago at all, in fact, in the garden of the Villalpando house. Three days ago. I only knew for a certainty when, after I told the story of that afternoon's fishing in one of the branches of the Grijalva, my fiancée forbade me ever to mention it again. I, of course, had never said that Mercedes Flores was, long ago, my fiancée. In fact, the story came to me suddenly and complete, and I decided to tell it only because the Villalpandos had become entangled in an irrational argument over the absence of animal life in the polluted waters of the Gulf. There must have still been something in my voice. Something clinging to her name."

Without making a sound, Joaquín stands up and leans against the doorframe. The waning quarter of the moon smiles at him from on high. The night is whole and intact. As he lights another cigarette, Joaquín asks himself how long it will take the doctor to recover from his own words. The worst thing that can happen to a man like Eduardo Oligochea is not remembering a story, but rather lacking enough self-awareness to tell it. Would he be able to look Joaquín in the eye afterward?

"Imagine what a coincidence, Buitrago. The first woman leaves but we remain stranded there." Eduardo, still inside the story of the first woman, has not had time to feel embarrassed. He is seventeen. He asks for a cigarette. His gaze is turned up toward the ceiling, vacant, lost, but he is not daydreaming anymore. There is something in his head. Joaquín recognizes the two vertical creases between his eyebrows: interest. The doctor is tying up some loose ends. Speculating. As in years past when he studied for an examination in anatomy, his concentration is total, the silence around him absolute. The two men are in the dark now.

"Matilda Burgos, do you remember that patient?" Joaquín nods doubtfully, fearing he has been discovered. "She is the very prototype of the first woman, Buitrago."

"How do you know?" The intrigue in Joaquín's eyes is real.

"My dear Buitrago, for a morphine addict you have a remarkable lack of imagination." The doctor's laughter makes the muscles tense in Joaquín's face and turns the saliva bitter in his mouth. He fears that Dr. Oligochea knows. He fears that his body has betrayed him, or his voice, the way he bends over as he sucks at the cigarette. He fears that Eduardo will never again have the candor of a stripling of seventeen. He fears, above all, the loss of Case 6353.

"Let's not be foolish, Buitrago. Both of us have survived a war that lasted ten years and we didn't do that by remembering women lost, women wasted."

"Yes."

For the first time since they began to meet, Joaquín is enjoying his company. There is something between them. A similarity. Despite the difference in their ages, temperaments, habits, futures, they both gravitate like freezing moths to the warm flame of thought.

"That is why you stalk her, isn't it?" he asks without looking at him, as though offhandedly. "Because she is the prototype of the first woman."

"No, Eduardo, that isn't why." But he goes no further.

Joaquín is waiting for a burst of triumphant laughter from his adversary's throat. The remark that leaves no doubt that the guess has hit its mark, the bomb's mechanism tripped. "I caught you, you old talker—I caught you at last." But what Eduardo Oligochea does is the following: in the darkness, groping, he opens his desk drawers. With the aid of a match he searches through a stack of file folders and comes to the one he wishes to find. He does all this in silence, unhurriedly and without anticipation, following a method that he knows by rote.

"Here it is. It's all yours, Joaquín. For twenty-four hours."

When the file passes from one man's hand to the other's, both avert their eyes. No one shall witness what is happening. It is an illegal act committed by two men still standing on the bank of the same river. Before passing through the door, not turning, Joaquín says:

"You, at least, were lucky enough that the second woman did love you."

A name. A birthplace. A date. All stories begin that way: Matilda Burgos. Papantla, Veracruz, 1885. "Have you ever seen men flying like birds, Joaquín?" He had only twenty-four hours to find out the rest.

2

~ঞ~

The husband of vanilla

ni mak'liti cac'xilam
coxo pamça qui nacu

[each time I see you
my heart leaps up]

Goyo Ja

In 1900, when Matilda Burgos arrived in the country's capital, the city ended at the Consulado River on the north and across the road from the Beneficencia Española, the insane asylum, on the south; the eastern limit of the city was marked by Jamaica, while the western part of the city stretched all the way to the Chapultepec forest. Electric tram lines already linked the pleasant villages of Tacubaya, Mixcoac, and San Angel to the bustling city. From early in the morning, the rush of people changed the direction of the breeze in the streets, and at night the incandescent lamps of the city's public lighting system protected the inhabitants of the well-to-do colonias, as they were called, and the scurrying of men and women who apparently never slept. As the century began, there were, according to the general census, 368,898 people living in the city. Matilda Burgos, at fifteen years of age, became number 368,899.

With her forehead pressed to the glass of the train window, Matilda looked out at the slow approach of the urban animal with a mixture of terror, amazement, and despair. It was the first time she had seen large buildings. At her wrists, her pulse raced, and a sudden rush of blood to the back of her brain gave her an ephemeral headache. Her hands, however, lying quietly in her lap, and her face, impassive at the spectacle of the city, did not betray her. She had decided to hide her fear. No one would see her cry. She bit her lips. As the train slowed and the sleeping passengers began to awaken and stir, her new solitude gleamed purple in her eyes. The memory of the smell of vanilla came to her suddenly and, just as suddenly, defeated her. A tear, before she could stop it, rolled down her cheek and was dammed at the corner of her mouth.

"Everything will be all right, don't worry." A low voice, soft and measured, woke her abruptly from her dream. Discreetly, trying to keep her from feeling embarrassed or ill at ease, the man with the white skin and aquiline nose was offering her his white handkerchief. Matilda took it. On one of the corners she saw the initials J.B. embroidered in coffee-colored thread. He smiled at her.

"Thank you, sir." The small-town accent that shaped the words came from far away. From her childhood. Then, in his arms, upon the withered male breast, Matilda cried in the city for the first time.

The interior of the National Library is filled with hushed whispers, monotonous echoes that bump into one another and then disappear into the porosity of the walls. Joaquín, whose figure glides through streets, banks, and shops with the movements of a man unable to fit into the machinery of the city, walks through the corridors of the library easily, comfortably, serenely—most unusual. In the reading room the only sound is the slow turning of pages and, from time to time, footsteps, the wooden clack of heels fading away unhurriedly into the distance. Before opening one of the seven books he has stacked on the table before him, Joaquín notices that the light of the morning sun makes whimsical geometrical figures on the floor. *Papantla.* The photographer hopes that this light will illuminate the story of the woman, every angle of her face, every mark that time has left on her knees, in her eyes. More than having her inside him and in darkness, Joaquín needs to have her around him, luminous. Like always, Joaquín needs a context in order to approach a woman. At forty-nine, he is still a man who falls in love as though he had all of time before him, and nothing else to do.

Totonacapan. Tajín. Tecolutla. After going over the names silently, the photographer writes them on the blue lines of his notebook. Behind each one, peeking over the hump of the letters, Matilda's playful eyes watch him as he starts a bit in shock and surprise and then contains himself. Each bit of information brings him that much closer to her. *The Totonacas arrived in the region of Tajín around the year 800 of our era. Some time later, in about the twelfth century and for reasons still unknown, the area was abandoned. The territory of Totonacapan extended from the banks of the Cazones River to the banks of the Antigua, and included, on the flanks of the Sierra Madre, the villages of Huauchinango, Zacatlán, Tetela, Zacapoaxtla, Tlatanquitepec, Teziutlán, Papantla, and Misantla.* The names suggested distant swamps, mud holes, malaria, fearsome epidemics, but little by little, as the books' descriptions increase and immense vegetation fills the space with variations of green, the fragrance of honey, sarsaparilla, pepper, copal, and vanilla transport him to what he would like to imagine as a part of the earthly paradise. In the drawings of Tierra Caliente, the hot land, the people of reason are shown riding horseback: their mulatto women are on foot, their bodies covered with simple white dresses; they are carrying water jugs on their heads. *The War of Independence suddenly broke out in the northern part of what was formerly Totonacapan and lasted until well into the twenties. Because the military rule in this area was unstable, the principle harbors and cities were taken and retaken several times. In 1812, there was a frustrated insurgent assault on Tuxpan. The next year the royalists took Tihuatlán, Tepetzintla, and Papantla. In 1816 they seized the important insurgent provisions center located in Boquilla de Piedras. Papantla was attacked again in 1819.*

Pedro Vega, Simón de la Cruz, and Joaquín Aguilar were prominent leaders, although the caudillo who emerged at last was Serafín Olarte, who brought together a number of indigenous troop contingents and maintained a steadfast defense, from his bastion in Coyuxquihui, against the colonial forces.

The names pile up; the names say nothing. The dates are swings on which Joaquín swings his long, dreary boredom, an expectancy filled with urgency. "When do you appear, Matilda? How long do I have to wait?" In the illustrations that accompany the chronicles and historical accounts, Papantla appears to be a peaceable village, though disorderly. The white houses, roofed with thatch or red tiles, are built in hollows and on rises with no apparent organization. Like all Mexican villages, Papantla has a town plaza on one of whose sides rises the spire of a church containing rows of wide wooden pews, a down-at-heels organ, the dust that has accumulated for all these many years. A herd of pigs that devours everything in its path, like some biblical plague, appears from time to time on the roads, which are otherwise peaceful and easy enough to travel. Joaquín sees it all, and then, with his nose in the books, counting with all his fingers, he ticks off the epidemics that scourged the populace: cholera in 1833, smallpox in 1830 and 1841. Then he counts off the number of businesses: seven main shops—groceries, dry goods shops, general stores, a liquor store—and a large number of stalls, establishments run out of lean-tos and windows, a restaurant or two, and several street vendors selling food at mealtimes. When a Spanish manufacturer of cigars is mentioned, Joaquín holds his breath, but when he sees that the man's name is not Burgos, he sighs disconsolately. Dances, cockfights, and billiard games are the village's favorite pastimes. *The authorities and inhabitants of Papantla absolutely repudiate the government of the United States of America, which is more than ever before claiming as its own the land of Mexico. They vow to share Mexico's fate forever, and to perish in its defense, sacrificing their fortunes, their families, and all that they hold sacred, as martyrs to their patriotism, and only over their dead bodies shall the enemies of Mexico's nationality and independence pass, to occupy the rubble and ruins that they shall leave in their wake. Only thus will they ever yield.* Joaquín cannot contain his laughter when he sees that despite the patriotic fervor of don Hilario Pérez y Olazo, the routes chosen by the American troops in their siege and occupation of Mexico City in 1847 left the Papantecos—ready for war, armed to the teeth with machetes and long guns of every sort imaginable—far from the battlelines.

And so, with a smile on his lips, he comes at last to the information he has been seeking: In 1857 or 1858 (the authors disagree on this detail), five hundred families, emigrating from Italy, arrived in the harbor of Tecolutla. The settlers were led by Giovanni Montessoro, and they took a boat up the Texquitipan River, near Agua Dulce, where they built their first settlement. *They were starving, and one of the Italians came to seek aid from the priest, and so families from the village went to them and took them food and medicine, and among other curious things they found an Italian cooking a turkey buzzard. When a Papanteco told him that that bird was not eaten, the Italian replied, "Tutte ave che vola a la tavola." One problem that bedevilled the Italians was the sand fleas, because all of them were covered with the tiny creatures but did not know what they were; the people from the village would speak to them, to tell them, but they did not understand. Finally, there was one who understood Spanish, and he told the others how to take them off. And all of them took up thorns from the orange trees, and lime, and they began to pick off the sacs of the sand fleas and cover them with lime and so they pulled them all off.* Some of the Italians were able to adapt to the coastal conditions, but others, beleaguered by malaria, insects, and heat, made their way to Cabezas del Carmen and into the interior, to the neighboring village of Papantla. The only one who understood Spanish and was not Italian was named Marcos Burgos. Bent over the table as though he were about to rise and flee, Joaquín hurriedly notes down the information. He is not certain why, does not know what his purpose in this is. His handwriting, neat and orderly on the first pages, becomes shaky, nervous, trembling in the last paragraph.

"I knew it!" an old man with a white beard exclaims with obvious delight at the other end of the table. "The days of these damned atheists' government are numbered!"

The old man, on the other side of the table from Joaquín, is holding the first page of the morning newspaper, whose headlines announce a new uprising in the southwest part of the country. The two men grin at each other like madmen, or fanatics. This is, without a doubt, one of the best days in Joaquín Buitrago's life.

They are standing in the shade of a chestnut tree. In the air, there is the whistling of the wind and the muted echo of the insane that are all around them. Joaquín asks her to close her eyes and put out her hands. Expecting another present, Matilda obeys without hesitation, like a child. A shock of hair crosses her face, from left to right. The tops of the clouds in the sky are gray. Surreptitiously, he takes a tiny vial out of his right jacket pocket and places it in her open palms. The liquid inside the glass is the color of India ink or dark-black chocolate.

"Vanilla," mutters Matilda the moment she opens her eyes. "It's vanilla. Shit vanilla."

When the cork is removed from the vial, the fragrance cuts the air like the blade of a sword. The confusion in her eyes is so real that Joaquín has to turn his back to her and look down at his shoes. Matilda, unseen, daubs a drop of the liquid behind her ears and on her wrists, as though it were perfume. It is.

Joaquín lets her talk.

"Vanilla is an orchid. Did you know that? *Xanat*, in the old language. I've talked to it, I know all the secrets of its pods. Its voice is a woman's voice. Just smelling it, even from a distance, I can tell whether it's wild vanilla, or a hybrid, or domesticated, or grown in a pot. The best is the domesticated. It should be planted during the waning moon in March and July. You do it like this. You bury one or two sprigs of it, about the thickness of your finger, alongside a coral tree, a mother-of-cocoa, a poinciana, a bird-of-paradise, or a ginger plant, and tie it very carefully to the trunk or the stalk, you know? Vanilla, although it feeds through the roots, needs, like a woman, to have a tree or strong stalk to twine around and hold it up so it won't die. For it to produce the pods, it has to be pollinated with a sharp piece of bamboo. The hands of Indian women, like my grandmother María de la Luz, are the best for that. It has to be cleaned three times a year. Three years later, between December 12 and February 2, the seed pods are harvested, still green. Paul would say that it was *planifolia*, that was its species, and that not even the Madagascar vanilla compared with the quality and fragrance of the black flowers of Papantla. If only somebody could describe the smell of vanilla! The sweetness of the root and the stupefaction of its smell mixed with copal. If only there were words. If only I could carry it with me always, tucked up under my skirt. But once you take it away from the trees, vanilla turns bitter, did you know that? Now the flower is no longer in the hands of Indians, but under the very watchful eyes of processors and politicians. Those men, they're white, mestizos, Europeans. They pay the ones who bring the harvest in from far away in the mountains only a few centavos, or they steal it from them at night. They are men of violence. They lay the pods out in huge drying areas in the patios of their houses and dry them in the sun, air them in the shade, and then dry them again. Following the poxcoyón system, they wrap the vanilla in straw mats and blankets and put it in the ovens and make it sweat, then they pick through it and choose the best and divide it into lots. The women play no part in this, you know, now, but the men that do it have to have very skillful eyes and hands and noses. Vanilla takes precision, perfection. My father was the best. My father knew that once it had dried, the vanilla had to rest for at least two months, and if there was no moisture in it after two months, then it was ready to be aired for another ninety days. My father knew how to cull the sprays, getting rid of the ones that were spotted or bruised or torn or split or soft, and there was nobody like him when it came to splitting out the pods. When he supervised the sheaving of the fifty black, almost crystallized pods at don Juventino Guerrero's processing plant, when the workers wrapped them in wax paper and packed them in tin boxes ready to be shipped in cedar crates to Europe, my father would sing them a nursery song, and he didn't give a hoot about the sarcasm. My father was crazy. My father, before he took to chuchiqui and lost everything including his dignity, he would baby that vanilla like it was a woman. The husband of the vanilla, that was my father. Santiago Burgos. But I'm crazy, Joaquín, so don't pay me any mind. Don't believe a word of this."

In the books that Joaquín consults in the National Library, "chuchiqui" is described as a moonshine brandy made from sugar cane, sapodilla bark, and grapevine—a concoction that would make any man go mad. *What does it taste like, what does it taste like, Santiago?* Santiago Burgos drank it for the first time in 1885, the same year Matilda was born, when an unusually dry season endangered all the vanilla plants in the area and his parents were killed in the Totonaca uprising organized and led by Antonio Díaz Manfort, a physician venerated as a saint. *It tastes like what death tastes like when it's in your mouth, Joaquín. It tastes like getting busted in the head. It tastes like finding her and letting her go. It tastes like life when it is over for you, hombre. It tastes like you and me, Joaquín.*

A few years before Matilda was born, thefts of the newly harvested vanilla pods became more and more frequent, and more bloody. Life, otherwise, continued on its accustomed course, giving little and then a little less.

"God will give us more," María de la Luz would say. María de la Luz was a woman who knew patience. But God, in those days, had gone deaf, or was bored. A short time later they began to receive offers to buy their land. At the time, people talked about co-ownership, which was a measure that was supposed to parcel out agricultural land to the various municipalities within the region, especially those in the hands of the Totonacas. Corruption, bad management, and the arbitrariness of the processes inflamed the spirits of the indigenous peoples in the region to such a degree that on December 30, 1885, when Antonio Díaz Manfort issued his manifesto of reply, seven thousand indigenous men followed him in insurrection. Marcos and María de la Luz Burgos were among them. The hundred and five national guardsmen stationed in Papantla finished off the rebels in less than four months. Of the children that Marcos and María de la Luz had had, one went first to Xalapa and then to Mexico City to learn medicine; only Santiago, the younger, remained in Papantla, finding it impossible, as he had since his early childhood, to be far from the fragrance of the vanilla.

Santiago, like his mother, was dark skinned, with wide eyes. He had inherited his nervous yet subdued movements from his immigrant father. His stubbornness and mercurial temperament, though, were his own. Even as a child Santiago might be seized by uncontrollable attacks of rage, caused by the slightest things: the climate, for example, the inevitability of mudholes in the rainy season, the withering sun of summer. After the rages, however, one could almost always find him resting in the hammock, his face peaceful. His tastes and desires might suddenly become obsessions. On the day in the municipal school when he learned to use a pencil, the discovery so delighted him that he spent days writing letters and messages to everyone he knew and not a few people invented by his feverish imagination. But it was only a small step from obsession to oblivion. Santiago was capable of spending weeks, or months, wandering through every inch of the woods and hills around his village, driven by the urge to dig up the treasures left by his father. Yet after two failed attempts, he never returned to the search. When he met Carmen, a mulatto woman who had come from the port city recently in search of a better place in which to take the rest cure for tuberculosis, Santiago pursued her with a fury, only to forget her the moment he stole the first kiss. Finally, the only woman who could hold him was Prudencia Lomas, a woman slightly older than he whose love for French poetry and the pleasures of the flesh led people to think her name had been given her in error. When Santiago married her, without her parents' blessing, Prudencia was pregnant with Matilda.

The smell of vanilla always had a calming effect on him. On April evenings, walking among the vanilla vines, he would think of eternity. As he planned the next year's plantings he might see on the tips of the leaves the smiling faces of María de la Luz's gods, the determination in the eyes of the young Marcos enlisting to sail from Puerto de Palos and leave Spain and all his former life behind. The admiration he felt for them was so sincere that it often seemed like love. The resentment and mediocrity of his own story, however, bound his heart inside. Besides planting vanilla, Santiago was not good at anything. His ambitions centered on producing a harvest as perfect as God Himself, or close to it. But to do that he needed his father's land and the ancestral knowledge of María de la Luz. When he finally rescued their bodies from the mud and blood of the wilderness, he did not weep. The next day he gave them a Christian burial at the far south end of the rows of vanilla plants, and immediately began to curse the government and God. Prudencia, with Matilda in her arms, watched him dig in the ground, and then witnessed the burial in silence. Santiago's rage, this time, was not fleeting. His anger took possession of the entire savannah of his heart, and there it lived through all the rest of the ten years of life that remained to him. The chuchiqui made the wait less burdensome, a bit less unbearable. *It tastes like wanting to die. It tastes for sure like dying, Joaquín. It tastes like a knifeblade, a nail, a whip, something they beat you with. It tastes like your tongue when it's motionless between your teeth.* What Matilda retained of her father was not his rage but rather the bitterness with which he sold his land and hired himself out as a day laborer at Juventino Guerrero's processing plant. What she always remembered of her mother were her arms around her, the slow beating of her heart at her right ear.

"If there were only another New World, another Papantla somewhere..." Those were Santiago Burgos' last words.

Family background (direct, atavistic, and collateral):

Is there, or has there been, in patient's family any person or persons suffering from symptoms associated with nervous conditions, epilepsy, insanity, hysteria, alcoholism, syphilis, or who has committed suicide or been an addict? *Patient's father was alcoholic and her mother, although she would not become inebriated, also drank. Patient's father died of alcohol; mother murdered.*

In the books, Joaquín feels safe. Among their pages there is a cathedral of smells in which everything has a name; there is a tunnel of voices where he can go to find clues, clouds. The organization of the stories gives him direction through the mysteries of the world. When no one is watching, he caresses the covers, sticks his nose between the brittle pages, inhales the odor of ink. If the city were a library, he would be a happy man. The drawings and photographs speak to him from distant places. There is always someone behind them. Someone who imagines, studies the surroundings, manipulates the light, and finally, when one would least expect it, gives the master stroke. A swift descent of the blade. The sword into the heart of the bull. The man's weariness, astonishment, or vertigo then remains there—simultaneously given shape and hidden—awaiting the second stroke, the definitive one. Joaquín has never been in Papantla, but he can move with increasing ease among its complex network of narrow streets bordered by white houses, among the pigs and chickens that trip up people walking. When he wearies of this, he rests under the colonial archway next to the church or sits on the steps leading up to the gazebo in the center of the plaza. If he pays attention he can make out, among all the other shadows, the shadow of Matilda. Her smell. There is something unnameable inside her, something that surrounds her and leaves everything in silence. Joaquín is taking notes. Over the years he has learned to mistrust his memory, mistrust himself.

El Tajín. Matilda's eyes are closed as she pronounces the name. She spreads her arms and twirls around once, twice, her skirt rising and blossoming out like an umbrella. The smile on her face is a smile of pleasure. The search for his father's buried treasures had led the young Santiago Burgos to the plains of Coatzintla, near the Cazones basin. There, making his way through the jungle on a mule, his lower legs protected by high leather boots, he entered the Tecolutla basin. When he saw the Pyramid of the Niches for the first time, Santiago did not know what to do. He and his mule stood motionless. He had heard people talk about the Totonaca ruins, but when he stood before them, all the descriptions seemed pale and imperfect. The beauty of the buildings made him realize that there were things in the world for which there were no words. Then a stroke of lightning split the sky in two and scattered purple particles through the air. The storm, when it came, forced him to pronounce one word, between his teeth: "Dios".

The photographer reads all the books. The first news of Tajín reached the world in 1785. That year, the *Gaceta de México* published an article of no more than two columns, signed by Diego Ruiz, a corporal on patrol duty in the jurisdiction of Papantla who, carrying out his duties for the Royal Tobacco Levy, discovered the ruins in the midst of the jungle. His descriptions, though filled with patent wonder and adorned with grandiloquent language, say little, really, about the timeless wound of the Totonaca stones. Years later, in 1804, Pedro Martínez, a Jesuit priest, now in exile in Italy, published his work entitled *Los antiguos monumentos de la arquitectura mexicana*, in which, correcting Diego Ruiz's figures, he stated that the main temple had 376 niches, not 342. In addition to being accompanied by detailed illustrations, his account, erudite yet at the same time tinged with nostalgia, attempted to decipher the calendrical meaning of the niches, the stelae, and the monuments. But of all the writings, perhaps none was as significant in planting the modern legend of Tajín in the European imagination as Baron Alexander von Humboldt's *Political Essay on the Kingdom of New Spain*. In von Humboldt's words, the architecture of Tajín was perfect; its beauty, ineffable; its age, as immemorial as mystery itself. The news of an unknown civilization, lost yet still intact in the middle of the Veracruzan jungle, attracted the attention of archaeologists, artists bored with the modern world, fevered autodidacts in search of ancestral wisdom, and every man and woman with an insatiable thirst for the exotic. As they made their difficult way to the ruins, most of them passed through Papantla to stock up on food, ask directions, and if necessary, hire a guide. In May of 1892, a French painter with astonished eyes found himself in the town plaza with Santiago Burgos, who, now stupefied with chuchiqui, offered the man his services. The Frenchman, exhausted but dressed to neat perfection in his wool suit, accepted the offer as though it were a blessing sent from heaven.

Before they departed, Santiago took the man home. There, drinking *aguardiente* and with Prudencia sitting on his lap, Santiago did not speak to the man about the ruins but instead described in minute detail the path of a lightning bolt which, after striking the very top of the main temple, had given Santiago new belief in God. When Santiago fell asleep on the table and the stench of days' worth of alcohol haloed his head, Prudencia pronounced, first shyly and then with uncommon firmness, the few words in French that remained in her memory from the days in which she had enjoyed its poetry. The amazement on the painter's red face was sincere. During the months it took to plan his excursion to the Americas, he had prepared himself for the discomforts of the voyage, the days in the burning Mexican sun, the lack of decent food, the primitivism of the inhabitants of the region, but his imagination had never foreseen that in Papantla he would come across a dark-skinned woman, caring for the three children she had borne, reciting French verse from memory.

"*Vous êtes la plus belle des Indiennes,*" he told her. And Prudencia, who took pride in having not a drop of indigenous blood in her veins, accepted the compliment with a new toast of aguardiente. At that moment she decided that both she and her children would accompany Santiago and the explorer into the jungle.

The journey was long and uncomfortable. The idea of taking his wife earned Santiago a new reputation: madman. Matilda, riding a horse for the first time, followed the pilgrims closely. The wonderment produced in her as she approached the ruins, which she unconsciously associated with the grandmother she had never known, took all hunger from her, and even thirst. When she spied the Pyramid of the Niches in the distance, Matilda, like her father years before, did not know what to do.

Some of the photographs that Joaquín sees in the National Library were taken in 1897 by the German photographer Teobert Maler. Others, most of them, come from the series that Hugo Breheme, another German, took in 1905. Joaquín, as though he were Matilda's very eyes, directs her attention to the details. More than on the monumental general panorama, he wants her to focus on the bas-reliefs swarming with a constant repetition of intertwined figures, the decoration of layered friezes of stone mosaic. When she is unsure what to look at, Joaquín points out the cornices, the little cells, the play of volumes that produces a dizzying dance of chiaroscuro in movement. "Look at the age of the stones, Matilda. Look at that carved column dedicated to the god of death. Examine the Xicalcoliuhqui frieze on the pyramid's central stairway. Did you know that only the Totonacas gave their idols smiles?"

Matilda climbed the stairs clutching her father's hand, her heartbeat rising to the very surface of her skin, in perspiration. When they reached the top, Santiago, still panting with the effort, fell to his knees on the stones, made the sign of the cross over his face, and forgetting the presence of his daughter, uncorked another bottle of chuchiqui. At that instant, clouds covered the face of the sun. Around them, spreading across the mountains and the basins, the jungle held its secrets. The silence, for one moment, was absolute. Matilda now loved her father hopelessly. When she finally stepped closer to him, trying to decipher the words that were issuing from his constantly moving lips, she realized that he was not saying anything.

As Joaquín wished, Matilda descended the steps alone, still filled with energy, curiosity. Leaving the steps behind, she inspected each and every one of the niches. Carefully, as though she were attempting to trace the stones into her skin, she ran her hands over the reliefs and intertwined figures. Hours later, with the light of sunset at her back, Matilda returned to the base of the pyramid. The surprise at not seeing her mother filled her with fear. Her imagination pictured gigantic unknown animals devouring her mother's body; then, immaterial gods, filled with fury, dragging her by the hair to the Gulf. Solitude, for the first time, took her hand and set a new expression of feigned bravery on her face. No one would see her cry. She bit her lips. Holding back her tears, she ran as fast as she could through the earthen corridors, climbed up onto the rocks, and when she could run no farther, remained there, looking out over the valley.

"I am alone," she told herself. The discovery made her think about the possibility of the existence of the devil. Then, without realizing it, she began to cry.

A shadow descends out of the distance and offers her, through time, an immaculate white handkerchief. J.B.

The echo of her mother's laughter immediately dispelled her loneliness. Following the sound on tiptoe, she came to the base of the column of death, where Prudencia and the French painter were amusing themselves in the hieroglyphics of their own caresses. Seized with happiness, careless of the consequences, Matilda rushed toward them. Her mother greeted her with outstretched arms, and then enveloped her in them. In her right ear, the slow beating of her mother's heart restored her calm.

Over the years, in the letters that crossed the Atlantic, from Paris to Calle Cinco de Mayo in the village of Papantla, the French painter always referred to Tajín with the solemnity of a revelation. Prudencia, who had made the mistake of falling in love at first sight with a Parisian dandy, never had the courage to answer his missives. The memory of that journey to Tajín finally faded into the hallucinations produced by the countless glasses of chuchiqui. Prudencia's body, however, took its placid place among the French painter's fondest memories. Her smiling face, the strange fragrance of her skin became the best metaphor for his days as an explorer in Mexico. Prudencia Lomas de Burgos. Even when he had forgotten her face, all it took was her name to soften the sharp edges of his old age.

There are other memories. Images of wild, unbridled happiness. Laughter whose echoes still make time's skin tingle. Days of carnival. Shrimp tamales with pumpkin and *atole morado*. *Tocotines*, the dances that the ancient ones had once danced. Confetti wars. Men flying like birds and landing in a rush in the open space before the church. Moors and Spaniards dancing to the rhythm of a drum and flute, in simulated combat. Who will win? Matilda describes the topography of Papantla as the surface of a wrinkled piece of paper. Her house is a niche for songbirds. The sky at night, a piece of black velvet punctured with the luminous holes of stars. *My father. Did I tell you about my father when he started believing in God again?*

Santiago Burgos disappeared two days before the spring equinox of 1900. The last time Prudencia saw him he was dressed in white and in a palm sling across his chest he carried two or three vanilla pods and two bottles of chuchiqui. The smile on his face was that of the man she had always known: honest, open, unworried. The first day of his absence she asked after him in the usual cantina and although she uncovered no clue to his whereabouts, she returned home without too much concern. Bad news, she was convinced, always traveled fast. The second day she washed and spruced up her children to attend the celebration in the center of Papantla. Before leaving the house, still thinking of Santiago, she took a little sip from his bottle of aguardiente. She, like Matilda, loved him hopelessly. Outside, the sky was implacably blue. When they came to the town plaza, the men had already planted the trunk of a tree in a six-foot hole they had dug in the grass in front of the church two days earlier. The priest had sprinkled holy water and then, amidst clouds of incense, praying and chanting, they had carried the trunk on their shoulders through the entire village. In the hole they threw aguardiente, flowers, incense, and even one or two chickens. Matilda witnessed the preparations with the indifference of a person accustomed to the spring ritual. After standing for a while on the tip of the tree, four birdmen, tied by their feet, would descend, spiraling slowly downward, until they came to earth once more. Each man represented one of the compass points, and the thirteen circles they made about the tree trunk represented the fifty-two years of the new solar period. The fifth man, meanwhile, played music and danced up above, and only at the end of the ceremony would he arch his body and look up at the sun at its zenith. But this time the birdmen were on no more than their fifth circuit of the trunk when Matilda, alerted by a cry of incredulity from Prudencia, raised her face to try to make out the reason for her mother's surprise. On the top of the trunk, a hundred feet above their heads, Santiago Burgos was dancing like a madman and, at the top of his lungs, screaming out the imprecations that his family and the community had heard from him only at the most fevered moments of his dipsomania. The government was to blame for everything. The vanilla processing plant was to blame for everything. Greed was to blame for everything. The oil companies were to blame for everything. "All of you are to blame for the death of vanilla!" His cries faded away into the air, and below, almost unable to hear him, the pleased and grateful crowd observed this unexpected spectacle. There were cheers. There were huzzahs. There were exclamations of chaotic delight. And there was the occasional pious matron who, realizing the danger Santiago was in, began to nervously finger the beads of her rosary. Prudencia clenched her jaw and Matilda, for the first time, felt pride in seeing her father so far above the things of the world.

Hours later, when forced by the people's pleas and threats Santiago finally came down, Prudencia realized that she had lost all hope of seeing him grow old. He was in a deplorable state. A three-day beard covered his shaken face. Stains of vomit and urine made dry lakebeds on his clothes. The smell of his body was not vanilla but rather perdition. A mob of the curious, attracted by his uninterrupted imprecations against the earthly and divine power that lay upon Papantla, surrounded him in the plaza. Professor Donato Márquez Azuara discreetly approached Prudencia and suggested that she take him back home at once.

"If alcoholic congestion doesn't kill him, the police will," he told her. Santiago was now talking about the ever more aggressive incursions of the Oil Fields Company into the lands surrounding the village. Then, half falling, half stumbling, Santiago informed them, still at the top of his lungs, of the process by which one hundred thirty thousand hectares of land had been concentrated into seven haciendas. Manuel Zorrilla had seized what had once been the property of Guadalupe Victoria and now owned thirty-three thousand hectares in Larios and Malpica; Pedro Tremari was the owner of twenty thousand hectares in Palma Sola, San Miguel, and San Lorenzo; Ana María Villegas Ocampo held twenty-four thousand in San Miguel del Rincón. His list of complaints grew. "All of you are to blame for the death of vanilla!" he screamed. The school teacher, Márquez, who a few years later, under the auspices of the Papanteco Democratic Club, would become editor of the newspaper *El Tábano,* "the bug that bites the beasts," carried him away. But by then, Santiago was crying.

The moment he saw him, the town's doctor diagnosed *delirium tremens*. There was little to be done. The only thing left for Prudencia to do was patiently await God's mercy. And God, like few other times in Santiago's life, granted it. After midnight, Santiago's breathing became peaceful once again. What Matilda remembers of this night is its smell. The sweet odor of vanilla mixed with the bitter stench of death. What she wants to forget is that on that night began the story of her future.

Knowing the precarious financial situation of the Burgoses, and Prudencia's own taste for alcohol, Márquez recommended that she find a home for her children.

"Who are the godparents of the older girl?"

"She doesn't have any," Prudencia replied. After thinking a while, she recalled the name of Santiago's brother, who lived, so far as she knew, in Mexico City. She had never met him and in fact had not the slightest idea of his fate, but once more placing her faith in God's mercy, she authorized don Donato to investigate and make contacts. While Santiago, jobless, struggled to recover, telegrams with terse questions and monosyllabic replies crisscrossed the western Sierra Madre. In August, all was prepared for Matilda to leave Papantla forever. Thanks to the schoolteacher's generosity, Prudencia was able to buy her a white dress, a new pair of shoes, and two pieces of white ribbon to tie up her braids. A rectangular suitcase held her apron, a skirt and a calico blouse, her rebozo, a little leather-bound Bible, and three pods of vanilla—a gift from Guerrero, the owner of the processing plant. Now enclosed forever in the hermetic world into which he allowed no one ever again to enter, Santiago watched her leave with no expression whatever on his face. Prudencia Lomas blessed her in silence. Matilda left her

house holding schoolteacher Márquez's hand; he took her on
horseback to Tezuitlán, and there he took the train with her
to the village of Oriental. From there, Matilda took the train
to Mexico City alone, her only company her suitcase and her
confusion.

"Have you ever seen men fly like birds, Joaquín?"

The librarian's voice startled him; he jumped.
"It's almost closing time, don Joaquín," she had said.
Nowhere but in the reading room of the Central Library did
anyone refer to him with the respectful "don." But from
seeing him wandering through the stacks, spending days
thumbing through old newspapers, the woman must think he
is a teacher at the National University or one of those
eccentric intellectuals that publish poems. If she only knew.
At seven in the evening, as he has done for the last four
days, Joaquín closes his notebook and tucks his pencil into
the right pocket of his shirt. Then, after putting his papers in
a dark leather portfolio, he bids good night to the librarian
with a slight inclination of his head. With his characteristic
slow pace, he walks out the front door and enters the tumult
of the city. Instead of taking the streetcar to Mixcoac, he
walks to the Colonia Santa María la Ribera. Today he pays
no attention to the sky. Today he moves forward with his eyes
fixed on the creases in the leather of his shoes. The city does
not exist. The noise and speed do not exist. In the chaos of
his head the only thing that exists is Matilda Burgos' solitude.
His right hand toys with the house key in his pants pocket.
He has not stood before the house since 1908, but were it not
for the voracity of the ivy and other vines and the unruly
growth of the plants in the garden, he would have to say that
behind the iron fence the facade, resembling a Swiss chalet,
looked just the same. Inside, however, everything is different.
The furniture is covered with white sheets, as though

underneath were corpses. Humidity has left iodine-colored stains on the wallpaper. The chandeliers have no bulbs in them. The dust on the piano has formed itself into immemorial maps, dunes, precipices. Since the death of his parents the house has been home only to ghosts without voice or desire. This is his inheritance: a house of the dead. The place is a minefield, a desolate, sterile plain on which armies have played at war. Will the buried bombs explode? Will grass ever grow here again? There was a war, yes, a long and bloody war. The house is just one of its many casualties. As he did when he was a boy, Joaquín gropes his way through the darkness of the hallways. He climbs the stairs and goes to what was once his room. A leak in the roof has made a lake on the mattress of what was once his bed. The noise of rats scurrying frantically back and forth forces him to watch where he steps. Even though he is not able to explore the house in Santa María de la Ribera carefully, Joaquín knows that it looks very much like the room he inhabits in La Castañeda. The smell of salt air and decay are the same. "I told you, papa, when all is said and done we're going to turn out to be just alike." The light of a firefly makes him blink. Joaquín could take possession of this place anytime, if he wanted to. The moment, according to the stipulations of his father's will, that a doctor certifies there is no morphine in his veins. The minute he marries, makes up his mind to put his faith in the future of the country, and throws his old Eastman in the trash.

Just as he has done for the last three days, Joaquín strikes a match and with it lights a cigarette and the oil lamp. Then, without pulling the sheets off the sofa in his bedroom, he sits down on the soft cushions of a train. The train's whistle hurts him, somewhere in his body. It is about to depart. Everything is about to happen. Joaquín knows, now, that he will never be able to return.

The girl at his side rests her forehead on the window, but even though her eyes are open she sees nothing. Her hands lie motionless in her lap, her ankles are crossed; there is no flirtatiousness in her. The photograph of a statue. Watching her out of the corner of his eye as he pretends to read the newspaper, Joaquín feels his heart leap up. The way she looks out at the world, the fragrance of her braids bring the word "nature" to his mind. There is something about her, something uncertain yet as sharp as the glint of a straight razor as its blade is tested by a murderer in the moonlight. Her will is stronger than her fear, stronger than her age. No one will see her cry. She bites her lip. Joaquín, suddenly, wants with all his heart for her to do it. Joaquín wants Matilda to rest. "Everything will turn out all right, don't worry." Wants Matilda to turn docile and flexible, like a vine. "I will care for you every day. I will protect you from the world." Joaquín wants to become a pichoco tree, a mother-of-cocoa, so that Matilda's vine can twine around his trunk and not wither away and die. "I will watch over you as you sleep. I will help you escape." Joaquín wants to be vanilla's husband.

In the station, standing beside her suitcase, Matilda sees the blurry reflection of her body in the polished mosaic walls. Her childhood is still marked by the cyclic, predictable rhythms of Papantla: the planting and harvest of the vanilla, the Holy Week celebrations, the light meal before six, the drunken binges of Santiago Burgos. Now, at fifteen, arriving in the city, she thinks for the first time about the future. Images of antediluvian animals and magnificent monsters pass through her head, followed by laughter and faces hidden behind mysterious veils. She has no money, and besides her uncle, who has the same name as her grandfather, she knows no one. She is intrigued by the rushing people all around her. Death. Life. The stories she has grown up with never mentioned lovers' assignations, employees' punctuality, ambition's intense haste.

"Matilda?" The person who hesitantly pronounces her name wears his hair slicked down with brilliantine, eyeglasses perched before his eyes. When she nods, the man gives her his hand to take, smiles. A wristwatch gleams on his left wrist.

"I am Marcos Burgos. Your uncle."

"Pleased to meet you." The words belong to schoolteacher Márquez. "That's what you say in the city when you meet someone for the first time," he had told her. She looks the man straight in the eyes. Her will is stronger than her fear, and it always will be.

"We're going to get along just fine. You'll see. We're going to make a good citizen out of you."

As they walk away, Joaquín observes them from a distance—behind the crowd of people, behind everything. Then, he waves goodbye. Every time he is near her, his heart leaps up.

The house is in darkness. On the ceiling of Joaquín's adolescence there are now, besides the old rivers and trees, people, faces. Their stories intertwine and unravel, flow together and, sometimes, crash at high speed. It is a web. One thing leads to another and yet there is no order whatsoever. There are no rules. The voices come from every direction, everywhere, and then disperse in all directions— inward, into his head, but also outward, outside, toward the city in which people are discussing the possibility of a worldwide recession, the end of the world, the advent of a new era, a different one. If there is one thing Joaquín has learned, it is that a mystery shields itself with another mystery. If there is one thing that Joaquín has learned, it is that great catastrophes always, always take place in people's bodies. He will survive.

"Every time I see you my heart leaps up." In his dream he is standing before her, inside the Insane Asylum, and they are accompanied by the noises of her ward. His heart leaps up. Joaquín is describing a mere biological fact, an organic function, a reflex. Now, returning from the confusion and bewilderment—the daze—of five days in the city, his weariness is so patent that he cannot even consider the possibility of seducing her.

"Really?"

Unable to speak, but with his eyes suddenly playful, light, Joaquín nods.

"Yes, really."

The madhouse—he had not realized this until now—is his sanctuary. The city's perpetual war fences it in completely.

3

Everything is language

They called me mad, and I called them mad,
and damn them, they outvoted me.

Nathaniel Lee

Inside. Commotion in the hallways. Smell of cigarettes. Screams and cries of desolation. Eduardo Oligochea puts a bookmark between the pages of his book before leaving the infirmary. The voices are coming from Imelda Salazar's cell. What are they saying? "The world is coming to an end. The plates are piled high with pride." Her eyes, like the wool shawl that she covers her head with, are black. She is down on her knees and, with her arms open like a cross, she is looking up toward the imaginary window through which sunlight pours. There is terror and hope in her eyes, determination in the words she speaks into the ears of the air. A sudden smell of sulfur makes her vomit and shiver uncontrollably. Her body bends into incredible angles, her empty hands reach out to clutch an invisible throat. The impurity comes from without. It is a plague of ants, the cavalry of an army in full attack, a storm. Satan. He hides in objects and once inside, tries to remain unseen as he destroys humility. The cadence of her prayers increases, the tone of her voice becomes shrill and piercing, like the calls of dolphins in the sea. The voices—what are the voices saying? "Everything must be destroyed. The plates, the clothes, the shoes—everything that is made in the factories of the devil." The beast's red skin approaches like a tide, and covers everything. He is here. *"Vade retro!"* The woman's eyes have rolled back in their sockets, the index fingers of her hands

73

are held across one another to make a cross. A viscous thread of drool hangs from the corner of her mouth. "Thou shalt have no power over me." Her groans travel through the halls and cells, and as though this space were a balloon filled with helium, it shatters into a thousand pieces. Everything is under the power of evil. Everything. There shall be no salvation.

By the time it is all over, night has fallen. Imelda lies in a pool of urine and tears. The only thing she can touch without feeling herself contaminated by the impurity of society is the mange-eaten skin of the dog that licks the scratches on her hands and brings her peace.

No. 6140
Imelda Salazar. Tlaltenango, Zacatecas, 1896.
Single. Teacher. Catholic. Weak constitution.
Precocious development in childhood, incomplete in puberty. Father, alcoholic; no knowledge of the rest of the family. 6 months ago, the patient came from Zacatecas to attend the College of the Holy Sacrament, intending to enter orders. She remained there 10 days, and was then sent to San Luis de la Paz, to another monastery administered by the College de la Paz, a filial monastery where she remained for 5 months. Due to her ailments she was not accepted, and was sent back to Zacatecas. At the first stop, she got off the train and returned to San Luis, and was then sent to Mexico City, now with several manifestations of extravagant behavior. Here, several doctors examined the patient and found her mentally alienated. Suffers from prolonged episodes, bouts of chaotic praying. Says that the dishes on which her food is served contain spiritual impurities (pride) and a marked smell of sulfur, which makes her throw the food on the floor, where she licks up the food in the company of a dog so that the dog will confer humility on her and thus counteract the impurities. Wishes to be called "Chucha." In her room,

has been startled by the "horrible vision of a diabolic
monster" which she scares away with a Magnificat.
Patient replies to the interrogatory correctly, has good
memory and orientation. Is only incoherent and delirious
when religious matters are mentioned. Remains apart
from the other inmates and refuses to take medications.
Weekly baths. Eats and sleeps well.

*Dementia with psychasthenia. Religious delirium.
Oligophrenia.*

Inside. Shyness. Voices barely audible. Eyes looking down
at the floor. "Do you know why you are here?" "*Yes.*"
Lucrecia Diez de Sollano de Sanciprián's black hair cascades
down her back like a waterfall. The corners of her shawl
twisted around her fingers. Immobility. When she raises her
eyes one senses defiance in them. A sword. As a well-
brought-up lady, she speaks only when she is spoken to; she
asks no questions, adds no unnecessary information. Behind
his desk, Eduardo shifts uneasily in his chair. Her voice
disorients him; her face brings to mind the image of a hawk
flying in concentric circles over its victim. The outward
tranquility of her body seems to be hung on a fragile
scaffolding. Her answers to Eduardo's first questions are
immediate, quick. Projectiles. It is clear that she has answered
them before, many times. Eduardo can find no way to control
that haste, that rapidity, that attitude of a woman with a long
list of things to do before the day is done. "You want me to
tell you the story of my life, do you not?" A vertical crease
appears between his eyebrows. "Yes." The sarcasm of her
smile disarms him. He is all ears.

No. 1482
Lucrecia Diez de Sollano de Sanciprián.
San Miguel de Allende, Guanajuato, 1874.
Married. Housewife. Catholic. Weak constitution.

"My parents. Don Vicente Diez de Sollano died at the

age of 60. My mother was Piedad de la Peza y Poza. The man, my father, was a very healthy man; he died of acute capillary bronchitis. My mother, who possessed a nervous constitution and very strong will, never had attacks. She died of an influenza that affected her intestine and heart.

"The man, my husband married at twenty. In the ten years that I lived with him I gave birth to eight children, of whom four are still living. Two strangled on the umbilical cord and two were stillborn from albuminuria. I also had four miscarriages because of the hard life I led with the man, my husband.

"I was born in 1874. At the age of six I had scarlet fever, but then I grew up healthy and robust. At fifteen my menses came on with no other disturbance or disorder. At that age I became nervous, and I married at seventeen. I was cured of my nerves and so I lived for four years in this good health, until, because of emotional distress and physical loss, when I was nursing a little girl who was very strong and healthy, the nervous state came on me again, from February to August. Afterward, I was perfectly fine, and five years later I had puerperal fever, which left me in an acute nervous state, which I cured myself of with distractions and travel. At that time, I took alcohol by prescription, and one might say that I perhaps unconsciously abused it.

"In 1899 I had an attack of dipsomania and Dr. Liceaga convinced me to admit myself to Quinta de Tlalpan. It was then that this attack due to the change of life, both emotionally and physically, occurred, because the man, my husband brought a woman home with him and since that time I have not lived on intimate terms with him and the emptiness of my soul has been reflected in my physical part. I did not drink another drop of wine until 1901, when I drank for

several days, entered La Canoa, where I remained for
three months, got out, and was perfectly fine until 1906,
when, because of having had excessive work and
emotional distress and dreadful quarrels, I drank again
for some days. Then I went back to La Canoa, and I got
out and I had an intestinal fever and I went back to La
Canoa where I remained for one year and five months. I
got out, and I was perfectly fine until September 29,
1911, when I went out and drank cognac and pulque and
went on drinking for a day and a half, noting that I am
not in the habit of drinking only one glass of wine or
pulque or beer, with the exception of when my nervous
state and emotional distress, physical losses and, above
all, the emptiness of soul reflected in my physical part,
as I have said, lead me to drink the first glass, for when
I am in full possession of my reason I bear terrible
things and do not lose the control I must have, given my
difficult situation and my exaggerated way of feeling
and being, and my passions overflow and I become
excited."

These notes were written by the patient herself, and
in them one can see her clear talent and facility for
putting into writing everything she thinks and feels.
Aside from her attacks of dipsomania, which she has
always tried to explain as the result of her emotional
distress, she seems to be normal; but closer analysis
reveals that there is a chronic state of manic excitement
more psychic than physical. There is not a day that she
does not have new ideas, new plans to carry out,
whether it be getting out of the asylum or following a
particular line of conduct with her husband, whom she
considers responsible for everything that happens to
her. Every day there is a new ailment of some kind, be
it a pain throughout an arm or leg lasting for a few
minutes or a spell of vertigo that makes her nauseated
all day, or a pain in her left ovary, or intermittent

hypersensitivity to smells, or, generally, a sense of anguish and malaise because she does not see her children or because she thinks that she will never leave this hospital. These symptoms suggest general hysteria, which is undoubtedly present, but on the other hand is the result of her chronic psychic excitement. The patient has been observed to write poetry for days on end, or letters to all her relatives, telling of the dolorous situation she is in; at other times, she devotes herself with true concentration to manual work, but in none of this is there continuity, or method. What gives her great enthusiasm today, tomorrow will disgust her. The patient realizes quite well what her character is, and attempts to correct it; she compares herself to "a spirited horse you have to ride with spurs" and is very difficult to break or to stop once it begins to gallop.

After careful examination, nothing found but a pain located in the left lower abdomen, near the left ovary, which inclines our diagnosis toward hysteria. Her sensitivity to touch and pain is somewhat exaggerated, as are her tendon reflexes. Aside from this, however, there are no abnormalities, no trace of alcohol poisoning. In conclusion, I will note that the patient eats and sleeps well, and that she is generally constipated. The patient's memory, both retrospective and prospective, is remarkable.

Dipsomania. Background of emotional insanity. Pensioner.

Inside. Files on the desk. Telegrams inquiring into the health of certain pensioners. Death certificates. Police reports from the sixth precinct. Eduardo Oligochea's hands lie inert on the stacks of papers. Behind his spectacles, his gaze vacant. The confusion and dullness of mind caused by all these case histories make certain winter afternoons unbearable. In December, everything is gray outside, inside. Sometimes, when he allows himself to be overcome by desolation and forgets his books, he doubts whether he will be able to find the correct names for each ailment. Sometimes, when he is weary of crossing out the old diagnoses at the bottom of the patient interrogatories, he wonders what hand will in turn scratch out his notations in the future. Sometimes the black sadness of a pair of eyes makes him think about his own "I." Eduardo Oligochea. Son of Jerónimo and Fuensanta, brother of Casimiro, Julieta, and Ramón. Resident of a bachelor's room in San Ildefonso in which there is no space for memories. Observer. Lover of the words that name things so that they can be seen from a distance and not touched. A studious, hard-working boy, at the head of his class in primary school. At thirteen, tormented by the fear of God. Medical student with government scholarship and ambition. The voices come in through every chink in his body and there they stay, inside, running through his veins, digging into the marrow of his bones. And then the images. Half-dressed women sniffing around the patios. Men with eyes bulging out of their sockets with terror. People reduced to skin and bones, like statues in the museum of the hanged. Sometimes the death toll makes him dizzy. Sometimes he can bear no more. To forget it all, he thinks about a blue sea, about the future, dressed in black and decorated with medals of honor, that awaits him on the other side of the ocean. He sees his name printed in gold letters on the first pages of books bound in leather. He sees Cecilia's white hands touching his forehead, embracing him, leaving her fragrance of gardenias. He sees the hesitant legs of their firstborn taking his first steps in the bowels of a distant country. And then he sees the hands of their second child. The Oligochea-Villalpando family. Then he laughs; he always ends by laughing at himself when he is alone and no one is watching and nothing that he does makes any sense.

Taking advantage of the shipment of five demented
persons which the governor of the Northern District of
Baja California sends via me to the General Asylum for
the Insane in this capital, I persuaded the Davis family
to give their consent to admit Santiago of the same last
name, who is completely alienated due to alcohol and
marijuana and is a true burden, bother, and mortification
to his poor family, which does not have the where-
withal to care for him in the manner his condition
requires, with the added circumstance that neither here
nor in the region nearer to them is there any
establishment suitable for his confinement.

Before being transferred to the new facilities of the General
Asylum for the Insane in 1910, the demented occupied a
privileged place in the bustling center of the city. The women,
in the Divino Salvador, and the men, in San Hipólito, were
often able to escape their confinement and walk the public
streets, where the cloud of their mental instability was easily
concealed amidst the comings and goings of the bustling
thoroughfare. Sometimes, overcome by the life they found
outside the hospital, they would return voluntarily, crying as
they sat on the edge of the fountains in the central garden.
Most of the time they would be led back by a policeman.
Those who managed to remain outside would take up their
posts at the doors of churches, begging for alms, or would
carry bales of sugar in the marketplaces in exchange for a
few tortillas, a couple of centavos, until death came upon
them as they lay on the sidewalks, in the dark alleyways of
Barrio de La Bolsa, or at the entrance of some pulquería.
Their skeletal, battered bodies, tattooed by the half-moons
of infected scars, shrouded in the stench of months-long-
accumulating filth, filled with words about to be spoken and
forever mute, found their final repose only on the aseptic
slabs of the morgue—as solitary and anonymous in death as
they had been in life. When the 848 mad men and women

were transported across the city and for the first time entered the buildings constructed on the former hacienda in Mixcoac, the possibility of visiting the outside world became remote. The confinement, this time, was real.

Inside. Their screams and moans, their letters, their eccentricities, and their filthiness no longer ravage the normal days of the new century, and only from time to time do they ruffle the peace of the nurses, the discipline of the supervisors, and the unshakable rationality of the doctors and residents. Their chaotic words, interrupted by stuttering or unwearying and ceaseless hallucinatory ravings, do, however, call up the beast of doubt inside his head. What if the outside world were actually ruled by the devil? And what if Sr. Sanciprián were really trying to confine his wife and her "exaggerated manner of feeling" only so that he could live in peace with his new lover? And what if Santiago Davis were right, and the future did not exist, and the country were on the verge of going straight to hell? Sometimes, on certain winter nights, the impassive life of the inmates can drive Eduardo Oligochea out of his mind. Sometimes his own uncertainty is so dark that all he can think about is the momentary pleasure of smoking a cigarette.

Under a moonless sky, where the cold prevails, the madhouse is as small and as hermetic as the inside of a nutshell. Eduardo walks down its hallways and gravel paths guided solely by memory, without need of lanterns or lamps. Then, as he does during the first hours of the morning, he makes a circuit of the wards, trying not to make any noise. There are women sleeping together, holding each other in the narrow space of the mattresses with the peaceful expression of those who have finally found an oasis. There are men lying on the floor like a rope with no knots in it, a sheet. The catatonics stare at the beams in the ceiling. Some melancholics are so weak and dispirited that only with difficulty can they make the effort to close their eyes and sleep. The furious, aided by chloroform and sedatives, win their own battles on the plains of dreams, and at least for a few hours can remove the helmet of their violence. There is whispering. Prayers that will not end with the light of day. Sentinels posted on the corners of deliriums, preparing themselves for evil's ever-punctual visitation. The walls are stained and smudged by the passage of nocturnal souls in purgatory, by the iodine ghosts of circular time. Fluttering rapidly just under the ceilings, the prophecies of the end of the world fly above the impassive heads of the inmates like an owl. There is never peace. A cigarette, Eduardo wishes with all his soul for a puff off a cigarette. In the pensioners' ward, lit by the flame of a candle, a law student searches among the bruises on his right forearm for a vein to put the needle in and feel the surge of morphine. His concentration is so complete that he does not distinguish the footsteps of the resident from among the formless noises of the night. After looking at his arm for a few minutes, he finally finds it. It is just the tiniest green-blue line, thin and fragile-looking, that crosses his inner arm. While the plunger inside the glass syringe slowly pushes the liquid into his body, the relief makes him raise his face to the immensity of the void, and he unexpectedly meets Dr. Oligochea's inexpressive eyes. The boy smiles, without interrupting what he is doing. When the operation is done, he rolls down his shirt sleeves.

"Everybody breaks the rules, doctor, everybody," he says, while he pulls on his socks and ties his shoes as though he were getting all dressed up for a graduation party. Eduardo has no desire to argue; he simply observes him indifferently. Addiction. Morphine. Fifty centigrams a day. Recently, the asylum has been overrun by a new type of madmen. These are not the starving campesinos whose visions of Indians shooting arrows down from among the clouds, at the right hand of God, make them feel part of an invincible army, or the unemployed day-laborers attacked by spells cast by inhuman forces which end up stealing their will and their reason, or the young women who want to be nuns, caught in the inextricable nets of the devil, or the girls from the provinces whose poverty, combined with their absolute lack of moral compass, has led them to the progressive paralysis inherent to the last stages of syphilis. The addicts are a group apart. They are generally, though not always, clerks, pharmacists, law students, medical students. People like him. People whose eyes he can look into without commiseration. Young men in coats, ties, and felt hats brought in by fathers or guardians who want to see them cured of the vice and cynicism of drugs.

"My poor boy no longer believes in anything, doctor," they would say sadly, shaking their heads. "He has no fear even of God."

Opium. Cocaine. Marijuana. Morphine. The boys always find a way to get them. That is the only thing they miss or ask for from outside.

"I am not one of those that think they're cows." The sudden loquacity puts Eduardo on the defensive. "I'm a flower."

The joke makes them both laugh. Then, closely following the boy and Imelda Solorzano's dog, Eduardo leaves the ward. The smell of marijuana drifts on the cold night air.

"Want one?" The filters of three cigarettes protrude from the pack. They are English.

They are at one end of the asylum, next to the cement walls that serve in spring as support to fragrant climbing roses. Eduardo takes one of the cigarettes and, his hands perfectly steady, lights a match. The light, from a distance, appears that of a firefly lost in the heart of winter.

"My father says that now the war is over, things are going to change." The murmur emerges at top speed out of the fragile cloister of the morphine. "The poor man thinks that the country is destined to find its due grandeur at last. 'Grandeur.' Have you heard that word? Everyone is using it nowadays. Nobody uses the needle but everyone seems to be delirious, have you noticed? I don't believe it. I don't even

believe the war is over. All a person has to do is open his eyes
to see the sharp claws and white fangs, still thirsty for blood."

The resident listens to the boy in silence, puffing on his
cigarette. He has the anger of youth on his lips. The
stubbornness. Now, after the chats with the photographer,
Eduardo has learned to recognize the voices of morphine.
He can hear them. He plunges into them, like a bucket into a
forgotten well, and comes out again surprised to have found
cool water. He rides their tail as though they were kites, and
from within them he sees the enormous distance that
separates them from the outside world. Then, he enters his
own jungle. He thinks about Mercedes, not about Cecilia.
And then about Joaquín. If this boy were not eighteen, twenty,
but instead forty-nine, he would know what they all know:
the war is never over. The siege of reality is ongoing. In life
there is pain, and beyond that, the kingdom of death. If the
boy were forty-nine years old he would know that, out of
decorum, certain truths are left unspoken, hidden away inside
one's veins so one can bear the passing of days. If he were
not eighteen, the novice morphine-addict would have to know
that lack of faith is not a continent only recently discovered
by the naive sailors of the twentieth century.

"Are you listening to me?" he asks.

"No. What were you saying?"

"I was saying that I do not believe in the boredom of the
future, that this. . . " he gestures at the needle-marks hidden
under the sleeves of his shirt, "is the only thing that can save
me from the absurd dreams of generals and presidents. I was
saying that people like you, doctor, are going to drive this
country straight to ruin."

In the night, only slight creaking.

Inside. Uncontrollable slaps. Loud curses that rip throats and
cartilage. The noise of skirts ripped apart by teeth. Bodies
wrestling. When the male nurses manage to set Roma

Camarena before the camera lens, the ends of her straight hair turn up and her face presents a smile tinged with sarcasm. In her round blue eyes there is a glint of victory, a personal triumph. After the flash, the wariness and twitching fear return. Taking advantage of the nurses' momentary distraction, the woman takes off running around the trunks of the chestnut trees. Sometimes it seems that she is playing hide-and-seek, happy. Sometimes she seems to be no more than seven years old. Her feet barely touch the dry grass. "My husband. It's all the fault of that pig of a husband of mine." The straitjacket restrains the movements of her upper body, but not of her head. "What did your husband do?" "He cheated on me. The wretch. The pig." Eduardo, trying to dodge the foul-smelling spray of her saliva, steps back. Three feet. Six feet. He is taking notes. "Yes, I can read and write. He likes whores, you know? The son of his bitch mother can only do it with whores." Unable to move her arms, the woman contents herself with launching spit and curses all around her. Her agitation smells of corn bread, of sweat diluted in orange-water, of a woman in heat. On her reddened skin there is neither peace nor repentance, just the throes of an anger that comes from inside, from her belly and even farther down. As the rage runs through her body, it leaves marks of fire; the veins in her neck are thick cords knotted with anger that escapes, later, in the tears that accompany the onset of wild, discordant laughter. "My parents? Whores drive him crazy. Everybody likes wallowing in pigsties." With one question and another, the resident manages to fill out the information that he has not yet obtained. Before retiring, he thinks he sees a playful wink from the woman's left eye. "You want to stick it to me, don't you, you little blondie?" Then, his disquiet reflected in the pallidness of his lips, he goes to his office, rolls a sheet of paper into the typewriter, and prepares to formulate his report. There are days when what is least interesting to him are the details of the private lives of the inmates. There are days like today, far removed from the world, when he would give anything for a chat, a human conversation. There are days when he almost misses Joaquín Buitrago.

No. 1473
Roma Camarena. Uriangato, Guanajuato, 1867.
Married. Housewife. Catholic. Average constitution. Can read and write.

Inmate is, according to her account, sick with jealousy because her husband has betrayed her many times. When she was admitted to the ward she was in a state of intense physical and psychic excitation. She could not keep still for a moment; she would move in all directions, run, dance, skip, jump. Night and day she would sing, often going almost instantly from happy to sad or from good humor to implacable rage. Her delirium was polymorphous, the clearest idea being that her husband had cheated on her and that she, in turn, had had her revenge by betraying him. Her delirium was characterized by association of ideas. She could not fix her attention for very long periods of time; her judgment and reasoning were not normal. It would appear that she was going to pursue a clear train of thought when another idea, different from the matter being thought about or discussed, would intervene, leading to terrible confusion. She exhibited auditory and visual hallucinations; her language was crude; her affective faculty was impaired to nonexistent. It was necessary to be constantly on the alert with her, for as soon as she saw persons of the opposite sex she would become extremely excited.

She remained in this condition for two months, after which time she has begun to show some improvement. She sleeps well; her physical and psychic excitation have diminished so greatly that it could be said that they no longer exist. She still has, however, great resentment against her husband, whom she cannot forgive for the offenses that, according to her, he has committed against her.

Intermittent madness. Violent jealousy. Manic onsets. Free and indigent.

Inside. There are words for which Eduardo Oligochea has a special predilection. The adjective "implacable," for example; the syllables of the word "delirium," pronounced one after another, which remind him of the artificial pearls of a necklace. He also likes the accent on the *e* in the adjective "hebephrenic," the rounded sobriety of the word "etiology." There are certain terms, on the other hand, that make him smile with an arrogance, a contemptuousness, that is hard to conceal: the diagnoses of "imbecility," "masturbatory psychosis," "fright," "reasoned madness." Every time he finds one of them at the bottom of the interrogatory, he puts question marks in the margin, and after discarding them, he adds a new term with his fountain pen. *Drug addiction, hysteria, schizophrenia.* These are the new names for those who have lost the desire to live. One of Dr. Oligochea's weaknesses is order. Both on his desk and in his head, things and words move to methodical rhythms; they follow patterns that are strict though haloed with harmony. Even when Eduardo Oligochea walks aimlessly through the city or inside the asylum, his steps give the impression that he knows exactly where he is going. The same can be said of his ideas.

The files. There are many cases of epilepsy, alcoholism, and neurosyphilis; their indisputable biological etiology leaves no doubt of the diagnosis. But there are other cases, many more, whose anomalous, often unique symptoms lead one into the temptation of new classifications and the scientific lucubrations of experts. In the hands of Dr. Oligochea, conditions described as onsets of moral insanity in perverted fin-de-siècle women or disobedient adolescent females are transformed, depending on the severity of the symptoms, into cases of hysteria or incipient schizophrenia, which in turn belong, along with various species of delirium, neurosis, and psychosis, to the plethora of illnesses of the constitution. In clear contrast to drug addiction and problems relating to menstruation, which are acquired mental ailments. Within the new categories, mental retardation and so-called idiocy fall under the heading of developmental or evolutionary mental illnesses. The incomprehensible logorrhea of patients over fifty becomes senile dementia, a clear example of the regressive or involutionary mental illnesses. The four large groups within which Eduardo fits his patients correspond to the Levi-Valensi system of classification, but he also has others that are still under debate. There is as yet little agreement. Since 1917, while others were arguing the feasibility of the new constitution and the rampant danger of the recent family-relations law making divorce in the country legal and thereby endangering the very foundation of the family, a mysterious group of doctors was meeting outside the usual large public forums, hoping to bring order to the language of psychiatry.

Dr. Agustín Torres, director of the Insane Asylum, had accepted the classification formulated in 1909 by the German psychiatrist Emil Kraepelin, in which mental illnesses are linked to precise physical injuries and not to ailments associated with that concept called "the soul." But despite recognizing the great advances in the formulation of a scientific etiology, Torres always favored the Tanzi system, because Tanzi included a greater diversity of ailments. After reading the arguments very carefully, and weighing the pros and cons of the various classificatory schemes, Eduardo has shown a certain predilection for the verbal scales of Levi-Valensi. There is something about the way he creates categories and subcategories that parallels Eduardo's own mental architecture. The symmetry, perhaps. The clarity.

The uniformity of criteria proposed by the classifications makes him breathe with relief. Eduardo can spend hours checking data without tiring. He opens books and notebooks filled with notes taken in class and then reviews the descriptions in the files. Everything is language. The teachers with whom he began to explore the labyrinth of the mind speak one language, and the patients confined within the walls of La Castañeda speak another. His job is to translate them, in order to find the invisible bridges that lead from one language to another, and cross them. The process is not only slow but also dangerous. There are areas of quicksand into which one can sink almost without a trace, slippery areas where one can lose one's footing, fall, and crack one's skull. In order to live inside hour after hour, five days a week, Eduardo Oligochea must learn to avoid the whirlwind of words, their shifting ground, their grasshopper-like leaps from leaf to leaf of reality. A hand is a hand. A syringe is a syringe. Tautology is the queen of his heart, the only monarch.

The few moments in which the resident falls on his face with language are when he is alone, in dreams, and more recently in the company of Joaquín Buitrago. On those occasions, his lack of knowledge of the new terrain and his consequent lack of caution help him to avoid accidents, fractures, but also fill him with dread and anguish. The dream that disturbs him the most has to do with wrong or misused words. Hardly has he closed his eyes when Mercedes' broad smile splits the darkness in two.

"I'm your man," she says after making love for the first time. "You're my woman, Eduardo."

Later, after a silence as sharp and white as light, Cecilia's face looks at him out of the mirror as she slowly brushes her long ash-colored hair.

"I am what you will never be, Eduardo," she says to him. The cadence of her voice, however, is not that of Mexico City; it is a coastal accent. It is then that Eduardo realizes that under the second woman hides the same painful promise as the first. When he wakes up, his head still spinning from the torpor of sleep, he rushes out of his room and, outside, turns his face up to the sky.

"I never wanted to be like you, Mercedes." The whisper is spoken to the clouds.

"You're wrong about that, too, Eduardo."

In order to describe Mercedes in his heart, he always uses his favorite words. The word "implacable" as a noun, for example.

Inside. Unhurried voices. Echoes from the past. Mariano García's hands, dark brown, callused, lie in his lap. Under his straw hat his hair is speckled with gray.

"From the land I have nothing, doctor, but from up above I have the sun, the wind, I have everything, just as He gave it to me. You don't believe me either, right, doctor?" Eduardo sits silently. "That's why I came here the first time, that is my story, the story nobody believes. Down there where I was working there was a war, and I was chased by the Villistas and the Carrancistas for no reason. There are Christians and Mexicans, both, riding around and shooting fire, and yesterday I saw an Arab, up in the air, in space, up where the bombs fly. I haven't been killed with those bullets because my Father is eternal and he told me that I, too, shall be eternal." He stops talking for a moment, cups his hand behind his ear, and listens intently to the whistling, howling wind of late January. "There is a wind, like being shot with a hypodermic syringe, that cleans everything, even a woman's body."

"What wind?"

"The wind that cleans everything."

Eduardo takes notes as the old man's voice moves on. His presence, so tiny on the chair, so ascetic, is filled with fragility and cracks. From time to time, while the old man

---

pronounces his sentences as though pulling a flower apart, petal by petal, Eduardo can hear the sand of his bones crumbling onto the floor and then fluttering chaotically in the noisy skeins of the wind. There is something in his voice, in the way his shoulders are stooped, that reminds Eduardo of his own grandfather. If they were not sitting here in the asylum, the old man's stories could pass for a conversation between old men inventing the past while the children gather around a fire.

"I am fifty-three years old now, and my Father tells me that I have been incarnating this earthly body for fifteen. My Father has also told me that a year from now I will take a woman, body to body, so now I console myself as Joseph consoled himself."

"How long has your heavenly Father been speaking to you?"

"Since He has used the cinematographer. But it is God the Father that speaks to me."

"Does he tell you anything else?"

"You won't believe me." He hesitates. "It's horrible."

"I'm all ears."

"He says that death will go on spreading across the plains and that there will be blood in plazas and gardens. He says that that money you have in your pocket is going to be worth less and less, and then nothing. He says that the city will grow so much that there won't be space for it on the earth. He says that the Indians playing around up there in space will come down one day, on the first day of the year, and bring the wind that cleans everything."

"But we all know that, don Mariano."

"It's that my Father talks to other people, too. Even to you, doctor. Have you heard him?"

"And when is all this going to happen?"

"Just before the world ends, doctor."

91

No. 6002

Mariano Garcia. Polotitlán, Mexico, 1857.

Tinsmith. Married. Catholic. Robust constitution. Normal development during childhood.

The person who brought the patient to the asylum says that that morning in Amecameca the patient balled his fist and hit General Tejeda. The patient does not believe he is ill. He says he converses with the King of Heaven and only takes orders from Him (which is why he will not allow himself to be examined), and that he needs to be released immediately. When he speaks with God he kneels. Delusions of grandeur, contradictory and incoherent hallucinations. His memory is abnormal; affectivity apparently diminished. When he speaks, his lips and eyelids quiver.

Progressive general paralysis.

Following orders from the supervisor, Mariano Garcia's room was searched. Four boxes of different sizes were found, containing, among other things, two large razors, approximately 50 used Gillette razor blades, a chisel, a large pair of tinsnips, a hammer, and a large number of iron bars of different sizes. The male nurse was asked why the patient had been allowed to have those iron bars and a room to himself, to which he replied that since he had only been working on the ward for a few days, he had not had time to notice what that room contained, and also that the patient, so far as he knew, had not received any treatment in the last two years. In view of this information, the patient was sent for and he said that he had been in the asylum for 12 years, that he had been brought in because he was a beggar, that he was not mad, but he had been kept in the neurosyphilis ward. He also said that since he had not felt that he was sick, he had not allowed himself to

be treated in any way and that he had collected the
iron bars little by little. Since the supervisor considered
what García said to be abnormal, he asked the doctor on
duty, Dr. Eduardo Oligochea, to perform a summary
examination in order to determine whether the patient
had any mental perturbation or disorder that would
justify his continued confinement. Dr. Oligochea stated
in writing that "the patient was in condition to return to
his family and society, and therefore I advise that he be
released." With the foregoing report, our finding is that
this individual has been held in this hospital for a long
period without justification. The case is considered
closed. [Signed.]

Inside. Eduardo's mind. After a period of rapid development
in the late nineteenth century, psychiatry went largely
disregarded by Mexican specialists until the late 1920s. They
had been distracted by the war, the lack of water, peace, food.
While the generals rehearsed new strategies for eliminating
the enemy, and the victors tried out new allegories in their
exercise of power, madness was as unnoticed as a beggar in
the center of a burning city. Later, when the time came to
think once again about the future of the country, about the
education and formation of new citizens, the insane and
homeless returned without any difficulty whatever to
classrooms and the chambers of political and intellectual
discussion. The image of their distorted faces, the smell of
their dirty clothes, and the abysmal conditions of their lives
became the topic of pleasant conversation among laypeople
and specialists alike. The mere mention of the future of the
city, the future of the country, cast over their blank
imaginations the shadows of the sick and ragged. The danger
these people presented to social order produced shivers of
terror and pleasure simultaneously. The terror of being
menaced and the pleasure of knowing that one was different

from them. Eduardo Oligochea, however, avoided talking about his patients. His silence stemmed not from the discretion expected of doctors, but rather from a sort of academic pride that prevented him from cheapening the knowledge he had acquired through long years of study, introducing it into the sort of inconsequential conversations that he often referred to as "lavatory gossip." The only occasions on which he allowed himself to discuss with others the ailments of the inmates in his care at the asylum was in academic forums, in a written presentation before an audience knowledgeable in the subject. Until he met Matilda Burgos, Eduardo had rarely discussed, much less shown, the content of his files. Until he met Joaquín, that is.

No. 6353

Matilda Burgos Lomas. Papantla, Veracruz, 1885.
No profession. Single. Catholic. Average constitution.
Precocious development during childhood. Father
alcoholic, mother murdered. Syphilitic ulcers. Running
sores. Blisters on the lower lip. Etherism. Wasserman
test negative.

The inmate is sarcastic and crude. She speaks too
much. She gives incoherent and interminable speeches
about her past. She describes herself as a beautiful, well
brought up woman, the queen of certain bordellos and
countless orgies. She says she worked as an artist in the
Fábregas Theater and in the Bonesi Opera. She suffers
from an eccentric imagination and has a clear tendency
to invent stories, which she never tires of telling. She
goes from one subject to another without pause.
Proclivity for using erudite terms, to which she attempts
to give another meaning. She explains her confinement
here as a consequence of the revenge of a group of
soldiers who came up to her in the street and demanded
sexual favors. Because of the hatred she has for soldiers,

she refused, and they had her sent to jail. Logorrhea.
Displays excessive mobility. Diminished affection.
Anomaly in her moral sense.

Moral insanity. Free and indigent. Nonviolent, first section.

"I thought you had left us, don Joaquín. What have you been doing?" The reserved, light tone of voice barely hides his sincere curiosity. There is a world someplace in the city, far from the asylum, that Eduardo knows nothing about. A private world that belongs only to Joaquín Buitrago. Confessions are never exhaustive, never completed. In the edifices of language there are always unlighted corridors, unforeseen stairways, cellars hidden behind locked doors whose keys slipped through the hole in the pocket of their only owner, the sovereign king of meanings. But there, sitting with Joaquín once more before him, puzzled and in pain at the same time, Eduardo realizes for the first time that those secret places are not hidden, like bulky objects under a shawl, but rather exposed to the world, protected only by their transparency. Joaquín had not hidden anything from him, but Eduardo had not yet known how to see.

"Personal matters, Eduardo, nothing important." After hesitating for a few moments the photographer decides to stand before his interlocutor. "But now I'm back."

Silence. Immobility. *Personal matters.* The two men are face to face, the unending noise of the mad enveloping them without touching them. *Nothing important.* Eduardo sinks into the wordless space where the words are; he is drowning. He does not know what to say. He wants to know. He thinks he has the right to know, but while he gradually convinces himself that Joaquín will not say anything else, his puzzlement and confusion grow; he has the sense that he has been mocked. Who is this man now?

"Matilda is still telling the same old stories," he murmurs

almost offhandedly, searching for the tone he used in their former complicity. Joaquín looks at him, his eyes dull, and then, without replying, turns his eyes toward one corner of the room. He lights a cigarette. He looks at him again. A shadow of dislike crosses his face.

"Perhaps they are the only stories that you know how to hear, Eduardo."

At 10:00 in the morning, inside the asylum, the photographer's words emerge into the air with the arrogance of bullets.

"The only thing I know how to hear?" The question exits his heart through his arteries and returns with the flow from his veins. Despite his outward tranquility, parts of his body shiver uncontrollably and without pause. The emotions which until now he has managed to keep neatly in order on the shelves in his head begin to grow restless. The sound of a bottle breaking. He feels rage. He wants to hear an explanation.

"What are you talking about, Buitrago? Have you not read her file? Look. Syphilitic ulcers. Running sores. Blisters on her lower lip. Ether inhalation. And have you not noticed her logorrhea? That is her story. The only story. The true story, not some romantic treacle, Joaquín. It's not that I don't know how to listen; it's that you're hearing voices that don't exist."

"The Wasserman test was negative."

"Of course. But all Matilda's symptoms indicate dementia. The logorrhea. The excitation and the nervous tics. The excessive and exaggerated mobility. The anomaly in her moral sense. Don't tell me that you think her stories are true. A woman like that working in the Fábregas Theater, in the Bonesi Opera? No. Impossible. What are you talking about, Buitrago?"

"Nothing, Eduardo. Really, I'm not talking about anything." Before turning his back to him, still indecisively, Joaquín adds: "Like all of them."

The sound of his shoes on the tile floors is lost in the noises of the asylum. On his back, as stooped as that of an old man's, there is some invisible burden, a mythological animal that clings to his neck and whispers secrets in his ear. Eduardo watches him walk away like a man watching a ship on the high seas. Then, still motionless, from his lighthouse, he sees the outstretched hands of Matilda Burgos when she spies the billowing sails of Joaquín Buitrago. The meeting of the two figures makes Eduardo shiver. Inside, in his cartilage and his organs, in the mass of heartbeats and fluids, under his fingernails, in the roots of his hair, Eduardo feels the spasm of incredulity and irritation that always sends him back to the stability of books. A hand is a hand. A desk is a desk. An empty room is an empty room. But Eduardo is thinking about another place.

"And you, doctor, what do you think about love stories?"

"What do you think about the future, doctor?"

"And you, Eduardo, do you know what the limits of pain are?"

At dawn, looking at the frost on the naked branches of the chestnut trees with a cup of steaming coffee in his hands, Eduardo Oligochea thinks that winter knows no compassion. The sunlight is still as timid as the color white. Across the frozen fields, covered with a transparent sheet of ice, there is a man walking barefoot. For a moment, Eduardo is about to run out to bring the inmate back into the ward. He knows that he can stop him, knows that he can lead him inside and prevent an attack of pneumonia. The man is most probably not able even to tell what time of day it is, what the temperature is, what the sensations of his body are, much less his emotions. But then, when the madman turns his face toward him, Eduardo cannot avoid being stunned. He is inside, trapped in his own deserted plane, in which the noise of the insane replaces the absence of his own voice. He is inside, hearing a murmur. "I am what you will never be able to be, Eduardo." A carriage without a driver, without reins, a man destined to die without leaving any traces, a man who has given in to oblivion or has voluntarily chosen rest. At that moment, with his eyes closed and the slightest of smiles on his lips, Eduardo Oligochea remembers that Sigmund Freud wrote *The Interpretation of Dreams* in exactly 1900.

4

Good manners

Without light, there is no possibility of hygiene, or public morality, or police, or security. Light frightens away the thief, moderates the intemperate, restrains the dissolute, and influences not only good appearances but also the development of good manners. The first thing the Creator did was light the chaos, and thereby give it order.

Rafael Arizpe
El alumbrado público ("Public Lighting"), *1900*

"You promised to tell me how a woman goes crazy, remember?"

"Yes." Matilda has answered him the same way more than once, but today, instead of offering him a forced and insincere smile, rolling her eyes, and toying with her hair, she stops and looks at him with no expression whatsoever on her face and her arms immobile at her sides. "But not now, tonight."

"Where?"

"There. Tonight." Her eyes turn first to Joaquín's room and then off into the windy horizon. Then there is only silence.

Waiting for her without being at all certain whether she will come, Joaquín observes his room apprehensively. As the minutes pass, then hours, the ceiling seems lower than usual, the angles of the corners widen and contract, creating asymmetrical shapes; the light given off by the oil lamp attenuates into darkness. The smell of the last days of winter fades into the air. Joaquín suddenly cannot breathe. He is sitting on the trunk that contains his treasures, little by little feeling the sensation that holds him to the floor and drives nails through the palms of his hands. It is hope. The fragility of hope, the forever imminent mockery of hope, the ever-punctual crucifixion of hope. From time to time, when he manages to forget about himself, Joaquín is certain that Matilda will come. Then, almost immediately, when a gust of air makes him tremble, he realizes that his skeleton is weak, that its wrapper of skin can do little to protect him against the icy weather of humanity. Joaquín cannot shelter any woman anymore. On the right wall of his room, the red dogs of melancholy are silent. A half-smoked cigarette hangs from his lips. In the smile that passes over his face there is no happiness, only pity. Joaquín is a man who knows weakness. *Matilda*. Her name flies in his mind like a moth around a flame. Light. Hope. Will it be worth the wait? He will wait.

When Matilda steps silently through his door, Joaquín immediately finds the reply. Yes. Somewhere in the world at that moment, there must be an animal leaping suddenly against the bars of its cage. Yes. Eager, once again caring nothing about the consequences, Joaquín lets her come in. It is impossible to see Matilda's eyes under the moonless, starless sky. It is impossible to approach her body. It is impossible to stop hearing her voice, suddenly as terse, odorless, and tasteless as water.

Mexico City. At first, she doesn't miss anything. The speed of events leaves her no time at all for nostalgia or home-sickness. The present becomes absolute. The past does not exist. Her days begin inside a large room with high ceilings and white walls; its smell of naphthalene and bleach suggest neatness, order. Matilda sleeps on a narrow iron bed and a mattress with cotton blankets. The only other objects in the room are the night table and the wardrobe in which she keeps her few personal possessions. An empty suitcase, a Bible with almost transparent pages, and three dry, odorless vanilla pods. There is a wooden crucifix above the head of the bed. Among all the novelties that fill her days, Matilda is especially fond of the green mosaics that cover the floor of her Tío Marcos' house. The first thing she does in the morning, the minute she wakes up, is put her bare feet on the smooth floor. The cold that stings her skin like long needles helps to remind her that her body no longer lives in Papantla. Here, for the first time, she has special clothes to sleep in at night, and as though every day were a holiday, she is made to wear shoes and tie white ribbons on her braids. Matilda, standing before the mirror, smiles. It is a smile of mistrust and amusement. So this is me. Before leaving her room she has to make the bed and be sure that everything is in its place, as neat and orderly as a museum. Then, seized with anxiety, she joins in the domestic habits of the Burgos family, her mind blank.

To reach the kitchen she has to go through the patio that separates her room from the main house. She walks carefully, trying to avoid slipping on the tiles wet from their morning washing. She still does not know the name of the birds that greet her from the seven cages hanging on the walls. Nor does she know the name of the white flowers on the bushes that mark the boundaries of the garden. She does, however, know by heart the name of the woman, her aunt, who is waiting for her in feverish activity at the kitchen's rectangular table. It is Tía Rosaura. The whiteness of her teeth is frightening. The loneliness of her eyes, surrounded by long black eyelashes, inspires something almost like pity in Matilda. Her copper-colored hair, gathered into a ponytail at the nape of her neck, makes Matilda think of a horse's mane. When she approaches her, watching her aunt's beautifully coordinated movements and the concentration on her face, Matilda is certain that she is a woman who does not know the pleasure of idleness. As soon as they see each other they exchange good mornings and, without pause, Rosaura motions toward the checked apron hanging on the clothes rack.

"You don't want to dirty your clothes, Matilda." They both smile.

The kitchen smells of orange juice and recently cut papaya, cantaloupe. Without waiting for orders, Matilda begins cutting the slices of fruit into small cubes, which her aunt serves up on big blue plates. They both work in silent synchronization, without looking at one another. Matilda and Rosaura do not ask each other questions about their pasts, their likes and dislikes, their chores. They treat each other with amiable caution, with the strategy of strangers who do not want to stop being strangers. Around them, going back and forth as busily as a little bee, the maid Jacinta cleans up after them. Besides the singing of the seven caged birds and the clacking of the knives on the wooden cutting boards, no sounds are to be heard in the house. Marcos and Rosaura Burgos have no children and when they sit, now, at the dining table, they exchange but few words. Some reference to the weather, a remark or two about the dangers of the city, how increasingly expensive everything is. Nothing more. Matilda's education begins in that way, in silence. There are the sounds of forks against the porcelain plates, burps screened behind white linen napkins, the discreet creaking of a chair. Without thinking about it, Matilda, with her hands under the tablecloth, begins to crack her knuckles. The endless boredom of breakfast makes her nervous. She has to wait. She has to behave herself. She cannot complain.

"The hands of a clock. Have you ever looked at them closely, Joaquín?"

Inside the Burgos house, time is measured by a clock with a copper pendulum. The clock strikes each time the big hand points up toward the ceiling and the little hand reaches one of the numbers on the clock's face, under the glass. There are twelve of them. Matilda soon realizes that the triangular slices that mark the hours on the long-case clock that dominates the parlor have specific, invariable names. A good citizen, a decent girl, a woman of good manners must begin by learning the exact name of the hours. There is the hour to rise, at five o'clock. The hour to bathe and dress and make the bed. The hour to make breakfast. The hour to sit at the table and wait for Tío Marcos to drink his orange juice, eat his fruit salad, and sip his steaming black coffee. The hour to clear the table, shake out the tablecloth, and put the chairs back in their places. The hour to take a basket and follow Tía Rosaura to the market. The hour to make lunch and wait for Tío Marcos to come back from his office at the hospital. The hour of the siesta. The hour to embroider tablecloths or mend skirts or socks beside her aunt, in silence. The hour to take lessons in citizenship and hygiene. The hour to learn the vowels. The hour to prepare dinner. The hour to pray. The hour to go to sleep. The hour to begin everything all over again, with no change whatsoever, in strict rhythm and order. Five o'clock in the morning. The hours. The repetition, at first, goes almost unnoticed. The order helps Matilda organize the vertigo caused by all the new things in her life in Mexico City. Then, as the days pass, chasing their tails yet never catching them, there suddenly appear the black seconds, the meaningless seconds in which the world disappears. The nameless seconds. Time goes from passing so quickly to not passing at all, and the air doesn't smell like anything. At those moments, the only thing Matilda has on her hands are ten knuckles. My bones. She caresses them. She cracks them. Only the sound of her bones cracking against each other has the power to assimilate, little by little, the syncopated rhythm of the city. Little by little. Reality.

"Where are you?" She still uses the formal *usted* with him.

"Here."

Joaquín Buitrago puts out his right hand and a crack of static electricity freezes it when it finds Matilda's hand in the darkness.

"Everything is a lie, Joaquín, you know?"

"Yes."

"Really, I don't remember anything," she murmurs. "Sometimes you go crazy from that, from not being able to remember, right?"

Yes, Joaquín answers, and as he does so he pulls his hand away. He knows very well. He knows very well what it is to have a lacuna in his head, under his skin, in the long marrow of all his bones. He knows about those solitary places where nothing has a name and the air is suddenly thin. He knows asphyxia. It has been twelve years now since he has been able to breathe.

This is the first night that Matilda, violating every rule of the institution, has slept in Joaquín's room. Lulled by her own words, Matilda has unintentionally left him alone again, abandoned on his narrow bed with his eyes open yet unable to say anything. He wonders whether she is dreaming. Are there dreams, he wonders, beyond reason? The woman is deeply asleep. Harried by insomnia, without a sorrow to his name, Joaquín sits on the side of the bed and watches her. It is hard to make out her face in the vast ocean of her hair. It is hard to imagine her body under the chaotic folds of her calico skirt, her feet in their black high-button shoes. The breath that rhythmically enters and leaves her half open mouth does not smell like vanilla; it does not smell like anything. Watching her sleep in the semidarkness, Joaquín can think only of the serenity of ropes, the disturbing immobility of daggers or pistols just before they find their mark. The sense of danger keeps him alert. A sudden wave of adrenaline forces him to stand up, light a cigarette, and pace nervously about the bed. It is 3:15 in the morning and there, in the trusting body of the woman, there is something throbbing blindly, without direction. The past. The future. He watches her. Few things have enthralled him as much as watching a woman sleep in peace.

"Any woman can make love, Joaquín. All it takes is two words, a little money, some promises, one or two lies. Those who can sleep beside a man who is awake, those are the ones that are hard to find, darling." It is the voice of Alberta, her sleepy yet always awake voice.

"Say the name of the street, Joaquín, and I will draw you a map of the city."

Matilda ventures out into the city's markets for the first time clutching Tía Rosaura's skirt. As soon as Tío Marcos rises from his chair and thanks them for the breakfast, before he leaves for his office, the women prepare for their daily trip to the market. Matilda awaits that moment with concealed eagerness. None of her movements or gestures as she picks up the plates, sets the chairs in their places around the table again, and smooths her blouse, give her away. No expression on her face betrays her. Once on the sidewalk, however, her eyes become eager. Darting here and there, with the voracity of the self-taught, her eyes open wide to capture everything. Every window, every cornice, every cloud, every color, every man and every woman that passes by her leave and indelible mark on her memory. "I remember everything, absolutely everything, Joaquín." Nothing escapes her, nothing. Matilda's sight at fifteen is absolute, and, like the present, total.

The days of February are scoured by incessant wind.

Joaquín no longer asks himself what he is looking for in Matilda Burgos. Now, the only thing that interests him is knowing with certainty what he has found in her. His few hours of sleep are light, spent hurriedly, as though he feared he was wasting time. There is urgency in the movements of his body, his reflexes. The moment he awakes, Joaquín puts his arm under his narrow bed, searching for the notebook with the thick black cover where night after night he transcribes some shadow of Matilda's life. Her mental state. Her condition. They are notes written rapidly, scribbled down without punctuation, staccato and disconnected phrases, fragments without apparent rhyme or reason that only he will be able to understand in the days and months to come. The shorthand of the emotions. The notes bring him back to life in the morning, give him a shake, a jolt that he believed was totally lost. In 1908, when Joaquín photographed Matilda for the first time, he never imagined that someday he would see her again; he never imagined that Matilda's life would one day be the key to his own. "What happened back then, Matilda? What happened to us?" Even his questions surprise him. Then, without pause, he gets up, plunges his face in the cold water of the washbowl, and, without drying off, steps outside his door so that he can feel the morning's cold wind. He is shivering. It's the plural: "What happened to us, Matilda?" The asylum is saturated with screams and cries, and none of them is the answer that he wants.

HYGIENE LESSONS BY MARCOS BURGOS

1. Wash your hands before and after eating, before and after using the toilet, before and after sleeping.
2. Remain constantly occupied in order to preserve mental hygiene. Idleness is the root of all evil.
3. Drink large amounts of boiled water in order to aid the digestion and prevent eventual dehydration. Do this especially in the dry months.

4. Avoid corsets and any tight clothing which may obstruct blood circulation.

5. Avoid using cosmetics and perfumes. Cosmetics harm the skin and perfumes cause neurasthenia and other nervous disorders.

6. Sleep a minimum of six and a maximum of eight hours per day.

7. Bathe three times a day during menstruation. In that time of the month, one must avoid any physical and intellectual effort which might cause dysfunction in the nervous system. This is especially recommended for young ladies whose delicate mental condition inclines them to outbursts and manias.

8. [The sentence that Matilda will never forget:] Decent women bathe every day before six o'clock in the morning, always.

When Marcos Burgos arrived in Mexico City, he kept his family name but rid himself of everything else. The process was almost immediate and also quite natural. When he learned to read and write, he had so ardently wished not to be what he was that, once he left Papantla, he dedicated himself with great diligence and discipline to creating himself anew. He did not invent a past for himself because he lacked the imagination for that, but he did decide to hide it with silence and, when silence was not enough, evasion. Using half-truths, he would mention, for example, that he was the son of Spanish immigrants whom fate and circumstances had forced to become vanilla processors in Veracruz. He never said, though, that his father had taken a local Indian woman for his wife, that he himself had grown up in a house with dirt floors, or that before coming to the capital he had worn shoes only on fiesta days. His seriousness, the cleanliness of his clothes, and, above all, the intelligence in his olive-colored eyes behind their gold-rimmed spectacles made his laconic stories credible. In his years as a student in the medical school, he was reputed to be a man of few words. Like all those who want to triumph over their past, Marcos developed a blind faith in the open possibilities of the future, the progress of the nation. To that project he devoted the greater part of his energies and almost all his writings. The title of the thesis with which he graduated from medical school in 1890 was "Mexico City Through the Lens of Hygiene." The relevance of the subject, the wealth of statistics, and his teachers' trust ensured that soon afterward, Marcos was offered a steady and quite honorable position in San Andrés Hospital.

Mexico City captivated him immediately. He liked the buildings and the palaces, the thin air of the high country, and the physical diversity of the pedestrians on the public streets. In the country's capital, too, Marcos could be anonymous. And at least at the beginning, being nameless was his most treasured blessing. In that situation, there was no ruin to hound him, no family whatsoever to make a claim on him. No one recognized him on the street; his face, alone amid the multitude, finally belonged to him alone. In that place, Marcos Burgos gave free rein to his will. The first thing he did was plan a schedule. From that moment on, he would rise at five in the morning and, after bathing, go over the day's lessons. He would drink coffee holding a book. At 6:30 he would leave for school and would not return until 2:30. Then, he would walk the seven blocks to the San Juan de Dios pharmacy, where he would put his medical knowledge to work dispensing elixirs, physics, and unguents in exact measurements. At 8:00 in the evening he would return to his boardinghouse for a hurried cup of chocolate and then cloister himself again in his room. Marcos would look up at the sky and enjoy the sunny days, but for the first four years he spent in the city he avoided, quite efficiently, any pleasure that might distract him from his objective, which was success. He did not visit parks or churches; he avoided going to the theater or meeting his fellow students in the fashionable watering-places; he did not write letters or pursue women, nor did he allow himself to be pursued by them. Thin, protected by faded wool sweaters in the winter or a simple cotton shirt in summer, with his ash-colored hair held in place with brilliantine and his gold-rimmed glasses, Marcos gave the appearance at eighteen of being a man of forty. People who saw him bury his head in the pages of borrowed books or pay excessive attention to his professors in class or the sick men and women in the pharmacy never recalled his poverty, only his determination. To describe Marcos Burgos, everyone used the future tense. It was always easier to guess where he was going than who he was.

Before having a name, Marcos was nobody. All the landlady of the boardinghouse where he rented a room wanted to know was that he was a student. The teachers paid attention only to his grades and the bright promise of his budding talent. His classmates' curiosity was satisfied with quick anecdotes and sudden changes of subject. Within a couple of months, Marcos had softened his coastal accent. After carefully observing his teachers, he imitated not just the way they dressed but also the weightlessness of their movements and their calm, peaceful gaze. Soon, everyone forgot that he was from Veracruz and at the same time agreed that he had a brilliant future. Marcos's presence, his self-assurance, commanded respect. Yet despite his affable, calm appearance, few approached him in order to cultivate his friendship. All around him there was a certain cautious distance, an invisible wall of self-sufficiency that separated him from others. Marcos postponed taking a wife. When that time came, just after completing his thesis, he rejected furtive affairs and mad passions. He met Rosaura in the home of one of his most beloved teachers. She was the youngest daughter. At twenty-four, and with very few physical attractions, she was, beyond the shadow of a doubt, an old maid. The sadness in her eyes was due to many years of waiting, and her voice clanked like the sound of empty clay water jugs bumping against one another. While her sisters and friends talked of engagements and planned their weddings, Rosaura would sit in one of the corners of her father's library reading Russian novels, and in the evenings, sitting at the piano, she would play classical melodies. When Marcos asked permission to court her, the entire family was grateful. Rosaura's peace, her good upbringing, and above all, her disinterest in sex laid the foundation for a marriage filled more with friendship than love. Marcos was always content with his choice.

At the hospital, he treated every sort of patient. His medical practice among the poor of the city confirmed his theories: all pathologies were directly related to a lack of hygiene, both mental and physical, in the lower classes. If the authorities truly believed in order and progress, he would often say, they would have to begin by making hygiene not a right but a civic duty. The design of the city would have to be in the hands of doctors, not architects with European, impractical ideas. Doctors, not politicians, would have to formulate strict urban legislation. His lectures in academic forums and the articles he published in the journal of the School of Medicine soon drew the attention of the bureaucrats in the Bureau of Public Health and Sanitation and, more especially, that of Eduardo Liceaga. All it took was one meeting, then letters of recommendation from three teachers, and in less than two months, in those final years of the nineteenth century, Marcos Burgos became a member of the Bureau.

The desperate telegrams from Donato Márquez arrived when he was inundated with work and at the pinnacle of his career. Marcos might have ignored all those messages from Papantla, but he did not. If he answered them, however, it was not out of nostalgia, and even less out of regret. What he thought one night when he found Rosaura alone, having nodded off in an armchair in the parlor with her sewing still in her hands, was that his wife needed company. Then, as the messages revealed his niece's terrible situation, he thought that with Matilda he could put all his theories into practice. In 1900, Marcos Burgos still believed that the civilizing influence of hygiene could transform even the most primitive of human beings into good citizens.

The book which had had the greatest influence on Marcos Burgos's social vision had been written by a friend of his, the attorney Julio Guerrero. Before its publication in 1901, Marcos had had numerous opportunities to read drafts of *The Genesis of Crime in Mexico: An Essay on Social Psychiatry*, which was finally published by Bouret Publishers, under the administration of Charles Bouret's widow. Like Marcos, Julio Guerrero believed that a series of cultural atavisms, or throwbacks, limited generally to the lower classes, were hindering the nation's progress and eventual glory. Their lack of hygiene and good work habits, the instability of their families, the promiscuity of their women, their excessive love of alcohol and other habit-forming substances, and even their custom of eating overly spicy food made this group a true threat to the country. The extreme, but natural, consequence of these atavisms could be seen in criminals, alcoholics, prostitutes, and the insane. Not so much a product of evolution, the general theory of which Charles Darwin had admirably put forth, these people constituted the most convincing proof of involution. The genetics of these individuals pointed not toward the future, but rather toward the past. All of them were savages—obtuse, stubborn, and only half-disguised primitives whose criminal instincts endangered their fellow citizens and, consequently, the entire nation. After long observation in the San Andrés Hospital, Marcos Burgos came to identify convincing signs of this biological tendency among his patients. In the battered and wounded bodies of accident victims, murderers, and thieves that came to be treated by him, there were recurrent stigmas: large jaws and ears, low foreheads, dark skin, small skulls with simple sutures, increased visual acuity and diminished sensitivity to pain. All his data confirmed the theory of criminal anthropology that had been coming into fashion since its formulator, the Italian Cesare Lombroso, first made it public in 1870. In fact, one of Marcos's numerous points of professional pride was that even before Lombroso had announced his theory at the Congress of Criminal Anthropology in 1886, he, Marcos, had already noted that in a large number of prostitutes in his care, there was a very great distance between the big toe and the other toes. The "prehensile foot," as it was known in zoological terms, was without a doubt a physical atavism which showed that its owner occupied a place closer to the apes than to evolved beings.

Julio Guerrero, however, was convinced that certain manipulations of the social environment might, if not erase, at least mitigate the malformations of biology. The economic strategy adopted by President Díaz was, to his mind, the one best suited to limit the dangerous influence of the atavistic multitude. Factories, he declared, would require and produce good citizens, responsible men able to support their families, good housewives, decent women. The only problem that had to be overcome was wages. So long as the average wage for a worker in Mexico City continued to be 37 centavos, the future would hang from a very thin thread. Enlightened, progressive, and pragmatic, Marcos Burgos also believed that so long as a bar of soap cost twenty-five percent of a worker's salary, the lower class's physical hygiene would not improve. Others, however, were neither so benevolent nor so optimistic. Journalist and poet Manuel Gutiérrez Nájera had other solutions in mind. "It is preferable," he wrote, "to see the corrupt succumb than to allow the good, the fit, to die. Criminals may be sick, but those who have contagious illnesses should be isolated. Those who may procreate sick children should be denied the pleasures of marriage and fatherhood or motherhood. Let us not put our lives in danger or support the extermination of the human race simply in order to protect the weak and the dangerous."

Both Marcos and Julio Guerrero read "Today's Plato," Gutiérrez Nájera's column in *El Universal*, with mistrust. First because of his incendiary language, which was more suitable to arrivistes than to a true scientist. Second because the poet, surely due to his own *maladie vitale,* neglected to provide the concrete evidence, statistics, and graphs that might validate his hypotheses. And third because of the irrational, and frankly impractical, consequences of his proposals. Although the doctors supported certain strategies of forced social isolation, they thought that if, rather than provide institutional methods for improving the deviant behavior of the coarse and unwashed, the society simply locked them all up, the entire country would have to become a jail. And there was no better place for breeding crime, promiscuity, and antisocial behavior than jails, prisons, and asylums. Punishment was important, confinement was important, but more important was correction. Julio Guerrero and Marcos Burgos, sipping their brandy, would discuss these and other writings in their libraries filled with evening light. In their view, the Bohemians, as they called poets, were as dangerous as the poor themselves. Lacking all ambition, living a life without fixed times or schedules, and ruled by a typically passionate temperament, these men did nothing but reproduce, and sometimes increase, the physical, mental, and emotional disorder of the lower classes, from which they had no doubt themselves come. The only difference was that they knew how to write, and that newspapers such as *El Universal* and *El Imparcial* had the questionable judgment to publish their writing. All the proof that was needed was one of those exaggerated poems filled with unwholesome passions and foreign influences. The solution to the social ills of the nation was unquestionably isolation, confinement. More and better jails, orphanages, insane asylums, and hospitals were unquestionably necessary in order to delimit the sphere of influence of society's sick and depraved. But that was only the beginning. Without the establishment of disciplined schools, hygiene programs, and job training, the reformation of society would be impossible.

"Correction, Julio, correction after punishment—that is the only way we shall ever transform this paralysis." At nightfall, when they said their farewells after editing documents and setting straight the world, the two friends were in the habit of giving each other a noisy embrace. The conviction that they held in their hands the means of creating a strong and civilized nation filled them with pride.

Marcos set about instructing and caring for his niece as though it were a professional as well as personal crusade. He labored with firmness, carefully avoiding pampering and sentimentalism. He labored untiringly, planning his strategies as though this were a war. Matilda soon became the very embodiment of the enemy who, more than defeated, had to be subjugated, convinced, domesticated, brought under the yoke of civilization. Like all the coarse and unwashed, Matilda's own genetic heritage worked against her, but at the dawn of the new century, Dr. Burgos was convinced that a proper environment, governed by discipline, hygiene, and education might at least soften, if not drastically change, the sharpest edges of her maligned nature. Guided by his own experience and taking himself as his example, Marcos believed he had found the secret for changing the destiny imposed by biology and with it, all reality. When he went to meet Matilda at the train station, he was planning to write an article presenting all the details of his feat. The slowness of the process and his own workload kept him from writing even the first sentence of his text.

"Did I tell you about my life among the doctors, Joaquín?"

Matilda met Columba Rivera one Friday, between the hour for siesta and the hour for darning socks. She remembers because that day, Tía Rosaura looked different. The loneliness in her eyes was the same, but the slight blush that had come to her cheeks gave her the appearance of a rose, something about to bloom or wither away. Matilda had never imagined that Tía Rosaura might be fragile. In the blue dress that she had arrived from Papantla in, the pearl-colored ribbons tying up her braids, Matilda stood ready to follow her aunt and uncle without even asking the reason for the sudden change in the daily schedule. Before leaving the house, just as he was putting on his hat before the mirror, Tío Marcos told her that they had found a job for her, something small. "Idleness is the root of all evil."

"It is a small thing, something that you can easily do during the day and that will allow you to come back here to sleep at night. In addition, you'll earn a little money."

Columba, like Tío Marcos, was a doctor. The second woman doctor in the country. An unmarried woman forty-three years old. She opened the door herself, and while she was hurriedly taking off her flowered apron she led them into the parlor where a pot of steaming chocolate and a plate of *pan dulce* awaited them on the parlor table. Columba's house was cold, and it was also dark. As soon as Matilda had taken a seat on the edge of one of the chairs, with her back straight and her ankles crossed, she took in every inch of Columba's body. Under the lace of her white blouse, buttoned perfectly up to the neck, could be made out two generous, flaccid breasts. Her white skin had the orange-amber patina of flower petals about to curl and wither. And her blond hair, salted with gray and caught up into a chignon at the nape of her neck, seemed dull and opaque. What most impressed Matilda was her face. First, the softness of her features and then, immediately, the contrast of the spectacles that covered her coffee-colored, almost green, and bulging eyes.

"Have you never seen a woman wearing eyeglasses?" Columba asked, half irritated, half amused.

"No," replied Matilda almost in a whisper, lowering her eyes.

While the others came to an agreement about her salary, her new responsibilities, and her new schedule as though she were not present, Matilda served the chocolate and passed around napkins just as she did at home, in the Burgos household. Columba praised her good manners. A half-hour later she herself led them through the corridors of the house in order to familiarize Matilda with her new environment and also calm any apprehension that her situation as a woman alone, without a husband, might cause Marcos Burgos. He had been very clear in that regard. If he allowed Matilda to work, it was not because the girl needed money; in that case he would have sent her to one of the cigar factories or dry goods stores downtown. What concerned him was that his niece acquire the discipline for work within a safe environment, without risks, in order so far as possible to reduce the effect of her deplorable genetic inheritance. Tío Marcos was convinced that besides hygiene, work was the most important civilizing agent, and that receiving a wage in exchange for services rendered, however symbolic that wage might be, fostered responsibility. Tío Marcos also believed that sending women to school was a waste of time and a bad investment, but that, out of respect for Columba, he did not say. Education not only crushed a woman's innate sense of abnegation and self-sacrifice, the best of the feminine virtues, but also produced legions of arrogant and useless females who, naturally, never found husbands. The most dreadful results, as could be seen in these very days, were those manlike women, those aberrations of nature who, mentally injured by their condition, insisted upon walking alone down the street and demanding their right to vote. Marcos Burgos was firmly convinced that the best that could happen to Matilda was learning to administer a house and acquiring a certain basic knowledge of firstaid by caring for a sick person. Columba sweetened the bargain, more to excuse the meagerness of the proposed salary than out of any desire of her own, with personal classes in grammar in the evening and, in addition, voice and piano lessons. At sixteen, never having visited the center of the city or its parks, Matilda became the housekeeper, maid, nurse, and companion of Dr. Columba Rivera.

Marcos Burgos, after a detailed inspection, approved of the house. The bedrooms were clean and orderly. The street door was tall and had good locks. The curtains that protected the interior from sunlight were also an obstacle to the lascivious eyes of vagabonds or coachman. Columba showed them the kitchen, the dining room, which boasted a long rectangular wooden table. They passed through the flowerless garden and then a room filled with books and then another, empty except for the piano. At last, they came to the bedroom where the patient lay, Columba's mother. Her mother had supported her throughout her studies and had been rendered paralyzed after a cerebral hemorrhage. Matilda's first reaction was fear. The old lady was asleep but her left eye was open, unseeing. Her thin gray hair barely covered the pinkish skin of her scalp. Her yellow skin, crisscrossed with wrinkles, seemed lifeless.

"Touch her," they told her.

Matilda slowly approached the sick woman's bed. Three steps, four. She hesitated. When she stood beside her, she had to force herself to put out her right hand and lay it on the old lady's left hand. At that moment, unexpectedly, the woman's bony fingers gripped her tightly. She tried to pull away but it was impossible. The chains of her destiny had just bound her forever. Matilda thought that it was the yoke of death, the stocks of misery.

"Look, Matilda," whispered Columba, "she likes you." The smile that covered her face was a smile of relief.

The years that Matilda worked for Columba and her mother flew past. "How do you measure time, Joaquín?" Almost without realizing it, Matilda learned to bathe the invalid, keep a home in perfect order, and haggle in the markets firmly but not without a touch of flirtatiousness. Her routine soon acquired the precision of a clock. Her face was transformed. The braids that had fallen over her shoulders since before she could remember gave way to a tight chignon at the base of her skull. Her hands learned to touch worldly possessions with no haste whatever, efficiently. The outbursts of happy sudden laughter were replaced by a sweet, domesticated, and invariable smile. Her body lost the ability to exude odors. Matilda forgot Papantla not out of an act of will but rather out of distraction. When Tío Marcos saw her eyes one winter morning in 1904, he was pleased with his work. The pupils that had once looked out with astonishment mixed with fear now moved cautiously, discreetly across the things of the world. It was then that he knew with certainty that science and discipline had once and for all defeated the alcoholic ghosts that had destroyed the lives of Santiago and Prudencia Burgos.

One spring night in 1905, those same eyes discovered the wounded body of Cástulo in the darkness of her room. The name alone makes her voice quiver. The name makes her voice fade away, little by little, into silence.

"Who is Cástulo, Matilda, who?"

"Cástulo Rodríguez is the scourge of the high and mighty, the wrath of the downtrodden. Me. You. Anyone."

It is 10:15. Matilda pushes the door of her room open with her knee and, at the same time, loosens the tight mass of her chignon. Often at this hour she goes over the imperfect tense, the future perfect, in her mind, or hums a piece by Mozart as she organizes her activities for the next day. She needs to buy rice, purchase more bandages and iodine in the pharmacy, change the dinner plates. When she is inside, as she turns the lock, she thinks about her good fortune, and at that moment, almost immediately, she becomes aware of the smell. It is a bittersweet smell that makes her nostrils flare and fills the room. Without moving, with no emotion whatsoever in her body, she fixes her eyes on the corners of the room and, after a few seconds, manages to make out a quivering form at the foot of her bed. In the darkness, the blood is even blacker, its odor even more penetrating. She should cry out, but she does not; she should run to the door and call for help but instead she approaches and brushes his forehead with the back of her hand. He has a fever. When the man finally opens his eyes, the light from his pupils illuminates the entire room. They show pleading, fear, exhaustion. But in the very center of the iris, there is temerity, daring, recklessness as well. Without a single word, the man puts out his arms and Matilda, bending over him, within his embrace, hears the beating of his heart without thinking of anything, without feeling. Tangled in his sweat-drenched hair there are pink peach-blossom petals. It is the beginning of spring and the man must have jumped the back wall to reach her room.

"This is not a maid's room..." It is the only thing the man manages to say before he falls unconscious.

"No," murmurs Matilda as her eyes take in the room, even though he can no longer hear her.

Just as she does with Columba's mother, Matilda lifts the man's body into the bed, skillfully removes his clothes, and with a cloth dipped in cold water cleans his arms, his underarms, his legs, his sex, his torso. His body is so thin that even in the darkness she can easily make out his ribs. When she turns him on his side to clean his back, she discovers the hole near the left shoulder blade through which the bittersweet blood of fear continues to well up. Without thinking, Matilda rushes to the kitchen and sterilizes two knives, then goes to the library to get an anatomy book. When she returns to the room, she lights the little oil lamp and puts a cloth wetted with chloroform over the man's nose and mouth. Closely following the instructions in the book, she makes a vertical incision over the wound, taking care not to perforate a lung. One inch, perhaps a little more. When the knife touches the metal of the bullet, she holds the wound open with her left hand and, with her right, extracts the bullet with a pair of tweezers. Then, with the same swiftness and firmness, she disinfects his wound with alcohol and, with strips torn from a white sheet, bandages it. It is not until she finishes, until she sees her apron covered with blood and the man's defenseless body lying on the bed, that she begins to cry. She does not know what she has done, she does not know where she has gotten the strength and the fearlessness; the only thing she understands, as an uncontrollable tremor shakes her body, is that the life of this man is in her hands.

The weeping, like all her movements during the operation, is not hers. It comes from somewhere else. There is a distance, a wide river between the weeping and herself, a river whose crystalline waters she cannot cross. Powerless in the face of the chaos of her sensations, Matilda sits quietly, watching him. Then, realizing that there is a naked man in her bed, she covers his body with blankets and begins to pray. Matilda Burgos has acted outside the law.

At dawn, when she gathers up the wounded man's clothing and begins to fold it, she discovers the note: "My name is Castulo Rodriguez and the government is to blame for what happens to me. I am the scurge of the high and mighty and the rath of the downtrodden. If you have the hart, join the struggle aginst dictatorship."

The misspellings make her smile. His name, too. Now more than ever, she is convinced that she did the right thing. Her Tío Marcos would never have given aid to a militant against the government, nor would Señora Columba. Medical science, after all, has its limits. Compassion should not be extended to just anyone. Before locking her room, Matilda touches his black hair and, as she does, his youth surprises her. Cástulo Rodríguez could not be more than eighteen. As she leaves, the first thing she notices in the gray March sky is a shapeless hole in the clouds through which she can see bright blue.

"Isn't it strange, Joaquín, that a person doesn't remember stretches of years and years and then can't forget the details of a single moment?"

Cástulo sleeps for hours, one day, two days, three. His rhythmic breathing is interrupted only from time to time by groans of pain, words broken or half-spoken. Shards of glass on the floor, echoes. Sometimes, when Matilda wipes off the sweat that the fever brings to his face, the boy looks as though he is about to smile. Matilda examines him closely in the darkness as though he were a thing, a possession. His body is as smooth as a newborn's. There is no hair on his chest, or arms, or legs. The pubic hair is downy, cottony, like angels' hair. There are angular scars on his knees and thighs, blue tattoos on the inside of his forearms. Two cats. His hands are disproportionately large, and they are as wrinkled and knotty as a wood floor mopped with water a thousand times. A raisin. Seeing his long arms, the firm muscles of his legs, it is easy to picture him escaping, running at full speed, leaping walls. No one would be able to catch him. Matilda cleans the wound twice a day and, to help the pain, injects him with small doses of morphine. She has learned all this during conversations with Tío Marcos and the distracted lessons given her by Columba. When the nights of fever give way to peaceful sleep, Matilda knows that Cástulo will survive. The only thing left for her to do now is wait.

Tía Rosaura had stopped inspecting her room sometime during the first year. The next four years of regular, predictable behavior bring no fear of sudden visits or unexpected intrusions by her aunt or uncle. Since Matilda has been earning a wage, she has chosen the fabric for her skirts, the quality of her shoes, her own bedtime. With Cástulo there, however, she takes additional precautions that no one notices. When she goes in or out she always locks the door. She does this to protect herself, but especially to protect him. There is something in the delicacy of his features, something in his pulse, something about that misspelled "hart" in his note that makes her trust him. Even without talking, even without knowing what crime or crimes he has committed, Matilda feels that she knows this boy better than she knows her Tío Marcos. His life is now in her hands. During the three days in which Cástulo's fate will be decided, Matilda walks through the hallways still feeling his embrace.

The embrace of Prudencia Lomas. Years before.

Matilda follows her usual routine, but the tension betrays her. In three days, she has more accidents than in the last five years. Two glasses broken in her aunt and uncle's house, the hem sewn crooked in Columba's silk skirt, a pan of water boiled dry on the stove. During these days, Matilda begins bumping into chairs, doors, windowsills. The landscape that had been so familiar, so eternal in her eyes, she now finds altered, skewed. Suddenly, there are corners she hadn't noticed before, spider webs, iodine-colored stains on the ceilings, cracked wineglasses. The afternoon she pauses to look at her face in the mirror, she realizes that she's trying to see reality through another person's eyes. "This is not a maid's room..." Cástulo's eyes are microscopes that enlarge the imperfections of the house, the imbalances of the entire city, injustice. Matilda, however, feels comfortable, relaxed with that vision. Her body does not have to keep its composure, her hands can fly. When she hears the sound of the third glass shattering at her feet, Matilda smiles without knowing why.

"You must be in love," murmurs Columba when she sees the yellow scorch mark of the iron on one of her white blouses. "Be careful, Matilda, that is the worst thing that can happen to woman."

Her voice, like Rosaura's, has the sound of hollow clay water jugs clinking against each other. For the first time, Matilda feels pity. So many years of study, so many books, and perhaps not a single embrace. Perhaps not a single heartbeat against her ear, transforming the rhythm of the world. Columba is not responsible for any of the lives she has saved. The prostitutes she treats at Morelos Hospital disgust her. When she examines their faces wasted by vice, when she spreads open their sexes infected with sores and chancres, the only thing that Columba can see is her fresh, perfect skin, the immaculate pink of her own sex. Dr. Rivera needs her patients as much as they need her care. Columba can only confirm the value of her own life by comparing it to the infection in other bodies. Syphilis always shows that she is right.

"You are a decent girl, Matilda. Do not forget that. The only thing that we women have is our good manners."

At night, leaning over Cástulo's defenseless body, Matilda whispers questions to him. "Where do you come from? Who is after you? What did you do, Cástulo?" She does this just to talk, without actually expecting any reply. In the novels that Matilda has read in Columba's house, the heroes are always men. Agile of mind and body, they overcome all obstacles to rescue the heroines at the last possible second. A speeding train. An old well disguised by dry leaves. The unbridled lust of a grandfather. Prison. Madness. Faced with Cástulo's frailty, Matilda is able to change the plot. In the hours of night that she spends at his side, her imagination glides through the air like a comet. She is unafraid. She will save him from all danger. She will discover the spell that holds him in thrall. She will capture and punish the enemy. Before stretching out on the floor beside his bed, before falling asleep, Matilda thinks that Columba was wrong, that they all are. Besides good manners, she has something more. Strength, for example. Intelligence enough to strike the fatal blow. Matilda clings to Cástulo like a detective who has accidentally come across irrefutable proof that an unjustly accused man is innocent. Cástulo presents the possibility for revenge.

On the third night, when Cástulo manages to raise his eyelids, albeit with difficulty, the light of his eyes illuminates the cloistered atmosphere.

"Thank you," he barely whispers. "Thank you for everything."

He gestures toward his bandages, the bed, the entire room. Matilda smiles, nods. Then, she hurries out of the room and comes back with a bowl of hot soup. The smell of chicken and cabbage and boiled carrots fills the air. Cástulo smiles, too. His best meal in years. His body is dreadfully weak. After the fourth spoonful, his eyes flutter closed once again. He has had enough.

"Tell Tina," he whispers, his voice quivering, using his last breath of air. "Tell her I'm all right."

"Where?"

"Mesones, number 35 Mesones."

After that, all is silence and darkness.

Joaquín catches his breath. There are events that he cannot forget, streets that will remain in his memory forever. Luminous punctures of light. Diamantina Vicario. A sudden attack of nerves makes him stutter. Number 35 Mesones. Without caring about Matilda's presence and without apology, Joaquín looks for his syringe and, with a band of rubber, ties his forearm. His skin is flaccid and yellow, and under it, an almost invisible spider web of discolored veins. His movements are hurried yet precise. Under the effect of the morphine, coincidences are less obvious, more distant. Coincidences. His calm after the injection is as unforeseen as his former disquiet. Fifty milligrams. Now squatting in the corner of his room, he makes her go on with the story of her life. He lights a cigarette. Inhales the smoke. He wants to hear the story. He wants to see them. Together. While Matilda's voice continues to fall, slow and impassive, into the darkened room, Joaquín does in fact manage to see them.

On the screen of his walls appears the image of Matilda walking from the Burgos house to Columba's house. It is a Saturday full of wind and dust. It is eight o'clock in the morning. The sky, in the distance, is blue. Matilda opens the front door again and steps out into the street with an empty basket on her arm. Without looking back, she walks toward the market, but she is going somewhere else. She has put on her navy-blue skirt, a white blouse, and over it, her best gray rebozo. Instead of her usual chignon, she has braided a pair of black braids that now fall over her breasts. When the whirlwinds of the street raise her skirt, her black high-button shoes can be seen. Matilda looks like a schoolteacher. She has never been on Calle Mesones and to find the house she is looking for she has to stop several times to ask directions. Past the hairdresser's. Next door to the pharmacist's. When she finally finds it, she knocks firmly on the door. She waits. The melody of a piano wafts through the window, under the door. It is Chopin's *Minute Waltz*. Joaquín recognizes it. When there is no response from within, she goes to the window and taps on the glass. Two, three times. From inside, a woman turns to look at her, her fingers still on the piano keys. She questions her with her eyes. Bother. Matilda raises her left hand, indicating that this is not some error, that she is looking specifically for her. The woman's only response is to signal Matilda to go back to the door.

"Are you Señorita Tina?" Matilda asks when the woman appears in the doorway. Diamantina Vicario nods silently, not certain whether to unlatch the door, not letting Matilda so much as peek inside.

"I have a message for you from Cástulo Rodríguez."

A smile, unpremeditated, comes across the woman's face. Her suspiciousness vanishes. Sticking her head out and looking up and down the street, recovering her composure a bit, she invites Matilda in.

"Did anyone follow you?" Matilda doesn't know what to answer.

The two women are on one side of a garden in which mint and epazote grow chaotically. Unmoving, unsure what must be said, the two women measure one another, trying to discover the limits of trust, the possibility of betrayal. Joaquín observes them through the magnifying glass of morphine. There is the long hair, streaked with gray, of his first woman. Lines of worry and quickly-consumed happiness cross her face. Joaquín puts out his hands, the tips of his fingers tenderly graze the lost skin. Behind her spectacles, her restless eyes, like those of a dark little mouse, have the same determination, the same intelligence that once half-frightened him. Diamantina must be almost forty. She has no children. Nothing around her. Before her, and as stunned as she is, is the other woman, whom Joaquín can recognize only by linking several almost ghostly pieces. The girl of twenty is still undecided whether to employ the measured formality of her house or the open amazement of her womanhood. Matilda still lacks personality. How many lives separate the two women? Joaquín is motionless, too, observing them with an idiotic, fixed smile.

"Cástulo is all right. He is in my house," she tells her tactfully. "He was injured but he is recovering."

"Who is looking after him?"

"I am."

Diamantina, giving a sigh of relief, thanks her. She invites her in for a cup of coffee and, at the same time, introduces herself. As Matilda follows her to the kitchen, she realizes that Diamantina has on overalls instead of a skirt. The wrinkles around her eyes are caused only by the way she laughs.

There are certain conversations that can only be held after a time of silence. On this March morning, Matilda and Diamantina look at each other, sometimes out of the corner of their eyes, with simultaneous interest and caution. What can be sensed in them is the warmth of their bodies and the intricate feminine gestures that illuminate the things about them. Complicity. Their hands have touched the same chocolate and tobacco skin, Cástulo's, and, when they touched his hair, they have both been surprised by his youth. The closeness they share there at the table is still untried, unproven. An undeveloped photograph. What Matilda thinks as she picks up her coffee cup and holds it just before her lips is that she would do almost anything to hear that piano music again, to see the woman bending over the keyboard as if the world had disappeared and there was no one but the air and herself on the face of the earth. What impresses her is the woman's absolute lack of vanity. Diamantina behaves as though her body were ethereal. Her careless clothes, her barely combed hair, the movements of her hands and legs shows that she has no intention of pleasing anyone or following the rules. Diamantina is the second woman in eyeglasses that Matilda has seen, but unlike Columba, she is a handsome woman, almost beautiful, graceful, full of life. The breeze comes through the open door and makes the women laugh, almost for no reason. For Diamantina, Matilda is a half-assembled jigsaw puzzle. What she does is hold back a few pieces so that later, when she has left, she can assemble them.

"Cástulo will be himself soon," she says as she is about to leave.

"I know, Matilda."

Joaquín captures that last image on his retina. Then he closes his eyes and feels the stabbing pain of the old, rusty pin under his fingernails. The sharp, fierce pain.

Two days later, Cástulo leaves. He does it the same way he came: at night, leaving in his wake the bittersweet smell of his blood. Without a word. Cástulo Rodríguez. Soon even his name will become a product of the imagination. After his departure, Matilda begins conscientiously and thoroughly cleaning her room. The novels she reads in Columba's house end differently. At the end, when everything is resolved, the hero and heroine become immortal in an embrace, a kiss. An orchestra playing in the background. Stars. While she washes down the walls and sloshes pails of cold water on the floor, Matilda scrutinizes every corner, to erase any trace of his presence. *Tabula rasa.* Then, she repeats his name over and over again, to leave it, too, clean, smooth, and soft. Finally, there is nothing, nothing: her reaction to Cástulo's absence confuses and bewilders her. With her emotions still in some disorder, and her hands red, she changes the sheets on the bed, shakes out the blankets, the pillows. It is then that she discovers the note. It is his handwriting. Everything Matilda knows about trust she learns in those days. "Thank you for all of this. You will soon here from us. C.R."

There are people who grow larger in their absence. In the months that follow his departure, Matilda never stops believing in Cástulo's promise. She knows very little about these people, almost nothing, but she nonetheless allows herself to take comfort in her memories. They must exist, they must be somewhere. There are rumors that even manage to penetrate the walls that protect the life of the Burgos family. Trains filled with slaves on their way to Valle Nacional. Hands, severed from Yaqui Indians, hanging from a pole in the possession of the governor of Sonora. Hospitals filled with putrefaction. Daily massacres. Matilda, however, continues with her day's routine. After the exhausting work of her two houses, the only thing that remains to her is the silent refuge of her room. Her solitude filled with ghosts, untold stories, words shattered like panes of glass. Some nights, she confuses the scratching of the opossums with Cástulo's footsteps. Some mornings, she is on the verge of going to find Señorita Tina again, but her duties will not allow it. The anxiety that comes over her in the markets, among the people of the street, fills her with fear. Some afternoons, the wind brings a nameless melody to her ears. In the city, suddenly she finds only questions.

Since the day she went to Calle Mesones, Matilda has fallen into the habit of taking little walks through the city when she goes out to shop for food. At first, her wanderings take her only two or three blocks, and even then she is apprehensive, looking from side to side, fearing that she will be recognized. Then, as she grows used to urban anonymity, her outings become somewhat more daring. Following in the footsteps of other people walking down the streets, Matilda visits the avenues near the Plaza Mayor. The distribution of the various trades, each in its own street, amazes her. There are blocks that sell only paper, others where black-suited professionals take photographs. There are shoemakers, little shops that tan leather, tailors with misspelled signs: *Tailor shop—Alteracions. Sutes and dresses made to order.* Matilda is especially drawn to the dry goods and fabric shops. Even without enough money to buy the fine cloth they sell, she steps into La Parisina just to touch the silks, run her hands over the rolls of merino wool, study the subtle transparency of the organzas, the laces. Sometimes, being careful not to be seen, she touches the fabric to her cheeks, her nose; the smell intoxicates her. The colors make her dream of an even brighter world. What she wants above all else in the world at those moments is a golden-yellow canopy over her bed. The same daydreams draw her to the windows of jewelry stores, and something similar happens to her when she spies the glistening white confections in the pastry shops. Her pleasure is not yet hierarchic. Even as she takes pleasure in her freedom, however, there is always a space in which she distractedly looks for Cástulo's face, Diamantina's blue overalls among the crowd.

Sometimes she kneels before the altars in the cathedral to pray for them. Wrapped in the fragrance of copal, with the flames of the candles reflected in her eyes, Matilda remembers their names in secret. Her expectancy grows, day by day. Sometimes she thinks that it is all futile, that the encounter will come at precisely the wrong time, when she has stopped waiting. Never, however, does she doubt that it will come. That certainty makes her whole life a series of signs given life only by her will. The pigeons send her messages as she walks. The clouds, the blue skies, certain children's shoes. Of all days, the event that she will never forget happens at the fountain in the Plaza Santo Domingo. Matilda sits down on the edge of the fountain, her upper body turned toward the right so that she can watch the water. White clouds floating in it. As she dreams about the ocean, the trembling silhouette of another face appears on the surface. It is the distorted face of an old woman, her hair cut short, her body half covered with a black shawl. Her eyes deep and black as tunnels. In that reflection, Matilda, without changing position, sees the lips move, and the arms.

"You are going to find everything you're looking for," she prophesies, "and then you're going to wind up like these."

When she ends, the two women smile as though they had both heard a joke. Matilda then turns to look at her. The old woman's toothless laughter fills her with fear. She has dirt crusted on her naked arms and suppurating sores on her ankles, which are only poorly covered by the tatters of a skirt. On the sling bag that crosses her chest there are food stains, and in the cotton sack hanging from her left shoulder Matilda sees pink porcelain heads and legs, skeins of artificial hair, broken dolls. The woman was no doubt referring to them. When Matilda hurries away from the old woman, there is no longer a smile on her face, only terror. The future, which she had never thought of, has brushed its hand across her head, and it makes her lose her way home.

Lost, trying to control her fear, "no one will see me cry, no one," Matilda turns corners without any idea of where she is. Then, without realizing, she is suddenly at the center of an irate, screaming crowd of people. In a tight group, some women rush nervously yet with determination into a pawnbroker's shop. Those waiting outside applaud and cheer. The commotion that makes Matilda's ears ring also, for some reason, brings her a bit of peace. Amidst the warmth of the bodies, Matilda feels not threatened but protected. Her face is like the others. Dark skin, low foreheads, large jaws and ears. Involution. Soon, a wave of energy makes her jump up and down and wave her arms like all the rest. The women have opened the windows on the second floor and, from the balcony, begin to throw sheets, candelabras, porcelain dinnerware, fancy gowns, and coins down into the crowd below. The riot is a fiesta. The only object that draws Matilda's attention is a mandolin which, passing from hand to hand, winds up smashed on the ground. She bends down to pick it up anyway, but as she is about to touch it, someone else's hand intervenes.

"You don't want this, Matilda." It is Cástulo's voice, his mandarin voice. His dark hair, his hard, lean body, his embrace. When she feels her own heartbeat as she inhales the tobacco smell of his body, Matilda realizes that she has never been separated from him, that no one can escape an embrace.

In Mexico City there are thirteen textile factories and more than five thousand operators work in them. Magdalena, Santa Teresa, Alpina, Hormiga, and Abeja are in San Angel

*and together have three thousand four hundred workers. They
pay only fifty cents a day to children and women. The biggest
factories, in the center of the city, are San Ildefonso and San
Antonio Abad. San Antonio Abad alone has one thousand
seven hundred workers and a capital investment of three and
half million pesos. The average salary is seventy centavos.
Depending on their skills, electricians, tram drivers, and
workers at the Ericsson telephone company earn as many as
two and a half pesos a day. The situation is different in the
cigar factories, where most of the workers are women. The
two thousand operators in El Buen Tono produce five and a
half billion cigarettes a year. With a capital investment of six
and a half million pesos, their sales produce a profit of five
million pesos per year. Yet a worker's salary is probably no
more than fifty centavos a day.* Cástulo Rodríguez remembers
every figure, every number perfectly, and as he pauses to
light a cigarette he turns his face to the people gathered
around the table to delight in his prodigious memory and the
information he brings them.

"This, as you can see, is a terrible injustice." His voice is
firm and, unlike his spelling, sure. "And that doesn't take
into account that there are other people, like Matilda here,
who earn barely twenty centavos a day in the cruelest sort of
slavery."

The Cause. The seven men and four women gathered at
number 35 Mesones to listen to Cástulo's reports refer to
everything they do, everything they say, everything they feel
as the Cause. The great Cause. Two of them know how to
read and write as well as Señorita Tina; all the others,
however, sign their notes with inked fingers. All speak well;
all have, beyond their voices, their tongues, a certain gift:
something like the crack of a whip in their speech, bringing
goosebumps to the skin and attracting sympathy. For one of
them, at least, Spanish is a second language. Like before, in
the riot at the pawnbroker's, Matilda feels protected, light,
filled with emotion, but when they try to convince her that

Tío Marcos is an agent of capitalism, a filthy pig, a member of the hated bourgeoisie, she finds she has to disagree. She has seen him work from sunup to sundown, seen him open the doors of his house at night to treat sick children. She has been present when he disinfects wounds and sets bones. She has lived in his house, where she has learned to read, write, listen to music, and behave like a lady.

"But what about your freedom?" they ask.

"You are my freedom." Her reply draws cheers and applause. Diamantina is now playing the piano again.

In the months they spend together, they do not tell each other the story of their lives. The past does not exist, the present is fleeting, and only the future is firm and fast. Using half-truths, Matilda mentions that she was born in Papantla, that she is the daughter of a man who lost his land and his dignity because of alcohol and the cruelty of Juventino Guerrero, the owner of the vanilla processing plant. The rest, she covers in silence, and when silence is not enough, disguises with evasions. Matilda rarely describes her life in the Burgos house. She does not mention that she has enough soap to bathe every day, that in the wardrobe closet of her room there are two pairs of shoes, three rebozos, cotton dresses, hats. Not even in the most intimate moments, the moments when she lies naked beside Cástulo's body, does she dare to untie the knot of their silences. Often, the effort leaves her confused. "Who is Matilda Burgos? *I* am Matilda Burgos." That pronoun, like many other things, is less and less firm, more and more unsettling.

Cástulo visits her at night. Like the first time, he comes over the back wall and, using the branches of the peach tree as a ladder, makes his way to her room without arousing suspicion. His affair with the doctor's niece gives him pangs of conscience, but also an almost perverse pleasure. The pleasure of nearness has, since the beginning, been interwoven with the thrill of committing an illegal act under the enemy's nose. A theft. There, in the back rooms of the world he wants to change, almost inside it yet irremediably outside, Cástulo lets his need take wings. The nearness, also since the beginning, is marked by murmurs, rashness. Illuminated by the flickering light from the oil lamp, the two lovers spend their first nights whispering inconsequential stories to each other, the footprints of the future. Mere inches separate their knees. Sheltered from the sunlight, far from the public thoroughfares, their courting is transparent, unambiguous. Matilda, ignoring Columba's advice, unbraids her hair and unbuttons her blouse. Cástulo's body is impregnated by the smell of tobacco that is left on him by his twelve hours standing before the machines in the Buen Tono factory: five and a half billion cigarettes a year. There are nicotine stains between the index and middle fingers of his right hand. A yellow-green half moon. Naked, he looks even younger, even more fragile. The bones of his clavicles and ribs look like low dunes on the desert of his skin. An embrace. A timeless crescendo of breathing. Their movements on the bed are minimal, as are their groans. With open eyes, spying on one another, they smile in silence. Trust. They have just begun to make out the shores of a peninsula; the continent lies farther on, hidden in the haze, though imperishable.

"What day is today?"

"Tuesday." The whisper tickles his left ear. "February, 1906."

"Always so precise, Matilda. I will remember that," he says before he closes his eyes and peacefully enters the cave of sleep, "later."

Cástulo is a man for whom sleeping is not a pleasure but an interruption. A bother. The quivering of his eyelids suggests that his eyes are closed from necessity, and that even so, as he lies on the bed with one arm around Matilda's waist, he is ready to get up, run out, and disappear into the streets. There are pursuits that never end. Duties. Watching his nervous, agitated sleep, Matilda tries to cross the space between her emotions and herself. The river is broad, and the waters cold. Everything over her head is white. In water up to her ankles, Matilda hesitates and then, without thinking, returns to her own bank. In the distance she can make out Cástulo's body floating, in flames, downriver. Before dawn, while he hurriedly pulls on his pants and shoes, he asks her something. He wants to know what he can do for her. It is the only way he knows to be necessary, useful.

"I want to hear Señorita Tina play the piano again," she says, "play with her."

Her answer makes him laugh. And stops him in his tracks. Watching her make the bed, dress, and braid her hair without looking at him, Cástulo realizes that there are places inside Matilda that he will never be able to enter. Closed doors. The discovery does not hurt him, but relieves him. Between a man and a woman certain distances make for happiness. When he says goodbye he does not say when he will return. Or whether. The February streets are covered with frost.

In the months they spend together, there is always haste, furtive absences, lies spoken brazenly and without a hint of shame. Matilda, who has never asked anything of Tío Marcos, today asks that she be allowed to take piano lessons. The surprise in his eyes is of gratification, triumph. The answer, however, is four days in coming. First he has to interview the teacher, inspect her house, weigh the costs. Diamantina Vicario. Number 35 Mesones. There, with this woman, Marcos Burgos makes the only decision that he will ever regret in his life. Despite the suspicions aroused in him by the absence of furniture in the parlor, the disorderliness of the garden, Marcos allows himself to be seduced and convinced by the word "charity," the word "civilization."

"Music," says Diamantina, "is the most sublime product of civilization. In addition, you would be doing an act of charity. My best students, the Mina girls, you must know them, are traveling, and as you will understand, my finances have been drastically reduced."

Marcos is a man who is always affected by adverbs well spoken. "Drastically." The development of his niece's artistic talent is a priority, and there is evidence to show that music sublimates even the most savage instincts of primitive animals. Evolution.

The first piece they play together is the national anthem.

At the Wednesday and Friday lessons, from four in the afternoon to seven in the evening, there are always more than just two people. In Diamantina's house there is always a coming and going. Men and women enter with alarming figures on their lips, news of new outrages, pamphlets printed in red and black. The newspaper that leaves black stains on their fingers is not *El Universal* or *El Imparcial,* but *El Hijo del Ahuizote,* in which, under the name Tina Vica, Diamantina publishes a column of criticism and jokes against the country's president, don Porfirio Díaz. Posada's playful skeletons make them laugh. The word "strike" is a passkey on their lips—it opens everything and closes everything they say. Because of their continual journeys into and out of Mexico City, Matilda realizes that only the very rich or the very poor travel in this country. Some for pleasure and others, of course, out of necessity. Then there are those others who, like her new friends, do it for the Cause. Sometimes Diamantina stuffs pamphlets in her black suitcase and disappears for one day, two, an entire weekend. Cástulo, without a suitcase, does the same. Neither informs anyone beforehand, neither mentions when they will be coming back. Or whether.

During these days, the name they give Matilda is "the Lady." "The little lady." She gathers up the newspapers lying about the house, the cans of paint, the pencils, she prepares coffee and, in the house's mismatched cups, serves it on a glass tray. It is she who finally cuts back the grass and weeds in the garden and prunes the geraniums. Thanks to her attentions, and with the help of some old curtains that she takes without permission from her uncle's house, some chrysanthemum bulbs, bleach, and soap, the house at number 35 Mesones is soon almost unrecognizable.

"Will you marry me, Matilda?" Diamantina asks her, laughing, as she inspects the dust-free piano, the impeccable kitchen, the room Matilda has turned into a study, with books on a bookshelf she has constructed from bricks and boards. Matilda, who had never thought about the possibility, blushes.

"You don't have to do all this, you know. The room you should claim is behind your eyes, inside your head. Women should enter into the kingdom of heaven with books, with music, not with brooms and dust rags, little lady. Wise up."

When Tina Vica disappears, Matilda misses her ringing laughter, her long strides across the tile floors, her hands flying over the ivory piano keys. Her sarcasm. There is a place under Matilda's skin which, in admiration, has the name Diamantina engraved in blue letters. An inner tattoo. Two hearts intertwined. Three.

In the months they spend together, there is a constant hole in the clouds through which one can see the blue sky of Mexico City. Aping the customs of the bourgeoisie, they ride bicycles to Chapultepec and, the women at least, wear bloomers, which inevitably attract the sidewise glances of passersby and sometimes cause ridiculous accidents. During Holy Week, however, they build grotesque cardboard effigies of don Porfirio and José Yves Limantour and burn them during the revelry of the San Judas celebrations. The men who work in the Renacimiento or Hidalgo theaters let them in the back door on opera nights, and for concerts. Thieves sell them imported liquor at less than half price. Anise. The owner of the Saldívar bookstore continues to lend them new books, poetry and political treatises. In the street, as they walk along, they pretend to be an isosceles triangle in motion. During these days, the three of them live on the edges of the world of wealth that simultaneously disgusts and seduces them. Happiness consists of putting their arms around each other's shoulders and knowing that they are safe, together. Happiness consists of kissing one another out of pure pleasure. On rainy afternoons, they do not use umbrellas. They live happily enough without money, and without any plan for the future except to change it. Uncomfortable yet expectant before the avatars of progress, they stroll through the city. There are many surprises. Sighs and exclamations of delight. When they walk under the incandescent lamps of the new public lighting, Cástulo asks aloud whether anyone has yet written an ode to Thomas Alva Edison. Telephones, trams, the networks of sewers, the pipes that bring water to the lavatory become the most profound and mysterious manifestations of God. What Cástulo likes most to do on his few free days is take the train to San Angel and walk among the textile factories. More than the city's palaces and monuments, even more than the moving picture show and the broad pavement of La Reforma, he admires the geometric sobriety of the factories, the smokestacks, the electricity. Nature tamed. Artifice. Will. Inside, arms move to the rhythm of the machines, all in unison. Inside, there is an almost military harmony that makes him think of the unlimited possibilities of work, organization. Cástulo pronounces the word "future" with the same vehemence, the same unshakable, unshrinking faith as Tío Marcos.

"The difference, little lady," Cástulo interrupts her, upset, "is that I believe that the fruits of labor must remain in our hands. We must take control of all this, take it over; only us, those who know, those who work, can carry the country forward. Into the future."

The months they spend together come to an end. June, 1906. The news of Cananea in the newspapers. The bare statistics of those killed by foreigners and the National Guard. At point-blank range. With the massacre and defeat at the Green Cananea Copper Company, Diamantina's wry sarcasm stops. In the summer she takes refuge inward, in a very dark and solitary place where only the sound of rain, a melody by Bach can be heard. Not even the angry debates in the House of Deputies lift her spirits. Cástulo insists that it is only the beginning, but for the first time Diamantina seems to fear facing the enemy. Then, in October, her face serious, her expression muted by a gravity that will never again leave her, she takes the train to Veracruz. Río Blanco. She does not allow Cástulo or Matilda to see her off at the station.

Why does she choose Joaquín? There is no longer anyone who can answer that.

Joaquín says goodbye to her once again on the platform full of people—long, long before everything. *Cultivate the imagination.* A light kiss on the lips. The lovers say goodbye without knowing when they will see each other again.

For the first time since he has been listening to her words, Joaquín asks Matilda to be quiet. A smear of oil spreads across the lake of his head that, when sunlight strikes it, is iridescent brown. He does not want to witness the end.

The liberal plan of 1906 demanded an eight-hour workday, the right to strike. In addition to democratic elections, it also demanded that their lands be restored to the indigenous communities. When Marcos Burgos heard about the manifesto, he thought they had lost their mind. A case of collective madness. And with it, he was convinced that neither discipline nor hygiene sufficed to mitigate the irrational instincts of the primitives with whom he shared this country. That same year, he purchased his first Ford. Matilda began to move through the hallways of the house like a ghost. She lost weight. Absence marked her face. On January 7, 1907, the news of Río Blanco came. Diamantina Vicario did not come back. The Great Cause. Dead bodies on exhibit. Marcos Burgos applauded the drastic measures taken by President Díaz to protect the future, good habits, the nation's sovereignty. Standing before the mirror in her room, Matilda cut off her braids. Then, without saying goodbye, she left the house. The only thing she took with her were three dry, odorless pods of vanilla. The adjective that Marcos used to describe his niece's actions was "ungrateful," but knowing that this was his personal defeat, he never employed the word in public.

"Matilda cannot go on sleeping in your room, don Joaquín. You know very well that that is not allowed." Dr. Oligochea's voice sounds restrained but triumphant. "This place has its rules. Think about it. It could cost you your job, or mine."

Joaquín does not answer, and avoids looking into his eyes as he lights a cigarette. For nineteen days, he has been imagining—quite accurately imagining, he now realizes—the doctor's reaction. First his anger and then the calculated threat, the challenge. Eduardo Oligochea is a man who seldom lets pass an opportunity to exercise his power.

"It is not worth risking your job for her, Joaquín. Your position is the only thing you have, after all, and the poor woman is mad. Stop acting the fool. You think that no one has noticed?"

"Don't worry, doctor."

The steps that take Joaquín to his room have the fragility of a man who has been wounded twice by the same error.

The next time he sees Matilda in the asylum gardens, he puts out his arm as though he were on a country walk, or in line for the motion picture theater.

"I want to ask you something," he says. "Did Cástulo ever tell you who was after him the night he came to your room?"

Matilda smiles. The sun on her hair like an ethereal crown.

"Yes." She takes his hands, touches his hair. "He said that it was chance. Nothing more."

It is March 21, 1921. And everything is in its place.

5

"The She-Devil"

This is the story that Matilda remembers on the train that takes them from Mixcoac to Mexico City. Outside. It is morning, and through the window the landscape seems illuminated by an unreal light. The cloudless sky is a limpid blue. Joaquín has taken one of her hands and clutches it as though it were an anchor. His face still does not know what to do with the happiness. Matilda does not look at him. In the window that protects them from the wind and cold, there are reflections, fragmentary images, colors superimposed on the frame of a static, inexorable time. This is the story that Matilda tells herself in silence as the two of them leave the madhouse behind, in oblivion. There are places that can only be entered by different doors, words that will not be shared with anyone.

"Are you dreaming?" Joaquín asks her.

"Yes."

The sound of coins falling into the little bank. The shadow of a kite on the sand. Bubbles and water about to boil. The staccato sounds of Morse code in telegraph offices. Two women laughing together. Her echoes. Matilda is inside them.

In 1903, the Mexican writer and diplomat Federico Gamboa published *Santa,* his most popular novel. Based on his own experiences and employing the resources of literary naturalism, Gamboa described in detail the fall into concupiscence of a girl from Chimalistac whose name alone, in the opinion of doña Elvira, the madame of the house, would ensure huge profits. The novel soon gained a reputation as "daring," and the educated men of the middle class paid willingly for the story, in order to see themselves reflected in its pages and to cleanse their hearts with belated forgiveness. Diamantina Vicario, on the other hand, was able to read it without paying, thanks to the loans from the owner of the Saldívar bookstore, and her only reaction was laughter. The simple moral of the story and its sensationalistic language brought her to her feet in the midst of her reading. Arms in the air, she heaped abuse upon the author.

"This man is an idiot," she would say to whoever would listen in the little parlor on Mesones. "Can you imagine putting French in the mouth of that stupid Santa's ghost in the preface!"

When, years later, Matilda Burgos had the opportunity to read the novel, she not only realized that Diamantina had been right but also became indignant herself. From that time forward, her *nom de guerre* was "the She-Devil."

A woman in ordinary dress and an unknown man. Of all the obsessions that emerged toward the end of the century, only prostitutes attained legendary status. Poets pitied them and praised them, in equal measure. Sculptors carved marble and wood with them in mind. Painters immortalized them. Doctors and lawyers created the first laws regulating the practice of prostitution in order to defend themselves from their danger and establish the rules of the game for their bodies. There were many who opposed this. Others who were in favor. Discussions were also carried on in medical journals, in the mute obscurity of memoranda, and in the narrow passageways of the palaces of justice. A fervor never known before filled each of these venues. Men in high positions, family men, and professionals of great prestige, who from the beginning had opposed the tacit acceptance of prostitution as embodied in the regulations, argued that the laws would lead eventually to uncontrollable epidemics of syphilis. In addition, allowing prostitution would lead men and women into ruin—men, by legitimizing their moral degeneration, and women, by not forcing them into decent work. Public health, the growth of the nation, and, most important of all, the survival of the human race depended on the eradication of the oldest profession in the world. The only alternative for avoiding contagion, both moral and physical, was targeting prostitution as a crime against good manners and the health of the nation. Dr. Manuel Alfaro, creator of the new legislation, used the same argument, however, to promote social tolerance. In his writings, prostitution was presented as a necessary evil. Recognizing that the authorities were totally unable to eradicate the vice, he pragmatically proposed that it be regulated in order to avoid worse ills, such as infection by venereal diseases, family dishonor, marital disputes, and even sodomy. And so, prostitutes were categorized as "public" if they lived in a house of prostitution, or "independent" if not. After they were enrolled in the official registry and given a medical examination, the madams would pay the authorities fees of eight, five, and three pesos per month for each girl of first, second, and third class, respectively. The independent ones, in turn, would pay fees of ten, five, and two pesos, likewise depending on their class. Once registered, the girl would receive her carnet, which contained her name, identification number, medical certificate, and photograph. If the doctors from Health Inspection discovered signs of illness, the girl would be sent to the Morelos Hospital before her identification booklet was returned to her. Police agents would see to the rest. And it was the police, spying on the clandestine couples entering hotels for assignations, who began their reports with the following formula: "A woman in ordinary dress and an unknown man." It was they who were in charge of the bureaucratic processes and also of protecting health and public order in any way they saw fit.

The first set of regulations was, however, a failure, and

led to the formulation of new laws in 1871, followed by others in 1889. The cause of social disorder and corruption was laid at the feet of a single figure: the "incompliant." These clandestine prostitutes who practiced their profession without registering and without paying the prescribed fees generally worked in unlicensed brothels or hotels such as the Bazar, the Refugio, and the San Agustín, where the police, thanks to modest sums of money, did not go. The incompliants' reputation for aggressiveness and arrogance was equaled only by their reputation for shrewdness. They would often go to public dances and even on country outings without being detected by the police. Many also practiced their profession in the streets or alongside church doors, aided by disguises. In late 1907, when Matilda made prostitution her profession, only the most scatterbrained or outright stupid, like Santa, bothered to register or expose themselves to the humiliation of the medical examination.

> *If prostitutes are not ferreted out, or if they have the assurance that the authorities will punish them with only a mild hand when they are caught, then why should they register? It is much more comfortable and financially beneficial not to obey the law, thereby avoiding any fee whatever, not to expose themselves to confinement in a hospital, and, lastly, not to have superiors that must be obeyed.*
> *Dr. Manuel Alfaro*
> *Chief of Health Inspection*

After leaving her uncle's house, Matilda Burgos walked aimlessly and without memory through the city, her fingers touching the three vanilla pods inside the pocket of her skirt. The thinness, the loneliness of the air without Diamantina made breathing difficult. "Wise up." The joy in her voice made Matilda unexpectedly turn her head. When she realized that there was no one there, she began to run, until shortness of breath and exhaustion made her knees week. She slept in plazas and at the side doors of churches. No one saw her cry. The city which had been a vigorous animal suddenly lost all its spirit. Matilda was silent, she hardly spoke a word. Cástulo found her one morning sitting in front of Diamantina's piano, motionless, staring into space. He spoke her name and when he received no reply, he approached her, embraced her. A statue. Rather than being warmed by him, Matilda transmitted her iciness to his body. He shivered. A flake of white paint fell from the ceiling onto her head. Matilda, who had always been so particular about cleanliness, made no effort to brush it away. Then, repeating her name without realizing it, Cástulo picked her up and, after climbing the stairs, laid her in Diamantina's bed, his urgency clear. The only thing Matilda did was crack her knuckles. Cástulo brought a pail of cold water, and as Matilda had done several months earlier for him, moistened a cloth and began to carefully and fearfully clean her body, as though it were a fragile, breakable object of great value. Naked, with her eyes open, Matilda offered no resistance. Cástulo threw her underclothes, stained with excrement and urine, in the trash. Then with iodine he disinfected her scratches, some raw, some scabbed over. They were on her legs, her arms, her neck, and even her cheeks. Her body resembled a field crisscrossed by newly dug ditches. With a brush, Cástulo managed to clean out the filth encrusted under her fingernails. He washed her irregularly chopped off hair, spread a cool balm on her cracked and chapped lips, and, with no modesty whatever, and skill learned even as he was doing it, he washed away the clotted blood that menstruation had left on her inner thighs. By the time he finished, Matilda was sleeping, and he lit a cigarette. The woman's absolute stillness made him curse don Porfirio Díaz once again.

Matilda woke up two days later as though nothing had ever happened. The blue sky of early morning illuminated her face. Cástulo was sleeping in a chair, his legs drawn up to his chest and a burned-out cigarette still hanging between the fingers of his right hand. Before she got up, her eyes swept the room. No matter how she tried, she found no trace of Diamantina. Her wardrobe was empty, the blankets that covered her bore none of her smell.

"Cástulo," she called him, "I'm cold, I need some clothes."

Surprised by her voice, unable at first to respond, Cástulo woke up and immediately ran from the room and returned with a flowered skirt and white blouse. In one hand he was carrying a still steaming bowl of cabbage soup.

"What happened?"

"I don't know." Matilda's hermitism was absolute.

Thus, Diamantina's absence belonged to her alone. She gathered up her memories and, one by one, put them away in a secret place. Then she closed the door and turned the latch of silence. "No one will see me cry. Ever." More than pain itself, Matilda feared other people's pity and compassion. Long ago, and no doubt without realizing it, she had decided to live with all her losses alone, without anyone else's company, sometimes even her own.

Both of them alone now, they became the endpoints of a straight line, never touching. The days when they had been an isosceles triangle lay forever in the past.

"I miss Diamantina," said Cástulo the last evening they spent together in the abandoned house.

"I do too," whispered Matilda, pronouncing her first words in several days. Then they looked into each other's eyes and found that they were empty. The evening light cast golden gleams on their hair.

Although he wanted to, Cástulo could not care for Matilda. He lived on the run, staying but a few steps ahead of his own death day after day. Without respite. But because he loved her, he offered to send her to live with some of his relatives, in San Mateo Atenco, and when Matilda declined his offer, he invited her to work with the Cause. She knew how to read and write, knew how to take care of the sick, and could lift the spirit of meetings with her piano playing.

"Matilda, you can be useful to the Cause," he told her. The woman's only reply was a silent smile; she couldn't do it, nor could she explain why. The last thing that occurred to him was suggesting that she find work in one of the city's textile or cigarette factories. Matilda promised him that she would do that, and before she said goodbye, she also assured him that she was going to survive.

"I want to give you something." He took a photograph of Diamantina out of one of his pockets and put it in her hands. The image was an old one. "I have that silly look on my face because I am thinking about you, my little Red. Tina." When she read the dedication, Matilda smiled softly. Diamantina had a deliciously easy way of lying. Her face in the photograph was concentrated on her hands, her fingers on the keyboard, nothing else. The rest was black, including her love for Cástulo, the pleasure of his sex. On the lower right corner of the picture were tiny initials: J.B. Before leaving Cástulo, she embraced him. The beating of his heart in her ears.

"You'll hear from me again," he assured her.

"I know."

Matilda and Cástulo never spoke of love.

The next day she went to Balderas and a short time later found a job as a machine operator on one of the production lines of the Buen Tono cigarette factory: thirty-five centavos a day for twelve hours' work. The smell of the tobacco always reminded her of Cástulo. For the first few days she made an effort to fix in her mind the features of his face as she mechanically went about her work, but as the time passed she completely forgot them. Just as the first time she had discovered his absence in the Burgos house, Cástulo

Rodríguez became just a name, another product of her imagination. In the cigarette factory, Matilda became sociable for the first time. More than a sudden change of temperament, her transformation was linked from the beginning to necessity. In order to survive in Mexico City at twenty-two years of age, a woman alone depended on the kindness, and sometimes charity, of others. In addition, Matilda looked so thin and worn, with her chopped-off hair and discreet smile, that her mere presence aroused tender sentiments in those around her. The women in the factory took to her. One of them rented her a cot in one corner of her room and another, discovering that she could read and write, invited her to share her beans and tortillas in exchange for a dozen love letters.

Matilda adapted quickly and with good humor to her new situation. Neither Esther Quintana and her two children, with whom Matilda lived, nor any other girls in Buen Tono ever heard her complain. Despite the comradeship and shared poverty, however, there were things, attitudes, that drew their attention. Differences. Matilda always said good morning and she washed every day at six in the morning, even when there was no soap. When Esther's children fell sick Matilda knew exactly which remedy to employ for them, and when they returned from the market, where they carried bundles for a couple of centavos, with their knees skinned and bloody, she treated them with a firm and efficient hand. Some nights, especially Sundays, she set aside half an hour to read them the news from the newspapers that they picked up off the street, and after rescuing a piece of slate from a pile of trash, she taught them their letters and, with a piece of chalk, how to join one to another to form words. Esther, a widow at twenty-four, her face worn, two teeth missing, watched Matilda as she arranged her few belongings neatly and planted geraniums in tin cans. She could not imagine, no matter how hard she tried, what it was that moved Matilda to try to pretty up a place that resisted all prettiness. Soon, neighbors began to present themselves at all hours with fevered children, husbands in the throes of *delirium tremens*, and daughters-in-law with fractures. Matilda, working as she had seen Tío Marcos do, touched their forehead, took their pulse, and, lacking a stethoscope, put her ear to their chest. Then, knowing that patent medicines were not within their means, she would recommend teas, unguents, or simple faith in God as she smiled and spoke encouraging words to them. Sometimes, when the sick person's condition had no cure that she could administer, she suggested that they go to the hospital or consult a professional doctor, but for the poor, hospitals and doctors' offices were places of perdition rather than health, and doctors had a reputation as police informants. On one occasion Matilda even helped a woman give birth in her kitchen. As thanks, her patients would bring her slivers of soap, little bags full of coffee brought in from family land in the provinces, sugar, colored yarn, rose water they had extracted themselves. She shared all of it with Esther and her two children, who, like everyone else, called her "the little doctor."

The only thing that Matilda refused to do during that time was talk about her life. When the workers in the factory began to talk about their courtships, their pregnancies and abandonments, Matilda would sit silent, blinking. The stories often moved her to grief. As for her, no one knew of a lovelorn man in her life, or even a relative. The girl seemed to have come out of nowhere. Without a past, as empty as a blank page, Matilda was known only for her warmth and kindliness, her good handwriting, and her knowledge of medicine. "The little doctor." What she herself most enjoyed was that she did not have to be anyone, or even be; she could walk in anonymity through the streets, without arousing suspicions. At birthday gatherings or fiestas organized for the Virgin of Guadalupe, she was the stranger at the table. Among the butchers and machine operators, the bearers, the tanners and water carriers, laughter was the true freedom. For a few hours they would forget about their work, their complaints, the miracles they prayed to God for. In the air filled with cigarette smoke and the smell of cheap alcohol, there was a sense of urgency: the urgent need for pleasure, companionship. In the revelry of those gatherings, men and women would often begin a silent courtship that later became an engagement and then, in time, marriage, although the marriages were never entered in the civil registry or the church records. The young women would wear earrings and, with slices of beets, accentuate the color of their cheeks. The men would move among them timidly, trying to feel out acceptance or rejection before going at the matter head-on. Matilda's happiness consisted of sharing her life with the kind of people Diamantina had spoken to her about. Her people. It was easy to imagine her there, moving among the children and men as though they were her own family, asking questions about their wages, their working conditions. It was easy to hear the growl of her laughter, the sound of her skirt brushing against the chairs. For Matilda, it was easy to live within the transparent ceremony of the dead woman in those days.

"If you go on like this you're going to wind up a nun, or something worse," Esther remarked to her one night as she mended a skirt. "You need a man, Matilda, someone to take care of you. You cannot go through life that way, alone, like some orphan. I'm not going to last forever."

"No, Esther, I don't need anyone." In her reply there was no arrogance, but only self-sufficiency, the assurance of having found the first permanent, stable niche in her life.

Among the workers at the cigarette factory sudden illness, even unforeseen death were not rare. The long hours of work during which the women had to remain standing caused varicose veins, chronic back pain. The closed atmosphere of the factory often produced incurable lung infections. And outside, during the dry months, there was always the threat of typhus. Pregnancies would leave the women as thin as a fruit sucked dry, and the loss of blood from abortions or even spontaneous miscarriages made them anemic. Emotional and spiritual mortifications also left their marks. Some of the women suffered from facial tics and uncontrollable bouts of weeping, while others would stutter or descend into melancholy. Abandonment and male infidelity often awakened homicidal desires. And then there were the dismissals, always sudden, surprising, and unexplained. All it took was the whim of a supervisor or the rumor that one of them had anarchist friends.

Matilda was dismissed for abandoning her post the day she had to take Esther to the hospital. Her friend had fainted at her machine, and then her body was racked by convulsions. When she awoke, her lips would not move; she could not talk, nor could she move the left side of her body. With the help of Esther's sons, Matilda carried her to the central hospital and there, the doctors gave her no hope of surviving. And if she should survive, Esther would be paralyzed, her mind gone. Death came but a week later.

In Mexico City, twelve percent of the women between fifteen and thirty years of age were prostitutes, or had been at some time. Many of them were orphans and single women, although there were also widows, married women, even women with children. They had been maids, seamstresses, washerwomen, machine operators, and street vendors, and they had probably never earned more than twenty-five centavos a day. Of those who bothered to answer the questions on the registry, half reported that they had been forced into prostitution by poverty, the other half by vice, or a certain personal propensity for the profession. The story that Matilda decided to tell the women she worked with was that she had been dishonored by a furtive love affair. Lying skillfully, she told of her seduction by a law student and, tears coming to her eyes, she related in detail his cruel abandonment of her and the inevitable expulsion from her family home. They had all told the same story since Santa made it famous, and they had all proven its efficacy. It softened the hearts and wallets of the men that paid them for their services, and also left the men convinced that fornication had actually been an act of charity. Thus, the morality of both the men and their whores remained unsullied.

> *The uterus and ovaries are centers of action reflected in the woman's brain. They may cause terrible illnesses and hitherto unknown passions.*
> Manuel Guillén
> Reflections on Woman's Hygiene During Puberty

Matilda began working as an "independent" first-class in unlicensed brothels. She worked at night, of course, and at dawn would return home, after first removing her makeup and changing her clothes. Esther's children refrained from asking questions, and the neighbors, aware of her obvious goings and comings, looked at her with sadness and understanding. Unemployed and with another woman's children to support, Matilda had made the only possible decision. Just as had happened in the cigar factory, the girls in the San Andrés Hotel immediately felt drawn to Matilda. They taught her to paint her eyes and lips, to take precautions so as not to be taken in by the police or thieves, and to sit in vinegar baths after each client in order to avoid infections. For the first time, Matilda began to smoke and drink alcohol, but in moderation. Her clients were clerks in offices and stores, soldiers, bureaucrats, students, and politicians. There were men who were so drunk that they paid her and then fell asleep on top of her. There were those who would barely enter the room, not even fully undress her, then turn her face-down on the dresser, raise her skirts, and penetrate her hurriedly, still standing. There were those who, before undressing, inquired in detail about her medical history. And those who, after finishing, licked at her nipples as though they were peaches. Some men paid her more for fellatio, and others if she would insert three fingers in their anus. Some, also for more money, put her on all fours and, squeezing her breasts, spread her legs and mounted her. There were some imaginative ones who asked her to assume contorted positions. Very few preferred her on top. Most, the great majority, were content for her to open her legs and let them push two, three times, before ejaculating gracelessly and in haste. The only ones that Matilda could not bear were those who wanted to chat.

"Secrets are for the confessional," she would say to them, and set to work. Her brusque manner with her clients and her generous erotic acrobatics soon earned her a certain reputation. The sobriquet "She-Devil," like all *noms de guerre,* was gained later, and in a real war.

Despite the sums of money that the brothel owners sent punctually to the police agents assigned to the Health Inspection office, raids were not infrequent. The instances of disorderly conduct that called for police presence were generally caused by drunks, who on paydays would think that they were the owners of if not the earth at least the whores' bodies. One Saturday in October, the San Andrés was full of medical students. Most of the women refused to entertain them because of the thinness of their wallets, but there were those who, thinking of a doctor's future, dreamed of securing a client for life. The trouble began when a boy, his face covered with pimples and thick tortoise-shell glasses, came out of his room half dressed, complaining loudly—the girl he had paid for a half-hour of sex was refusing him her services. The owner of the house came upstairs to find out what was going on, and a couple of the girls, among them Matilda, followed him. Naked but now on her feet, her face red with rage and the small blue veins in her temples throbbing, the woman made it clear that the boy was trying to get something for nothing.

"He wants an around the world for the same price," she

said indignantly, rushing up to the boy with her fists doubled. The owner tried unsuccessfully to stop her, and soon the boy's friends and the whores were engaged in a pitched battle, with broken bottles, screams, and black eyes. When the two agents from Health Inspection arrived, they got rid of the students immediately and were about to arrest the prostitute, who, despite being naked and tousled, still had a little necklace of paste diamonds around her neck. It was then that Matilda stepped in and, using the same eloquent voice she had heard often in the parlor on Mesones, pronounced an improvised speech on justice, workers' rights, and the authorities' lack of compassion. The coarse laughter of one of the agents infuriated the naked girl, and with a strength lent by adrenaline, she picked up a chair and broke it over his head. The second agent took out a pistol and aimed it at the girl. The other prostitutes, meanwhile, armed themselves with bottles.

"If you do it," said Matilda, now fearless, "we will first kill you where you stand and then file a complaint against you at the Ministry of Justice."

Matilda's words helped increase the fear already beginning to be felt by the police officers. It was the first time they had faced a whorehouse in open rebellion. When they finally decided to leave, the naked girl threw her arms around Matilda's neck. Her sweaty blond hair smelled of gardenias.

"You were like the devil himself, Matilda," said one of the girls as she lit a cigarette. Others were pouring beer, still trembling in excitement from the ruckus.

"You mean the devil *her*self," corrected another.

"Just call me the she-devil," said Matilda.

Her triumph over the students first and the police agents later filled her with pride, and was the event out of which her legend was born. Meanwhile, she was still embracing the white, naked body of the girl whose love of the necklace of false gems had earned her the sobriquet "the Diamantina."

Matilda would have done anything to pronounce that name once more. The name. That morning, the house quiet and empty of clients, the two women slept in the same bed, their legs wound about each other like braids.

"La Gaditana" was not so fortunate. In Federico Gamboa's novel, Santa was able to understand the none-too-subtle insinuations of La Gaditana only through the explanations given her by, among other men, a blind pianist. Thus, thanks to the timely intervention of a man, Santa was able to decipher the erotic content of pelvises pressed together during dance lessons, kisses left by La Gaditana on her still warm clothing. Then, naturally, Santa reacted with disgust. When the "She-Devil" and La Diamantina read this passage together, they not only howled with laughter but also made love on the pages of the book. Poor ambassador Gamboa, so cosmopolitan and so lacking in imagination!

Matilda repeated the name of her lover constantly, at the least provocation. When she had her naked at her side, she slowly counted the vertebrae along her spine; watching over her sleep, she leaned over her mouth to drink up the airy ghosts that set her breast in motion. A woman. Her presence, like her name, illuminated everything around her. With La Diamantina beside her, even the little room with yellow walls and very little furniture seemed a true home. The sheets were softer, the bed more welcoming, and their bodies theirs alone. An island of white. Matilda embraced her. The golden hair between her legs suddenly like a forest from the nearness of the observing eye. La Diamantina slept without fear of anything, without even blinking. Her trust was infinite. In the morning, Matilda washed her feet and ankles and untangled her golden curls. Then, with her fingers, she anointed her with perfume smelling of gardenias and helped her on with her underclothes and clothing. When they were ready to go out, Matilda told her they were going to the city authorities to file a complaint against the Health Inspection agents. Though surprised, La Diamantina concealed her astonishment and stepped out into the street, holding the She-Devil's hand, head high. Matilda Burgos had met her equal.

Thanks to the constant disputes over jurisdiction between the authorities of the Distrito Federal and those of Health Inspection, the complaint by the two rebellious women was registered in the official books as No. 151423. Ligia Morales, alias La Diamantina, made an official complaint about the excessive force used by agent Gregorio Uribe when Uribe illegally tried to arrest her. As proof, she included a medical certificate attesting to a broken arm, scratches, and a case of nerves. The agent was called to testify. Timid, using an excessively deferential tone of voice and choice of words, and with his hands motionless on his knees, Gregorio Uribe took the occasion to say, first, that the city's incompliants were not only increasingly numerous but also more arrogant and coarse. The pauses in his testimony showed rage, humiliation. Knowing that the district government would set them free in exchange for a simple promise of their regeneration, these women would insult agents from Health Inspection, utilizing the vulgar language common to their profession and, more recently, physical force as well. The only example needed was what occurred in the San Andrés Hotel, to which Gregorio Uribe had been called as a representative of the law, owing to one of those dust-ups also typical of those brothels. According to his testimony, as he was about to place the so-called Diamantina under arrest and take her to Health Inspection, the individual had insulted and threatened him, her and the other woman, the She-Devil. Fearing to make a grave error that might cost him his job, the agent simply reported the incident and left the premises. In addition, he wished to say that the medical certificate presented by the plaintiff was totally false and that the complaint was simply one more of the numerous acts of slander perpetrated by the prostitutes in order to discredit not just the agents but Health Inspection itself, passing themselves off as victims rather than what they really were, women outside the law, common criminals, and no doubt lost souls as well.

Although after examining the evidence the district authorities decided to dismiss the charges against the agent, they also decided to set La Diamantina free. The first decision was expected, but the second became a cause for celebration among the whores in the San Andrés Hotel and other houses of prostitution nearby.

The She-Devil and La Diamantina had fallen into the habit of strolling through the city during their free time, in the hours of daylight. As soon as they awoke in the morning, they would choose simple skirts and blouses, gray rebozos, tortoise-shell combs, and when they were dressed they would step out the door of the hotel as though they planned never to return. First they would walk to the market to buy food for Esther's children, and then, after leaving their purchases in the room Matilda rented for the youngsters, they would make their plans for the day. Sometimes they would go to Chapultepec and lie on their backs on the grass, trying to pick out animals and faces in the tall white clouds. Sometimes they would be content to walk through the busy streets in the center of the city, admiring the colorful placards and their bodies reflected in the storefront windows. La Diamantina had a weakness for jewelry shops. Motionless, with her eyes and mouth open, she would stare at the sapphires, rubies, and emeralds as though they were long-lost children whom she had just found again. The sighs torn from her breast by the gleams of diamonds behind the glass were only comparable to those provoked by her lovemaking in the She-Devil's bed. Matilda, holding back her laughter, would have to pull her away by the arm to continue their stroll. Other times, they would walk down the sidewalk along Reforma, admiring the carriages that drove by. At least once they visited the natural history museum and took in the insects, fossils, and stones on exhibition as though the two of them were medical students or budding scientists. There, however, La Diamantina grew bored. Nor did she pay much attention to the monumental sculptures of unsmiling "Indians" at the National Museum of Artillery. When the two of them discovered that their favorite place was the Plaza Santo Domingo, they gave each other a hug beside the fountain and then went into the church to give thanks to God. Matilda enjoyed having a companion, a "buddy," but she enjoyed her new freedom even more. Freed from the prison of the Burgoses, the little parlor on Mesones, the room in Balderas, she found that the streets had become her only home, the blue sky of Mexico City the only roof she liked over her head. It was in this way that she discovered her true homeland.

Some evenings, before she started working, when the women would gather in the parlor around the piano, waiting for clients, Matilda and Ligia would rehearse dance steps as the music played. Soon the practice begun as a game took on the air of a performance. Ligia would put on a white silk tunic through which one could see her naked body and, barefoot, with tiny Castile roses in her hair, she would dance about the room with long steps, her arms outstretched as though she were searching for something, someone, that eluded her. Matilda, naked as well, but wearing a purple tunic, would then burst into the room with brusque movements, twirling on one foot, as though she were a top. At that point, the chords of the music would grow harsh and almost discordant. At last, the purple tunic would completely cover the fallen body, knotted into the shape of a fetus, in the white tunic. Ligia suggested that they name the piece "The Embrace of Syphilis," but Matilda preferred a more generic title: "Illness." Some of the clients, especially those who gave themselves airs as poets or artists, began to come to the house earlier. One of them, a thin man with bony hands and a permanently lighted cigarette in his lips, offered them his services as a painter one night, free of charge, in exchange for their own services, and the girls agreed.

From the beginning, Santos Trujillo admired their daring and their talent. The first afternoon that the three of them met, he applauded their selection of costume and also the strange but suggestive dance they had chosen to perform. What they had to change from the outset, however, was its title.

"That name 'Illness' is not only morbid, it will never seize anyone's imagination, Ligia. Why don't you change it, call the piece 'The Nymphs' or 'The Odalisques'?" At this suggestion, La Diamantina put her index finger into her open mouth as a sign of her disgust.

"But Ligia, 'The Nymphs' or 'The Odalisques' will stir men's loins," he said, trying to convince her.

"Who told you that we do this for men, Santos? If they want to come, let them come, and let them *come*, too, if they want to, but this is for the girls, you understand?"

In addition to "Illness," Ligia and Matilda also created "Jail," "Hospital," "Neurasthenia," and "Rules." When Santos begged them to at least use adjectives or a second name, such as "Delirium" for example, Matilda informed him that nothing *they* did would ever have such a ridiculous word in it.

"That word should be removed from the dictionaries," she said, refusing to discuss the matter further.

In all else, they were more flexible. They accepted the colored lights that Santos included in the spectacle, and also agreed to combine live piano music with phonograph recordings. For reasons they never managed to explain, both of them had a particular weakness for oboes. Santos also added enormous pictures painted by him. They were done with aggressive brushstrokes in electric colors, and they portrayed distorted faces that could only be made out at a distance. These were his most intimate and least fully realized paintings, and they worked perfectly for the women's spectacle. As a lark, La Diamantina wanted to perform a parody of Santa, and she convinced Ligia to do it. While she herself went about transforming the stupid, provincial heroine into a fine lady with dragon's wings, Matilda became a man in a tuxedo, whose naivete and ignorance of the demimonde earned him the nickname "The Idiot." None of their pieces produced more laughter and applause among the spectators, and it was thanks to this one that they found work in La Modernidad.

The owner of the bordello, a fallen aristocrat whose only weakness was dressing as a woman, went to see them one night at the express invitation of Santos Trujillo. His black tuxedo, the large curl he had pasted to his forehead with brilliantine, his monocle, his bright red lips, and the cigarette holder he used to smoke gold-tipped cigarettes attracted the attention of the clientele that night. The smell of the place and the vulgarity of its furnishings disgusted him so much that he was about to leave before seeing the performance, but as soon as the women appeared and bowed to the audience, pronouncing their *noms de guerre* proudly, Madame Porfiria, as he liked to be called, was enthralled. Immediately, never taking his eyes off them, he began to calculate the possible earnings they might bring him. When they were done, Santos introduced them, and instead of going upstairs to the rooms with some client, they went off with their eccentric new friend. As they left, they realized that they would never return. The lights of the city shone brightly, casting yellow circles on the sidewalks. Full moons. Their solitary midnight footsteps filled their bodies with echoes and the taste of salt. Kisses like strolls in the park. Feet in step. Porfiria offered them champagne.

La Modernidad was a nondescript house located out on the road to Salto del Agua. Nothing about its traditional facade suggested that within its cement-and-stone walls, behind its wrought-iron balconies, there was another world. The salon, whose *pièce de resistance* was a grand piano, had a floor of black and white squares of marble in a classic chessboard pattern. The drapery that fell in a cascade from the ceiling was blue velvet. On the walls, one could make out fragments of intertwined naked bodies. More than drawings, or frescos, these were lines that crisscrossed the painted walls like the marks of a seamstress's pattern, and they acquired form and body only if they were seen from afar. In addition to Santos Trujillo's paintings, the house contained some drawings by Julio Ruelas in which satyrs, nymphs, and young men engaged in orgies. A copy of his painting *The Dominatrix* occupied a special place above the piano. Like the girls of the house, a naked woman, dressed only in a hat and black stockings to her knees, was lashing a pig who not only had a monkey on his back but also was forced to run in a circle in the earth around her. The eternal battle of the sexes! Sketches for some of Angel Zárragas' androgynous Christs hung on the walls of the stairway. There was also a marble copy of *Malgré-tout,* the sculpture by Jesús Contreras that had won the Prix d'Or at the World's Fair in Paris in 1900. There were also, however, sprays of peacock feathers, little statues of suspect Maya provenance, and bas-reliefs of the figure of Cuauhtémoc which, combined with the imaginative lighting of the salon, gave the place an air of exoticism that was quite the rage just then. The girls' rooms were on the second floor, as was customary in the city's brothels. Matilda and Ligia tried to conceal their aston-ishment and delight when they saw the silk draperies, the cut-crystal chandeliers, the gold-leaf-framed mirrors on the walls, and the exuberance of chinoiserie, but they could not. Like children, they began to touch things with trembling hands, to bring their noses to the bouquets of tuberoses, to see if they were real. Porfiria smiled.

"Each of you will have your own room. But if you want to sleep together, that's none of my concern."

Matilda and Ligia continued to offer performances whose names in French, English, or Nahuatl reflected the influence of La Modernidad. None, however, ever surpassed the success of their parody of Santa. Matilda, whose tuxedo for the part of The Idiot was most flattering, decided to cut off her hair, so as to look more the part of a man. Wearing dark pants always, and with no jewels or perfume anywhere on her body, the She-Devil began to gain a reputation as an androgyne. Ligia, in turn, combined her love for diamonds with tunics in a pre-Hispanic style to create a personality that was at once exotic and avant-garde. Between the two of them, and thanks to the advertising that both Santos and Porfiria strategically disseminated throughout the city's select circles, La Modernidad's profits doubled. At ten o'clock, the arrivals began: high-ranking bureaucrats in search of something to combat the boredom of their everyday lives; foreign investors with a desire to try something authentically Mexican; theater directors and actors; poets wearied by long nights alone and white swans; fashionable showgirls and minor actresses; architects who had just returned from Paris; generals with a taste for something as fierce as battle; famous painters addicted to ether; wealthy married couples attracted by the possibility of experiences outside the bounds of "polite" society. All applauded. All, beginning at ten o'clock at night, felt that they were part of another world, another society. Refined yet daring, elegant yet broad-minded, all felt free, almost loquacious, liberated from the tight corset imposed by society. When the performance was done, they greeted Porfiria and then, champagne glasses in hand, set about looking as modern as their bodies and the color of their skin allowed. Conversations in French were common, as were cigarettes rolled with hashish, pills of opium, and water-pipes for smoking marijuana. Meanwhile, those interested in sex chose a woman and disappeared upstairs. From the beginning, Matilda and Ligia drew the attention of certain couples. Some paid to witness a scene of lesbian love, while others, fewer in number, came to La Modernidad to take part in an almost intimate, family-like orgy. And of course there were the men who came for those "girls" who, like Porfiria, only dressed as women without belonging to that gender. La Modernidad was a place filled with corridors where no desire was forbidden.

The eternal, cruel history of the sexes in their alternating and inevitable approach and withdrawal: approaching one another with a kiss, a caress, and a promise, only to withdraw from one another with ingratitude, spite, and tears!
  Federico Gamboa, Santa

Both Ligia and Matilda soon became aficionados of good wine, imported cigars, and water-pipes for marijuana. Before beginning to work on any new project, they would drink black coffee from Veracruz and inhale the bittersweet smoke of the narcotic. Then, taking over the entire parlor, they would try out new melodies on the phonograph and plot out ever more erotic and daring librettos. Porfiria, on the rare days when she got up before two o'clock in the afternoon, would sit in one of the armchairs and accompany the two women, sniffing from time to time at the smelling-salts she kept always with her in a small mother-of-pearl box. If her spirits allowed, she might even dance with the girls in her Chinese robe and unshaven legs. When, on the other hand, the two women woke up devoid of inspiration, they would not even attempt to get out of bed. Instead, they would puff once or twice on the water-pipe and lie in bed, kissing and cuddling and whispering stories to one another. *Diamantina.* Matilda would repeat the name each time her lover shed a tear over some episode in her past life. Ligia, who had become a true daughter of happiness and joy, and a princess of the night, had not had a happy childhood. Her memories were many, and she would sometimes not be able to express them for the dryness of her mouth, the result of the marijuana. To solve the problem and encourage her to go on, Matilda would get up and bring in a bottle of champagne. Without order, in a sequence whose logic was apparent only to her, her experiences would appear and disappear and intertwine, forming a capricious collage, a labyrinth without doors, a kaleidoscope. Ligia would describe days without food and then, without transition, the pawing and scuffling that would move from slaps on the backside to silent masturbations bringing on wet orgasms on her father's lap. Ligia might spend hours describing the color and texture of the little chamber-pot that she kept under her bed when she was a girl, but only seconds talking about the afternoon sunsets that made her think about the end of the world. She would also tell Matilda about her days in the orphanage for girls, where she was sent after her mother died, or about the afternoons when, after confessing imaginary sins, a young priest would open the door of the confessional, seat her on his lap with her back to him, spread her legs, and penetrate her hurriedly, without her even moving. Often as she recounted the stories of sexual encounters (which she was much given to doing), Ligia would wind up spreading Matilda's legs and slipping her fingers into her lover's wet vagina. Then, seized by a frenzy that tended to increase as the days went on, she would lie face-down on the bed and plead with Matilda to kiss her, there, or put something in her. Matilda, repeating the name "Diamantina" over and over again, would comply. One morning when they decided to remain alone in bed without opening the curtains, Ligia told her what, judging by the seriousness of her voice, seemed to be the key that would allow Matilda to unlock the secrets of her life at last. It was the story of a seduction by a telegraph operator whose betrayal and ultimate abandonment had broken her heart. Matilda's eyes were sad as she listened to the story, but then Diamantina broke into howls of laughter. It was like a slap in the face.

"That story is still as effective as ever, isn't it, She-Devil?"

Ligia had to bring her an entire box of Havana cigars before Matilda would forgive her.

Like the first Diamantina, the second could lie with ease and conviction. The difference between them was that Ligia's lies were dark, more the product of machination than imagination. Matilda could never disentangle her past. Before her eyes, Ligia's life lay like a palimpsest at whose center there was nothing; she could see only her figure walking through a valley with bright light but no plants. La Diamantina changed the story of her life no fewer than seven times. The orphanage became a boarding house, and then the boarding house became a back room in a rich family's residence, and that room in turn became a classroom in which a Frenchman recently arrived from the Côte d'Ivoire taught her to make strange, guttural sounds. Sometimes her past had been unbearable, sometimes a paradise of purity to which she longed to return. Her father had been a thief, a tailor, a disgraced priest, a professor of mathematics, a poet. Her mother, a washerwoman, had also been of the evangelical faith, traveled to the United States, and been murdered wearing the family jewels. Sometimes, watching her act or dance or laugh among the clients, Matilda imagined that Ligia was a house full of stairways that led nowhere. And when one looked out the windows, there was only the empty blue of sterility. Matilda loved Ligia as she had loved her father, hopelessly. Often she put her ear to her lips, hoping to find wisdom, and just as on that day when she had done the same with her father at the top of the pyramid, she discovered that she was saying nothing. The words had become meaningless sounds, syllables which once spoken vanished into the air.

The spectacle of their ballets devoured everything, and became their only reality. Both during them and when they were done, Ligia constantly "struck poses." Moving her eyes and hands with the studied perfection of clockwork, or the delicacy of a mannequin, Ligia would behave as though the eyes of the world were mirrors, or display-windows. The only thing that brought a true gleam to her eyes were the diamonds, now real, that dangled from her ears and at her throat. "Diamantina." Matilda went on pronouncing her name as though it were a talisman, her only salvation, but as often happens when a word is repeated many times, in time it lost its meaning and its power. At that point, she went on saying it for that very reason. Someday, the name would bring up no memory whatever; someday, when she heard it on other lips, she would have to think for one or two seconds before associating it with something real; someday, when she herself pronounced it, she would shiver with cold.

The day when, looking into Ligia's eyes, she discovered someone else in them, she laughed. It was a man with dark skin and presumptuous manners, a liquor merchant with a certain weakness for gambling. He attended the horse races at the Jockey Club and the boxing matches on the top floor of a certain club, La Casa de los Azulejos, where, more than winning or losing money, he liked to feel the rush of adrenaline that freed him from his routine. Which he also felt with Ligia. He courted her with colored gems and horseback rides through Parque La Marqueza, with silk dresses and tickets for Teatro Arbeu, with nights of frenzied sex and the vague promise to get out of the city.

"So he is 'el Jarameño,' eh?" Matilda asked her as she watched her folding clothes and putting her jewelry boxes in a suitcase. Her voice was filled not so much with anger as with sarcasm.

"Well, it's every whore's dream, isn't it? You should do the same thing. La Modernidad is not going to last forever."

"That story is still effective as ever, Ligia, but remember the ending. 'El Jarameño' winds up feeling contempt for Santa and the poor woman ends up in an operating room in the company of a blind pianist," she answered.

"You, She-Devil, don't believe in love," Ligia purred sweetly as she caressed the tip of her chin.

When Matilda watched her descend the staircase and cross the salon where they had performed their parody of Santa so many times, she could only repeat her name again and again until, not crying, she turned her into yet another figment of her imagination. Porfiria put her arms around her and smoothed her hair. Then she tried to lift her spirits with phonograph records, silly jokes, and the whiskey that she saved for special occasions.

"The same thing always happens. And I ought to know." The two of them were in the same large chair, their arms around each other, looking up at the ceiling. "I'll tell you, the real dictatorship is a married couple. Under the pretext of children, they shove us aside as if we were contagious."

Matilda nodded, recognizing the truth of what Porfiria said, and then got up. Then she did something she had not dared to do for a long time. She sat at the piano and, timidly at first and then totally absorbed, played the first piece she had played with the first Diamantina. The chords of the national anthem echoed so sadly in the rooms that it seemed the entire country had been lost. The war had ended and Matilda found herself, as always, among the defeated.

"You should have a good cry," murmured Porfiria, without daring to look at her.

"Have you ever noticed that all mistakes begin with a name?" That was her only answer. Then she played a catchy song from a zarzuela. After that, silence. At the end, there was nothing left.

"How does one come to be a photographer of whores?"

The question came out of nowhere, out of the amusement and brazenness that always accompany emptiness. In the man's frightened eyes, Matilda saw for the first time the gleam of pain, his pain, both his own and others' through him. It was a rusty pin, a bed covered by a yellow canopy, a place whose only reason for existence was that it not be shared. Joaquín Buitrago's pupils grew small and closed their doors. That was what it was all about: see without being seen. The name for that was solitude. Matilda, who had been moved by nothing after the departure of the second Diamantina, was moved. His body was proof enough of the cataclysm he had been through. The man was a loser and like her, another soldier in the legion of the defeated.

"Once, many years ago, you took a photograph of me." The words are barely whispered into his right ear. A secret told on a train. A revelation.

"I know," Joaquín tells her, his eyes open, scanning the lines of her throat as though they were stepping-stones.

In the train station, they move in unison, slowly. Holding hands, not looking back, they walk away from the groups greeting each other loudly, from couples hugging one another tightly. Matilda had been fifteen the first time she tried to see the reflection of her body in the same tiled walls.

"Everything will be all right," the photographer tells her. Then they walk on in silence through the streets of the city.

6

A map

His name is Paul Kamàck. His hobby is lost causes. The moment she sees his small, sunken blue eyes, Matilda knows that. And she confirms it when she unwraps the package he has placed in her hands immediately after introducing himself, taking off his hat, and begging her pardon for his forwardness. It is a length of purple silk.

"I saw you several days ago in La Parisina," he explains, staring at her hairline, where her forehead ends. "I believe you like this. Six yards."

What she will always remember about him is the ease with which he talks about numbers and dates, figures. His concentration when he looks at something. During this time in her life, Matilda does not know that living inside an empty name has left a gleam in her eye and an unusual softness in her body. When they see her pass by, wrapped in her own world, men in the street find her beautiful, unreachable. Paul Kamàck is one of them. A foreigner.

"Is this a love story?" His voice echoes through the dark house.

"Yes." Her reply does as well.

The madwoman and the morphine addict sprawl on armchairs in the salon. The white sheets that have protected the furniture for years and years are lying on the floor, in a pile, like a white island with mountains.

"I don't like love stories."

"Nor do I."

The words fly through the air like owls. A fluttering of wings.

Matilda says she wishes she had met Paul Kamàck years ago. Before. Somewhere else. The story would have been different. Once upon a time. Long long ago. How to start? Paul could convert inches into centimeters instantly, in his head. Fahrenheit into Centigrade. Pounds into kilos. Feet into meters. In those days it was not unusual to run across an engineer from the United States. There were hundreds of them drawing maps, identifying mines, planning the route for railway lines, building factories. They could be recognized by their austere suits and the way they looked at things. Unlike doctors, their hands were rough and weathered. They were explorers in a foreign land, adventurers who altered the surface of the earth, men with the ability to move the horizon from one place to another. Matilda called him Pablo from the beginning, and she forgot his last name.

Paul Kamàck became interested in Mexico for the first time when, still a student, he attended the World Columbian Exposition in Chicago in 1893. What captured his interest was not the calculated exoticism of the materials, but rather the statistics that presented the country as a perennial horn of plenty. That was for him! In addition to the open invitation to Anglo-Saxon immigration, there were pictures that showed the vast natural resources waiting for investors, the increases in textile production, and the country's advances in the field of hygiene. The wizards of progress who were in charge of portraying Mexico also had the shrewd idea of including geographical, mining, and hydrological charts of the country. Paul paid little attention to the information that described the quantity and quality of monuments and public buildings in Mexico City, and he also ignored everything about the artists and intellectuals of the time. Instead, he carefully examined the diverse climatological regions, the networks of rivers, and the systems of communication, especially the telegraphs and railways. Then, outside the fairgrounds, he set about investigating the kind and number of investors who were already profiting from the country's wealth. When he found Rockefellers and Guggenheims among the names of these men, the word "Mexico" began to hold a special place in his mind. An altar.

Like Matilda, Pablo arrived at the central railway station in Mexico City for the first time in 1900. But he came not via Veracruz, but rather Laredo. It was also his first time in a foreign country. Other than his knowledge of engineering, his fascination for bridges, and an unlimited faith in the possibilities of progress, Pablo brought nothing with him. Years earlier, his Hungarian parents had arrived in Boston with nothing but hope, and after only a generation, now living in Chicago, they had a professional in the family. He saw no reason why the same thing should not happen in Mexico.

Although he tried to be objective and not make unflattering comparisons, nothing that he saw could hold its own against the great works of engineering that had transformed the urban spaces of Chicago and New York. Nowhere did he see anything like the suspension bridge designed by James Eads to cross the Mississippi, which had become the very symbol of St. Louis; nothing like the Brooklyn Bridge that, thanks to the Roebling family investment, spanned the East River to Manhattan. In Mexico there were no architects like Louis Sullivan and William LeBaron Jenney, creators of skyscrapers like those that had begun to be built in Chicago after the Great Fire of 1871. But far from disappointing him, these discoveries increased Paul Kamàck's faith in the possibility of making great, rapid profits in Mexico. Without much money, but careful of appearances, he took a room in the Hotel Regis, in the very heart of the city, and like many immigrants he presented himself in several offices without invitation or contact, showing only his business card: Paul Kamàck, engineer. The symmetrical letters were black.

He scrutinized the sewers and probed the buildings, weighing their quality. Notebook in hand, he made sketches and wrote down important dates. He spent entire mornings at the Mexican Natural History Society reading articles, or in the Mexican Society for Geography and Statistics. It was there that, for the first time, he learned of the Real de Minas de Nuestra Señora de la Purísima Concepción de Guadalupe de los Álamos de los Catorce, or "Catorce," as it was called. The article that drew his attention described a conflict among certain scientists in Mexico City because of the splitting of a meteorite that had been found in the area. The area's name was La Descubridora, "The Discoverer." A land of great mineral wealth. Smiling at his find, he carefully analyzed a mining report that appeared in the society's Bulletin in 1872. It was signed by engineer José María Gómez del Campo, and it was titled "Report on Mining in the State of San Luis Potosí. Catorce." Paul learned that there were six veins being worked in this area, in a total of forty mines; La Purísima was the largest. The veins were of native silver and the silver was found in several forms: layers, clumps, flakes, filaments, felt-like fibers, knotty grape-like knuckly clusters, dendritic clusters, blue ash, and a fine powder. The profits were huge. In ninety-six years of constant exploitation, total production was estimated at 163,360,552 pesos. The owners of the mines lived not on the site where the mining took place, but rather in nearby villages, and they hired engineers. The emotion Paul felt run through his body was like electricity. Diligently, in a firm hand, he copied out the information, and when he was done he left the reading room to walk—aimlessly, anywhere. He needed a drink to put his thoughts in order and calm his excitement. That night he went to the National Theater, where he heard a concert by the Polish pianist Ignace Paderewski. Paderewski's interpretation of Schubert's impromptu and Chopin's berceuse only increased his faith in the country's progress. In his own progress.

In Mexico, unlike in Chicago, his blond hair and engineering title opened the doors to aristocratic houses and certain circles of professionals on the rise. The marriageable daughters of attorneys, doctors, and businessmen looked at him with hopeful eyes while their fathers, after weighing his manners and his future, offered him glasses of imported whiskey and praised his Spanish, thinking about the benefits of racial mixing. Paul had grown up speaking Hungarian as well as English; he had learned Italian among the immigrant families in his neighborhood, and he had mastered Spanish in courses he took after the 1893 Exposition. Pablo, however, had eyes only for his own future. The society señoritas he invited to the opera seemed dull and uncultured, languorous, pale. Their skeletons seemed to be held together by thin threads, and their talcum-covered skin had a doubtful whitish cast. On their smooth, soft hands there was no trace of any labor. On the train that took him back to Laredo after two months in the capital, there was no Mexican woman at his side.

Before he left the country, he got off at the Vanegas station. The dry landscape, covered with plants whose names he did not know, looked to him like paradise itself. In the dry wind that ruffled his hair he could almost smell the silver many meters below ground. The mines' names made his head spin, as though he were dreaming. La Purísima. The Philosopher's Stone. The Hog Burrow Shaft. Santa Edwige. Pablo decided to walk the twelve kilometers to Catorce, even though the town had had its own station since 1888 and the Potrero-Cedral line was in service. He wanted to not only see but literally touch the ground with his own feet, with his whole body. A full moon. He had never been in a semi-desert region before, and the vastness of the place, bathed by a high, glaring sun, filled his head with images. He carried his explorer's rucksack, a compass, and a couple of lemons to quench his thirst. Despite the fact that his future was bringing him to Catorce, he forgot about it during his journey. Time stopped. As though he were inside a fishbowl, he could hear his own breathing and the noisy rushing of the blood as it left his heart and flowed through his veins. His body, its urges, distracted him. He wanted to make love to the very earth. When he finally arrived at Real de Catorce, his eyes tired and his clothes covered with dust, he realized that during his trek he had found his destiny. He would die here, his bones would be preserved inside a cave. The only thing he needed was to find the woman who would give him the last embrace before he closed his eyes and finally rested in peace.

In two days Pablo Kamàck was able to gather all the information he needed. In addition to walking through the town and visiting its churches, bullring, hospital, and the grand houses on Avenida Independencia, one of which, number 1003, was a true mansion, he paid a visit to the archives in the municipal offices. Catorce, he wrote in his notebook, lay fifty-eight leagues north of the state capital, at 23 degrees 33 minutes 20 seconds north latitude, 1 degree 17 minutes 40 seconds west of the Mexico City meridian, at 2992 rods above sea level and 790 above the Valley of Matehuala. Due to its altitude, the climate was cool. The city was divided into four districts or wards, and the following barrios: Charquillas, Venadito, Puerto del Palillo, Tierra-Blanca, Hediondilla, Camposanto, and Las Tuzas. It had five bridges: Purísima, Tierra-Blanca, San José, Hediondilla, and Guadalupe. Among the family names he encountered were the Coghlans and the de la Mazas, and, in passing, don Vicente Irizar Aróstegui, who, having taken charge of some of the business dealings of the de la Mazas, earned a salary of five thousand pesos per year. Pablo was about to go when a clerk in the city offices approached the table where he was copying down notes as fast as he could. The clerk was bringing him some papers. They were the "Geognostic Map of the Restoration Company Lands," drawn by David Coghlan, and the "Mineral and Geological Map of the District of Catorce, San Luis Potosí State, 1885," also by Coghlan. The documents took his breath away and, just as he had felt in the Geographic Society reading room, a jolt of electricity ran up his spine. Besides bridges, there was nothing in the world that Pablo loved as much as well-drawn maps in which all of reality was measured and reduced to scale. In silence, he copied the maps on blank paper.

This is the story written on the lines of a map of Real de Catorce.

Paul returned to Real again in the summer of 1902 and later, in the fall of 1905, he revisited Mexico City. In Catorce he met don Francisco M. Coghlan, who, after a brief conversation, invited Paul to be a guest in his mansion on Avenida Independencia. That generosity was unusual. What the old miner liked best about Paul was not the knowledge that he made much of in his after-dinner conversations, or the mass of technological innovation he brought from the United States, or even his determination to succeed and become wealthy. What convinced the old gentleman to open the doors of his house, offer the stranger friendship and a job, was something else. The young man's energy, first of all, but more than anything the steely gleam that the desert imparted to his eye. Don Francisco recognized it immediately. It was the same gleam that had been in his father's eye (and which had never changed) when, in 1885, he had taken over the Santa Ana Mining Corporation. Although he was not its proprietor, David Coghlan was equally as diligent, equally as pigheaded, and equally as filled with the faith, comparable only to his faith in God, that he could improve the conditions in the mine and correct the problems that plagued it. In the first four years, he not only leveled the floors of the tunnels, opened new shafts and adits and built a railway line to extract the ore at low cost, but also managed to attract capital investment of four hundred thousand pesos. Then, in the next six years, he installed an electric generator in Santa Ana when there were no more than two electric windlasses in the entire United States. He also installed steam-driven Dow water pumps capable of lifting water a thousand feet at over five hundred gallons per second. Under his firm hand, Santa Ana became one of the richest mines in Mexico. The profits were so great that they not only enriched the mine's owners, the de la Maza family, but also filled his pockets, decorously of course, as well. The money filled him with pride, but no emotion was as evident as happiness, or was more abundant. Simple, whole, peaceful. Just thinking that he had struggled body to body, hand to hand, against a harsh and hostile nature made him smile. He had courted the mine shrewdly and ingeniously, he had subjected it to his will little by little, with work, steam, and electricity, and at last, when Santa Ana opened its generous entrails to him, the triumph was like fireworks. In 1895, when President Díaz and an entourage made up of Romero Rubio, Fernández Leal, and González Cosío, government ministers all, came to the mines for a visit, the fireworks were real. David Coghlan loved the desert because it was his wiliest opponent. When Pablo decided to tell don Francisco the story of his first trek from Vanegas to Catorce, his voice was grave and crystalline, and his discreet gestures were those of a man recounting a revelation. Then, smiling, the old man realized that he had not made a mistake. Kamàck, like him and like his father before him, would die here. Happy. In the middle of the desert. With nothing but an old map in his hands. His eyes were those of a man in love.

Paul, however, could not stay. His destiny, if he had one, would have to wait.

In 1905, rather than returning by train via Laredo, Paul boarded a steamship in New Orleans and sailed to Veracruz. Weariness and a bout of the influenza forced him to remain for several days in Mexico City, which seemed, at least to him, ostentatious and not at all attractive. But he was here, empty, as it were, with no goal in mind at all. His wife and only child had died in childbirth, and if he had decided to return to Catorce it was less in search of a fortune and more on account of the lunar landscape that had once so captivated him. His grief had been unbearable, and all he wanted to do was die. He could imagine no other way to find rest. Those who bothered to listen to him were told that he was in search of his destiny. The few who saw him board ship with one suitcase full of books and another crammed with scientific instruments realized that he would never be coming back. Paul was returning to his nation, his homeland—the real one.

His illness forced him to unpack his bags and spend whole afternoons sitting in a chair watching the crowds through the dirty windows of his boarding house. Sometimes, with nothing else to do, he would thumb through books of design or trace drawings of bridges on blank paper. Most of the time he studied the map of Mexico drawn by General Carlos Pacheco, or the many sketches made by the geographer Antonio García Cubas. His eyes, at those times, were like a man's eyes gazing upon a woman's body. Sometimes, when his humor and his energies allowed it, he would go out for a short walk with his walking-stick and his broad-brimmed hat. In the streets there were beggars, workers returning from work, students walking in groups and smoking cigarettes, a scurrying attorney. Few attracted his attention. The first time he saw her, Matilda was carrying a heavy basket filled with fruit and other purchases from the market. Her quick steps and the lightness of her body made him think that this was a woman who was strong, accustomed to work. That was why he followed her to Santo Domingo Plaza, where she sat on the edge of the fountain. Then he saw her run off, quickly and apparently without a fixed destination. He would never have recalled her face had it not been that the woman, standing in the middle of a riot in front of a pawnbroker's, passed over food and jewels and chose to bend down for a broken mandolin with no strings. Silly girl. Moments later, he saw her embrace someone in the crowd. And it was then, in that embrace, that her face became immortal. The nearness was absolute. The man and the woman were suddenly somewhere else. The absolute isolation of that embrace made Paul feel both envy and longing. The strength of his emotions made him lower his eyes and return to his room. His destiny was on this moon, and it was his and no one else's.

By the second time he saw her, he had forgotten her. He was walking along in front of the shop-windows of La Parisina and his eye caught the figure of a woman caressing the bolts of silk as though they were a beloved body. He stopped. He entered the shop and asked how much the organza and taffeta cost while he watched the woman out of the corner of his eye. When one of the clerks addressed her by name and politely but firmly asked her to leave the store, he realized that this was not the first time the woman had done this. It was then that he recognized her face. The woman from the embrace had a weakness for silk. Two pieces of the puzzle became three with the mention of her name. Matilda. Matilda Burgos. It was not until three days later that he bought the six yards of fabric, but then, no matter how he searched for her in the streets and byways of the city, he could not find her.

The three years he spent in Catorce before deciding to return to Mexico City were spent working underground. He struggled against the inevitable, because only in that struggle could he recognize his own human face. Despite the death of Francisco Coghlan in 1903 from a disease of the liver, Paul took up residence in the same cold room that he had been given in the mansion on Independencia. During this period of his life, few heard him speak and no one ever heard him laugh. With the univocal strength of a man who has lost everything in life, Pablo had no objective except taking silver out of the mines. With no friend but the ghosts of don Francisco and don Francisco's father, the mapmaker, he waged a war to the death against nature. Nature, this time, came heavily armed. The Dolores mine was like a headstrong woman leery of being the object of his attentions. Paul courted it with all his engineering skill and wisdom. He dug new shafts, set the old steam-driven water pumps and electric windlasses to work again. He made contact with the Vidal Cervantes corporation. But everything ground to a halt for lack of capital. Within a few years, Catorce had become unreal. Most of the mineworkers sought better luck in the north, in the mines in Cohauila and Arizona, and the village was reduced to a formless group of hopeful, stubborn men living among other men who had no hope left whatever. Not even the hope of leaving. In 1908, when, without family or prospects or happiness, Pablo decided to go to the Vanegas station and take the Laredo-Mexico City train, his spirits were still somewhat buoyed by the mad idea of finding among the businessmen of Mexico City one who would entrust him with a small amount of capital. As he left behind the Valley of Matehuala, he realized that the love he felt for that landscape was the strongest emotion of his life. The only emotion. Not his dead wife and not his stillborn son, not engineering and not even his desire to amass a fortune of his own—none of them were as sure and clear as his desire to see Catorce as he had seen it that first time. He was forty years old, and it had been three years since he had touched a woman.

He knew that he was not likely to find anyone willing to share their capital, knew that the profit to be made from commerce was much greater than that to be dug out of mines, knew everything that he had to know, but hope is an animal always searching for a waterhole.

What he did not know was that he would see the woman again. He immediately remembered her name, as though it had never left his mind. To her long strides and strong-boned frame had now been added an aura of emptiness, a pair of dark eyes that looked only inward. Matilda was walking through the city as though she were already in the desert. This time he followed her at a distance until he saw her enter La Modernidad. He watched her for days. Then, after buying the six yards of purple silk for the second time, he walked up to her in the street.

"I saw you several days ago in La Parisina," he said, never taking his eyes off her hairline, where her forehead ended. "I thought you might like this. Six yards."

"I see you like lost causes," declared the woman, still smiling.

"Yes."

"I do, too."

But the love story does not begin there.

Sun-bright days and moonless nights had to pass.

Surprise, astonishment, and mistrust had to pass.

Rain.

The feeling of wanting to run, run.

The future. The past. And the time that lies between them.

In order to reach the embrace, they had to get past themselves.

Paul Kamàck opens the door to La Modernidad. Inside, under blue lights, Matilda's body is twisting and contorting during the performance of what they have titled "Immensity." The applause and the suddenly brighter lights interrupt his concentration. He is on the verge of loving her already. Then, at the end, when no one is left on the stage, she decides to go over to him still covered with makeup and praise. The loser. She takes his hand and leads him through the people to the spot where Porfiria is holding court, under the painting of the Dominatrix. Pablo's eyes smile. She is on the verge of loving him already.

"So the story is still as effective as ever after all, eh, my little she-devil?"

Not understanding, Paul extends his hand.

"I suppose this is another 'Jarameño,'" Porfiria says, still laughing.

In the room, Paul watches how Matilda unbuttons her dress as though this were some new, untried technology. He does not help her. Then he watches as she unbuttons her shoes. The stockings fall little by little, becoming a black roll under her fingertips. Suddenly, Pablo is once again a boy watching in amazement as his father puts broken puppets back together, cuts out pieces of wood, strikes the hammer exactly on the head of each nail. In her petticoats, she steps toward him. Her breasts are full, as is her smile. Her waist is probably about twenty-nine inches. The curve of her hips is about seventy degrees. Shoe size, 7. The black triangle at her pubis is equilateral. The warmth of her nearness. Matilda takes off his wool jacket and vest, then unbuttons his pants. Paul lets her. Then a piece of yellowing paper falls out of his pocket.

"It's a map," he says, trying to snatch it away from her.

Matilda unfolds the paper and puts it in the center of the bed. She kneels on the mattress like a child. There are no more than eight inches, now four, between them. His face is gilded by the sun of the Valley of Matehuala, by the fear that he is witnessing a miracle. Matilda turns her face to him and says, without really meaning anything by it:

"This is where I'm going to live with you, eh?"

The embrace that precedes the lovemaking, the embrace that culminates in lovemaking, is as warm as a breeze, as dark as a mine. A photograph.

"Don't go on."

In the coach of the train, Pablo talks about the Valley of Matehuala as though it belonged to him. His homeland. Through the window he points out to her the zigzagging row of creosote bushes, the flowers of the barrel-shaped melon cactus, yellow, red, the thorns of the garambullo. There are cactuses as tall and stiff as priests and nopal trees exactly as José María Velasco painted them. Pitahayas. Guayules.

"The air," he says, "the air is blue. The horizon is a line that cuts your heart in two. A hawk."

When they arrive in San Luis Potosí, he asks her not to

look at it, it is not worth the trouble. In San Luis, a man and a woman can only embrace sadly, he tells her, embraces that do not deserve the name. Embraces that are not embraces. In the Vanegas station, he almost begs her to walk the twelve kilometers with him along the tracks. A ritual. If she had met him before, in another place, Matilda would not remember the name she remembers as she walks among the sharp leaves of the creosote bushes and the little pebbles that once belonged to the sea. Sometimes, when she turns to look at him, she wishes with all her heart that her eyes would discover the face of Diamantina, the first one. A Bach melody. In the desert, time stops and emotions become confused. How long has it been since she has seen her? How long has it been since she has wanted to? Paul Kamàck. His name produces the first real tenderness in her entire life. The only thing he asks as they enter the short, narrow streets of Catorce is that she never give him a child. Matilda agrees to that.

Love cannot be told. Love is evil. It is made of insipid gestures and habits hard to break. Love is the years that pass, one after another, unvarying. In the desert, love is a plain on which nothing grows, a mine that spits out silver from time to time, a parish priest who is dying, a constant scarcity of water. Love is what is under the tongue when it is dry, the thing beside one's footsteps when they are unheard. Love is a weeping willow in one corner of the Venado cemetery and the open ruins of the Diezmo building beside the town hall. Love is a popular song, or perhaps not quite a song at all.

> *The silver mines of Catorce*
> *will surely break your heart*
> *because every one of them, my friend*
> *is all closed down and dark.*

As I passed by Potrero
they asked where I was bound for.
"I'm going to look for work, friend,
in the mines up farther north."

Day after day, Matilda and Pablo saw whole families leave the town. They realized that a revolution was going on only when mobs began carrying off the machinery, silently dismantling the steam pumps and windlasses. Then silence fell. The only ones who did not stop coming were the pilgrims in search of the miracles of San Francisco de Real de Catorce. Work. Health. Peace. And water, especially water. Thanks to those things, the Santa Ana trains continued running. Then there were the others, the *huicholes* coming in for their annual harvest of the peyote during the winter months. But these had no need even of railways. The miners and merchants who had once amassed substantial fortunes in Catorce left behind not a single charitable foundation or convent or public work or fountain or piece of art. With their passing, all that remained was the riddled earth and the ghost of the machinery, with its decay-ridden teeth.

The hopeful remembered. The hopeless wanted only to forget. Once, when Catorce was the center of the world, the celebrations had been lavish. In 1901, for the inauguration of the Ogorrio tunnel that joined the mines of Catorce to those of Potrero and Refugio, a happy crowd congregated to celebrate the proud achievements of engineering without knowing that there would be no more after that. The 2270 meters excavated underground led the way not into the future, but only into darkness. The Lavín Theater had been the setting for works whose characters, such as Opinion, Justice, and Better Materials, had inspired the audience's applause. When there was life in Catorce, when struggling for an increase in wages or better working conditions made sense, there were even strikes such as the one that halted production at La Concepción in 1900 and forced the town's cantinas to close down. People read the news in *The Catorce Echo* and *Public Opinion,* in *The Voice of the People* and *The Lever.* But in 1909 the last attempt to maintain contact with the outside world had been *The Flu.* Now there was only the parched earth and a cloudless sky. No way to find out that outside, in the rest of the country, everything was the same. For Pablo Kamàck and Matilda Burgos, that was enough. In the ruins of Catorce, the two of them could at last find rest.

Pablo speaks very little, and when he does, his words are full of the names of the mines. Ana. Edwige, Concepción. In the desert, language becomes as tenuous and ephemeral as memory. The vastness floods one's breast and leaves no room for anything else. Matilda, during these years, learns all the strategies of silence. In the winter, she and Pablo, like the *huicholes,* comb the land in search of peyote flowers. The nine alkaloids of the peyote transport them to other places and then, to only this place. Pablo walks across the bridges that he has constructed in his imagination for years. There, over the waters of the Tuxpan River, between the villages of Tampico and Tuxpan, there is a steel structure that withstands the onslaughts of time and hurricanes. Another very similar structure, simple but monumental, stretches across the waters of the Grijalva as well. Construction begins on both banks and, as time goes on, the supports and concrete piers link up in the middle. The joined hands of progress. A group of engineers and another larger group of workers observe the slow transformation of the horizon. Then, during the inauguration, the fireworks, the painters under the arches and the photographers enthralled with the geometry of space— all these are authentic. Once his mission is done, Pablo always returns to the mines of Catorce. Down in the entrails of Santa Ana, he passes through the chamber where the four boilers, the reservoirs of water and coal, the windlass, and the conveyor belt with its tower and pulleys are located, all in perfect condition. The walls are cement and stone, the ceilings iron. He is 156 meters underground. He goes on descending, and he comes to the pump room, where he watches the compressed-air hammers work. He is 306 meters—1181 feet—under ground. There is the sound of engines and dynamos among the minerals, and the muted crunching of his own footsteps. The miracle of technology takes his breath away. The miracle of the earth split open. He climbs. Ascends. Returns. Then there appear the roots of the creosote tree, and after that, the sun. A coral snake makes tiny dunes in the loose earth. Beside it, only Pablo's footprints.

Matilda, on the other hand, sees nothing. Under the influence of the peyote she sees nothing. Besides the blue sky, she sees nothing. She is inside Paul Kamàck's eyes.

He has three scars on his right leg and one, half-moon shaped, on his left ankle. There are two dark moles on each of his shoulder blades. When he smiles, two small asymmetrical indentations form in his cheeks. The soft down that covers arms, chest, legs, and back is golden. He sleeps on his left arm. His feet are cold. He is not interested in knowing anything else.

"Don't go on."

The strangers arrived during the winter with cameras and hightop boots. Two men. They set up the camp about 100 yards from the railway station, with the permission of the mayor. At night they would sit around a fire, and during the day they explored the surroundings. The moment they arrived, they began taking notes and making drawings in notebooks with white pages and blue covers. They had brought two pewter pots with them to brew coffee, and bars of soap that they bathed with out in the underbrush. To each other, though they had trouble with the pronunciation, they would repeat the word "Wirikúta" and the word "Tsinurita." Their eyes thirsted after wonders. When the procession of *huicholes* came, they joined it, and melting into the crowd, they took photos and transcribed songs. "*Qué bonitas colinas, qué bonitas colinas, tan verdes aquí donde estamos. Ahora ni siquiera siento, ni siquiera siento que quiero irme a mi rancho. Porque todos somos, todos somos los niños, todos somos los hijos de una flor de brillantes colores, de una encendida flor. Y aquí no hay nadie que lamente lo que somos.*" When they discovered Paul and Matilda among them, they invited them into their camp. They wanted to hear stories, legends, tales of apparitions. They wanted to fill their ears with wonders. One was a photographer and the other an engineer turned amateur anthropologist. Both were working for the Ministry of Education and their job was to discover the continent of the past and plant the flag of the Revolution in its center. It was through them that Matilda and Pablo learned of the new winds that were blowing through the nation, the new spirit that was animating it. When the men left, their mules were loaded down with the timeless dream of Real de Catorce. From that time on, there would be no refuge. Now there would be no salvation.

Here there is no one to lament what we are.

Pablo is exhausted. He no longer has the strength to find another place. For days, he makes detailed plans for his own end. First he goes to Venado, and then, when he cannot find the dynamite, he decides to go to Matehuala so as not to have to see the ugly face of San Luis Potosí. All this he does on foot, buffeted by the wind. When he returns, his skin is covered by brown splotches, his hair is yellow. His eyes have turned gray, almost white. Colorless. It is 3:00 in the afternoon. Around the table where they have shared rattlesnake meat, prickly pear, sips of silence and parsley tea, the only thing he can ask of her is forgiveness. He will leave her absolutely alone and without a heart.

"I am going to die, Matilda," he whispers. She hears him without blinking, without any movement at all. Distance. Then, the words fade away little by little. The only thing she can hear while she watches his lips moving is her own breathing, the air going in and coming out her lips, the calm beating of her veins, and the grinding of her white teeth. Over and over again. The mechanical sounds of her body, like blows of a hammer. Over and over again. She is inside a fishbowl, far away, somewhere else. There the colors are brighter, the wind cooler, and there is no grief.

"I am going to kill myself, Matilda."

When she sees him stand up and push his chair back, she remains seated. Then the male figure walks through the door, and the woman watches his body move away and grow small in the distance. Later, she can make out just his hat beyond the rise of a small hill, and then she sees nothing anymore. The sky over Catorce is cobalt blue. When she hears the distant boom of the explosion, there are three stars above her head. Behind her, where she cannot see it, the circle of the full moon is orange.

The next morning.

Matilda goes into her house and looks at it as she has never looked at it before. The walls are adobe, the floors dirt. On the woodstove there is a little oil lamp, its wick still lighted. At the bottom of a tin bucket there are two plates, a pitcher, a pot, all of clay. All with food crusted on them. The only table in the place is square, the wood old. The bed is a straw mattress covered with cotton sheets. Above the right side of the headboard is a photograph of a bridge, dark waters flowing under the metal structure, and behind, the pointed cupolas of the buildings. Paul Kamàck. Matilda folds the shawls hanging from nails, the shirts, the gray rebozo. Calmly, neatly, she puts all of it in the leather suitcases. The air that enters and leaves her mouth is calm. Not thinking about it, following the rhythm of her body, she pours oil on the floors and, from the door, throws in a lighted match. The flames she watches as she sits on a rock make her smile. The only thing she is still holding in her hands is the purple silk, six yards. It takes her three whole days to unravel the threads, one by one, and scatter them into the skeins of the air. Blue.

Outside: desert: inside. The difference is nil.

When Matilda comes to, it is 1918, and her name is still Matilda Burgos. The sounds that come in through the hospital windows where she finds herself are the sounds of a city. She recognizes them by their speed. A woman dressed in white informs her that she is in a convent in San Luis Potosí. Then come the questions. The replies. Softly, unsure of herself, Matilda says that she lived ten years in an adobe house in the barrio known as Camposanto. Someone takes notes. Then, when she assures them that her husband was an engineer, the son of a Hungarian couple named Kamàck, her interlocutors raise their eyes, look at each other, and smile discreetly.

"No one has lived in Camposanto since before the revolution," they tell her. "In the censuses, there is no family named Kamàck," they add.

Matilda's only answer is to sit up in her bed and ask them to help her get to Mexico City. She wants to leave as soon as possible, she doesn't want to see the ugly face of San Luis Potosí. She begs them.

"Who is the president of the republic?"

"I don't know," she answers after trying unsuccessfully to remember.

"How old are you?"

"Twenty-four," she answers, guessing incorrectly.

"How much is two plus two?"

"Four." That response wins her her freedom.

In the train on the way back to the capital, the only thing she hears is the echo of the explosion; the only thing she sees through the train windows are the flames that sent her life up in smoke; the only thing she touches is the map of Catorce on which, many years ago, a faceless and voiceless man made her a promise that she has forgotten.

"No one believed me. I told them so many times and no one believed me. When I got to Mexico City I told them I had come from the desert and no one, not a single soul, believed me."

"I believe you."

The answer makes them both laugh. As though there were anyone who cared what Joaquín Buitrago believed or didn't believe! Here, in this house full of sheets and darkness, there is no one to lament what they are, what they were, what they will someday be.

"The flames, Joaquín. Have you ever seen a house on fire?"

Joaquín's only answer is to approach her and, hesitantly, pull her face down to his thin chest. Another embrace.

"Yes."

"When?"

"Right now."

7

A method with no doors

Matilda Burgos and Joaquín Buitrago have missed all the grand historic occasions. When the Revolution broke out, she was in the midst of a love made of barrel-shaped cactuses and blue air, and he was in the wavering daze of morphine. On the day Pascual Orozco took Ciudad Juárez, neither of them was aware of it, or of the exact day on which Porfirio Díaz fled into exile on the *Ypiranga* bound for Paris, on his lips that prophetic phrase: "They have unchained the tiger; let's see whether they can tame it." Neither of them was part of the crowd that celebrated the entrance of Francisco Madero into Mexico City, and none of the bullets of the Ten Tragic Days in 1913 wounded them. They never saw Victoriano Huerta in any cantina whatsoever, and although they heard the rumors and witnessed the chaos, they did not bother to read the newspapers with the headlines about the American invasion. When Emiliano Zapata and Francisco Villa offered each other the presidential chair, each making a show of good manners, Matilda was absorbed in watching the bubbles of water about to boil in a clay pot and Joaquín was using his head only to call up again the cruel ghost of Alberta. Neither of them saw the trucks filled with furniture belonging to those who were leaving the country forever, or witnessed the dismantling of the grand houses along Reforma. Neither of them caught typhus or went for food to the aid stations that the constitutional government had organized around the city. The days during which the generals, professionals, and other important men of the country met in Querétaro to draft a new constitution, Matilda spent with Pablo inspecting a rusty steam pump, while Joaquín was in the common ward of a hospital due to a lack of narcotics. In all that time, the photographer never went out searching for revolutionaries or their female camp followers or massacres; instead, he devoted himself to taking photographs of absences. A chair, the wrinkled outline in the seat of someone who just got up. A cup of coffee with a dark lip-print on the rim. An empty swing seat still moving. The half-open pages of a book. A lighted cigarette. For Matilda, on the other hand, the Revolution was reduced to two foreigners gathering information. A suicide. The absence of sound. Both were forever on the wet, messy banks of history, ready to slip and fall out of its spell and yet always inside it. Very much inside it.

In 1921, walking through the city, they find things not very different. They know the name of the president, and remember that he has only one arm. They know that there are groups of young teachers in a few corners of the country who are giving classes in grammar and hygiene. Matilda knows that there are anarchists in the capital and other industrial centers trying to form unions. Cástulo. The word "justice" is much in vogue, the word "equality," the word "progress." A year ago Zapata was assassinated, and soon Villa will be shot down, not on the horse that made him famous but rather in a black car on the outskirts of Parral. People are listening to *Varita de nardo*. Hand in hand, walking tentatively, aimlessly, Matilda and Joaquín are two jarring notes in the concerto of the new city; they concentrate only on other things. This is the jewelry store where La Diamantina, the second one, sighed in longing before the emeralds. This door behind which there is now a shoe store was the one that each, or both, once opened to find themselves dazzled by the lack of artifice of a woman who wore spectacles. This is the fountain where Matilda first heard the voice of her destiny. That was where the morgue once was, where Joaquín took his first photographs of death. In that house adorned with a black bow Matilda lived for seven years under the rules of a man she never knew and a woman whose name she no longer remembers. May they rest in peace. Here is La Parisina. That place there, which is now called Progreso, once bore the name La Modernidad. On the map of their sentimental city, the monuments are transparent and the scale varies widely. Matilda and Joaquín do not like to cry.

What they do, these days, is put the house in Santa María de Ribera to rights again. They have already gotten rid of all the ghostly sheets, and now they take brooms, feather dusters, and mops and clean the floors, the ceilings with their iodine-colored stains, and the corners thick with spider webs. Joaquín has managed to get the electricity connected and, with inexpert hands, Matilda has mended the old drapes and reclaimed the garden. Little by little, the house has become habitable once again. But everything is different. By mutual accord they have taken the mattresses smelling of mold and humidity and, with the crystal, the porcelain dinnerware, the silverware, and the Persian rugs, given it all to the rag man. All they have kept of the house's furnishings is a rectangular mahogany table, two chairs, and a large armchair. All the rest they have cut up for firewood.

"Louis XV coming up. Walnut or cedar this time, Matilda?" Joaquín asks with fevered eyes. His activities induce excitement in him. There are entire days when they are no more than a couple of children, two termites delightedly destroying everything around them. The shouts by which they communicate from room to room, or the howls of laughter that certain objects inspire in them, a picture with the whitish face of Porfirio Díaz, for example, keep the neighbors on the alert. The only things they have not touched are the books in the library, the piano, and the dark draperies that keep out the outside. At nightfall, lit by the flickering flames in the fireplace, they lie down beside each other with their clothes on and exchange hurtful words. Although they embrace one another and cuddle each other almost ravenously, their touching is not sexual. The caresses of one another's hair or the kisses on the forehead or cheeks wear the halo of familiarity. Exhaustion leaves dark circles under their eyes, dried-out skin, but does not lead to sleep. When dawn comes, they are still awake, and it is only then that, on Joaquín's schedule, the two of them can finally rest. In peace.

In the empty, clean house, the echo of their voices resembles a constant prayer, religious words. Joaquín and Matilda never caress one another.

The day the money he obtained from his photographic studies runs out, Joaquín bathes by pouring buckets of cold water over himself and he dresses in his only black suit. Among the papers that his father left untidily in his desk drawers, Joaquín finds the will and the address of the family attorney. Outside, in the street, without telling Matilda that he is leaving, he hails a taxi to take him to the center of the city. The office is on the third floor of a building on Calle Bolívar. Arturo Loayza. The gold letters on the door, the sound of telephones, and the rapid click of the secretary's high heels almost give him a headache. When the prim young attorney sees him, his surprise is sincere, unfeigned. Joaquín is a man from the past, a man about whom many alarming stories have been told among his circle of acquaintances, a man whom everyone believed dead or vanished.

"Forgive my surprise, Mr. Buitrago, but you will surely understand. We have had no word from you in years. Many years. And now suddenly...I need some time to analyze the documents and see what we can do for you."

In addition to the house in Santa María there are bank accounts, properties in Cuernavaca, land that has become part of the barrio now known as La Condesa, investments in textile factories, and documents that attest to ownership of a pharmacy. Joaquín knows that to obtain these things, all he needs is a medical certificate. The cursed morphine. The only doctor he knows is Eduardo Oligochea. While he waits, he goes over to the window and looks down at the coming and

going of automobiles in the narrow streets, and he is swept
by a wave of nostalgia. When did all this change? The
sunlight passes through the clouds and then, sullied,
adulterated, falls almost exhausted on the streets. Large
colorless islands. A blue that is almost gray prevents him
from seeing the old face of the sky.

"As you know, my father, may he rest in peace, handled
all of your father's business matters. Everything seems to be
in order. If you like, we can discuss the things that need to be
discussed over a drink at La Opera." The young man's eyes
have a slight greenish cast; his voice, the studied insistence
of ambition. "You would be my guest, of course. It will be
my pleasure."

In addition to the profitable business, the attorney is
motivated by a sincere curiosity. They must be about the same
age, they are the scions of similar families. His memories of
Joaquín are limited to a couple of parties, some family
gathering in the country where his slim, sullen figure easily
slips away and vanishes. Then as he watches him out of the
corner of his eye as they walk down Bolívar, other events
come to his mind. One in particular. There is music by Liszt
on the piano, the sound of glasses clinking and discreet
whispers when Joaquín approaches the pianist. His eyes have
seen no one else. "Call me Diamantina." Everyone heard her.
The woman's presumption caused one or two women to break
into nervous giggles and more than one man to clear his
throat. She was a nameless little schoolteacher whose
spectacles and grimy taffeta skirt aroused the unmuted
criticism of some women. "Brazen." "The daughter of a
painter—a *house* painter, of course." A person who looked
Joaquín up and down, took him in from head to toe, with
arrogance and disdain, as though she belonged to his same
class. The woman who lured him away from medicine. The
steely, concentrated face that appeared in his first
photographs, which his mother tried to destroy. His perdition.
Arturo Loayza has a special weakness for men who allow

themselves to be consumed by passion for a woman. He wants to know. Wants to know what he feels. In his comfortable life, with his wife and three children, a house in Colonia Roma and an office in the center of the city, the only activities that make the adrenaline flow in his veins are bullfights, a game of poker, a soccer game. Money. Aside from that, he is ruled by routine, his concern about the eventual illnesses of his children, the slight boredom of a bed shared with the same woman for more than ten uninterrupted years now. Joaquín, suddenly, is his anti-mirror. The burnished glass in which sometimes, especially on those interminable Sunday afternoons, he would like to see himself. He wants to know.

"It is a great deal of money," he tells him, "almost a fortune. Do you know that?"

"Yes."

Joaquín is totally out of place in La Opera. He detests the rich upholstery, the ceilings with their rococo details, the waiters in their black suits. The way they speak to him: don Arturo. The sudden respect he acquires from simply sitting at the man's table. His nervousness begins to subside only with the first glass of whiskey. If only someone could bring him a hypodermic syringe on one of those little trays! Accustomed to the low voice of Matilda, the lonely vastness of all the rooms he is living in, he is stung as though by darts by the sounds and crowded furniture of La Opera. Arturo is too close. He can smell the lavender-scented cologne at his collar, see the exquisite perfection of his white hands. Two golden handcuffs: the wedding band on his left hand and the professional ring on the right. There is a coffee-colored thread visible on an edge of his lapel.

"My father had great esteem for your family. I was just a boy when the accident occurred. We were so sorry. But we did not see you at the funeral." The pause is intentional. With the passing of time, the attorney has learned to ask questions with great tact.

"No, I wasn't there."

The liquor that makes Arturo's head feel light does no more than sharpen the protective strategies that Joaquín has developed. It is as though each of his sentences were punctuated by a period. New paragraph. The turning of the last page of a book. There is nothing else to say.

"I understand that you went into photography, Joaquín."

"Yes. Photography."

Arturo is not used to monosyllables. In the places he frequents, it is difficult to stop the soliloquy of men who, lightheaded with drink, describe their triumphs, their conquests, and the long path of their future without thinking of anyone else. But Joaquín's silence, far from dispelling Arturo's curiosity, piques it. He has read too much poetry in his leisure hours. Joaquín's worn, haggard face and his long hair occasion in him something very much like envy. The photographer knows it. With the passing of time he has become accustomed to people's disdain for him, their contempt sometimes, but he is also aware, especially after his conversations with Dr. Oligochea, that some of the details of his life can feed the imagination of a certain kind of successful man. The only thing he has to do is avoid revealing the most shameful incidents. His stories must not include vomiting, clothes covered with excrement, the number of needle-marks on his arms, the times he has waked up in pools of his own urine. Any allusions to morphine must be accompanied by words that are part-spiritual, part-modern. Phrases such as "the loss of traditional values," for example, or "this cold industrial madness" immediately assure him the compassion and complicity of his interlocutors. Disenchantment, disillusionment is in vogue these days. Touching upon it is an index of intelligence, the mark of a refined spirit. Without it, the others would not be able to justify progress. Their own. Among certain successful men, losers are beautiful beings, not to mention essential in the complicated interactions of modern life.

"What we are going to need, and you must not take this in the wrong way, Joaquín, is a medical certificate. It is a clause in the will."

"I'll bring it to you in a few days," he assures him.

"So your addiction has been cured," the attorney ventures, hesitatingly. "Forgive me for being so blunt, but those are the exact words used in the document, 'cured of his addiction.'"

"Yes, don Arturo. Morphine. But everything is in order now. Everything."

The two men smile.

"The country is in need of artists now. Without you, our nation might have glory but no soul, no substance. Perhaps one of these days you might show me some of your photographs and we might even be able to do something for you there. If you would allow me, of course."

When Joaquín takes his leave, he does so courteously, carefully. Then, in the street, he cannot keep himself from bursting out laughing. "Artists." The constant noise of an explosion in the middle of the desert prevents him from hearing the sound that issues from his own throat. "What we can do for you."

I will care for you day after day. I will protect you from the world. I will help you escape.

Joaquín finds Matilda sitting at the upright piano, her eyes glazed over, staring into nothingness, and her hands motionless on the ivory keys. Two drops of fevered sweat hang on her forehead. The tension in her body is visible only in her jugular vein. The moment he arrives, the vacancy of her eyes is filled. When she cries out his name, the happiness wells up from somewhere else. *Joaquín!* The embraces to which they have become accustomed protect them from reality. A wall. Only in her embrace, hearing the beating of her heart under her blouse, can Joaquín control the shaking of his knees and the urge to vomit. The outside world always overwhelms him, crushes him, wounds him. Then he runs to his old room.

This time, before he leaves, he tells Matilda he is going out. He is not sure how long he will be gone. He has many affairs to attend to, documents, certificates. The only possibility of helping Matilda depends now on the good will, or ambition, of Eduardo Oligochea. In his journey to Mixcoac, he goes over the pleas, the supplications, the slight hint of threat. Finally, he commends himself to chance. And chance, for the only time in his life, shows its best face. Dr. Oligochea is going through one of his most boring days. The wards full of naked women and paralytic men bring him nothing but weariness, ennui. The words he exchanges with supervisors and nurses leave him cold, unmoved. No one has any stories to tell. No one can jolt him out of his self-absorption and withdrawal. When he spies the figure of Joaquín walking across one of the patios, approaching him, the sigh that escapes his lips is one of relief. Within the madhouse, Joaquín is rational. Feeling that he is safe at last, that he is bathed in peace, Joaquín greets him as though he had never left. The shouting and screaming of the institution echoes in his ears like great chords of music, a triumphant march.

"I knew you'd be back, Buitrago."

"And here I am."

They are in the infirmary, in the tiny cubicle that both of them insist on calling his "office" and that now has a sign that says "Surgery Section." They are in the same places: Eduardo behind his desk, Joaquín on the edge of a wooden chair, tense. Neither of them mentions the name of Matilda Burgos. With his habitual false starts and rambling, Joaquín little by little discloses the reason for his return. He describes his house, the amounts of money, the pharmacy. At each revelation, the vertical creases between the doctor's eyes grow more pronounced. His surprise is genuine. There are things his imagination is incapable of fabricating for itself. Joaquín's story, the story that the doctor has wanted to hear from the beginning, with its beginning, middle, and end, now emerges with astounding clarity and naturalness. The photographer of the insane is the son of a doctor of great renown, almost a legend. He attended the San Carlos Academy after meeting Diamantina Vicario. He was in Rome from 1897 to 1900. He was part of the group that congregated around Agustín Casasola. Suddenly, everything begins to fit. His manners. The delicate movements of his body. The impression he gives of an aristocrat gone to seed. The vocabulary with which he seduces the people he meets. Pieces of the puzzle. A game of chess. He is offering him half of everything that will come to him in exchange for a certificate which states, in writing, that there is not a trace of morphine in his organism.

"But you haven't freed yourself from that vice, Joaquín."

"And that is why I need your signature, Eduardo."

It is the bargain of his life, the opportunity that has always been denied him. With less than half of what he is being offered today, he could cross the Atlantic and take courses with Emil Kraepelin himself in Germany. Then, after returning, he would not have to marry Cecilia Villalpando. No more Sundays *en famille* discussing the quality of the water in the Grijalva River. No more scorn from the silk merchant. Respectability, at last. Triumph. Men seeking to get ahead are always the easiest to bribe. He knows at once that he will sign, but he also knows that he will make him wait. His reputation is at stake, his pride, and, above all, the exercise of power, his own power. They will have to sign before a notary, and he wants to see Joaquín again.

"In a week or two I will have some time free," he tells him. "I'll take the document to your house personally."

Joaquín takes advantage of his return to the asylum to pick up the brass trunk in which he keeps all the bits and pieces of his life. Photographs. The rest can stay where it is. The little two-burner stove, the rickety cot, the pewter pan in which he prepared his almond infusion. On the shadow-dappled landscape, on the abode walls, there is a new color. It is the amber tone of hope. His crucifixion.

Each time he returns to the city, Joaquín cannot breathe. The paleness of his skin is accentuated and his body resembles a frayed rope about to break. The effort unties the knots inside him. One by one. Trembling, his face covered with bitter-tasting sweat, Joaquín walks, but without being able to control the movements of his legs, his hands. A St. Sebastian wounded by the arrows of reality. A puppet without any strings. Only when he is within Matilda's embrace, hearing the sounds of his body, does calm return. Little by little. Then he goes up to his room and ties a shoelace around his arm. His movements are quick, sure. His body is shadowed by bruises like clouds, twilights on the skin of a man's horizon. When the morphine can finally run through his veins, the universe reorganizes. Peace.

The only place in the house where Joaquín injects himself with the narcotic is his old room, the room of his adolescence. When the knots are tight again inside his body, he lies back on the floor and looks at the cracks in the ceiling. The trees and rivers are still there, the faces, the webs of light. The River of Passion. The Tagus. The Amazon. Corozo palms. Huisaches. Olive trees. Diamantina, Alberta, Eduardo Oligochea, Matilda. One thing leads to another, one name to the next. With the same lamp he has used to find his vein, he now projects a yellow circle on the ceiling. He is seeking the center of everything, the first-born knot that ties all the other ropes in their places. But he does not find it. The structure is capricious, and it obeys only its own rules. There is no beginning, there is no end. A swamp filled with bones.

Matilda amuses herself by looking at the photographs, her back leaning against the windows in the entry hall. The sunlight paints arabesques in her flowing hair and leaves a pink tone on her lips. The pictures are intimate tableaus of some isolated place in society, of nature, of bodies. Matilda looks at them but she does not understand them. Despite their nightly conversations and their embraces, there are certain limits they never cross during the hours of daylight. The distance, however, is not uncomfortable, but rather natural. It is an intimate part of their bodies, their eyes, the way they move, absentmindedly, timidly, through the rooms of the house. Matilda makes no comment whatever about the photographs but after looking at them she looks at Joaquín with more astonishment than curiosity. Recognition. Identification.

"Joaquín, you have to talk to me." Matilda illuminates his face with the lamp and shows him the photograph of Diamantina she has brought. When he sees it, a smile is sculpted on the photographer's lips.

"The great Cause," he murmurs. "The wind that sweeps clean. The first woman."

The sound of a drop of water somewhere in the house, in Morse code. Everything else is motionless.

"You want to know what it feels like, too, Matilda?"

Sitting beside him, playing with the threads of smoke from his cigarette, Matilda forgets to answer.

"I miss her," she whispers.

"So do I."

"You have to talk to me, Joaquín," she repeats softly, trying to convince him.

"It was you that promised to tell me a long, long story, remember?"

"We have all the time in the world," the madwoman says. They both smile, and silence snuggles down between their bodies.

Alberta's name takes a long time to come, but when it does, Joaquín squints as though he were in full glaring sunlight. It is ten o'clock at night. Matilda is playing with the images printed on paper as though they were playing cards, lottery tickets. *Le jeu est fait, mesdames, messieurs.* That is Alberta, the *lady*, with short chestnut-colored hair. A stole over her shoulders and a cigarette-holder between her lips. The *bell* that can be seen at a distance in the bell tower of the convent with its wet, yellow walls. The *spider* that dies under the sole of her blue shoe. The *arrows* laid across her flat, white belly, like a still more feminine version of St. Sebastian. The *water jug* balanced on her head as though she were an Indian woman of the tropics. The *pear* of her naked hips and thighs on a table. The *hand* covering her pubis, to guard it from another's gaze. The *devil* in her deep, coffee-colored, unpredictable eyes. The *drunk* she sits down next to on some forgotten sidewalk. The *moon* caressing her body while her body floats on the waters of a black river. The incandescent *sun* of her sex. The still living, still bleeding *heart* she holds on her open palms, as though it were a toy. The *brave man* that dared to follow her down the streets of Rome without looking back. His figure, behind the camera, never appears. Joaquín, who amuses himself placing imaginary pebbles on an infinite chessboard, cannot win. *Le jeu est fait. C'est fait.*

They are on the bank of a river and Alberta has just told him that if he wants to, he can die in peace. Her gestures are not those of abandonment but of exasperation. There are slaps like butterflies, screams that rip throats, ears.

"If you want to become a photographer who's famous in your country, then leave me alone," she mutters between her clenched teeth. Joaquín is abandoning her. He has told her that there are medals waiting for him, scholarships, trips to the United States, books with his name printed in ornate letters, exhibits. He cannot throw it all away for a woman.

"Not even for you, Alberta," he says. He has told her that to be happy, all he needs are a lens, a darkroom, the chemicals that reveal the never-before-seen images to the eyes of the world. He has told her that he snores, that at night he pulls all the sheets over him, that he can never arrive at an appointment on time. He has told her that there is a purpose to his life—one grand, clear purpose.

"I'll send for you," he murmurs. "Later."

And the Roman working woman who has led him through hidden streets, bars smelling of harsh wine, endless sunsets, lights a match and holds it under the palm of her hand.

"I curse the day I met you, Joaquín Buitrago. I curse your father and your mother, the children you will not have, the women unlucky enough to sleep beside you. I curse your house, the streets you will walk both night and day, the skies that will cloud your head. You will never triumph, never succeed. I curse your eyes, which do not know how to see. This burn I owe to you, Joaquín. This burn is going to hurt you for the rest of your days."

Standing a yard from her, watching her yet not daring to say a word, he concentrates on the flow of the water, the sky, the night, the infinite. The match's flame is a firefly in the darkness. Joaquín picks up his boots, his jacket, his hat, and turning, he thinks that he will not allow himself to be consumed by passion for a woman.

Joaquín looks at his cracked hands, smiles.

"There is no mark, you see?" His voice is low, almost inaudible, ironic.

"Go on." Just those two words, nothing else.

Alberta. Joaquín always pronounces her name as if for the first time. A rat scurrying from his mouth. He is sitting on the side of his bed, the morning light is falling on his vertebrae, along his spine. When he wakes up, he puts out his arm, his eyes still closed. The arm passes over the wrinkles in the sheets slowly, once, twice. He opens his eyes slowly, fractionally, just until he can make out the body, the porosity of its soft skin under his fingers.

"Our first fight, Joaquín," says Alberta with unusual lightness. They both smile, though not a happy smile. Joaquín is on top of her, covering her wounded hands with his, and their bodies intertwine in silence. The four hands together, motionless, just above her head.

"Now I will never be able to forget you, Alberta," says Joaquín in a tone of mute reproach, the tone of someone who has committed a fatal error.

A Sunday. There are the hurrying footsteps of children on the uneven paving stones of the street. Men greeting one another. The squeaking of a bicycle.

"I know," the woman laughs. Joaquín, sentimental, had returned to the bank of the river for her. He had washed her naked feet with the cold water of the river and then dried them with his jacket. Everything in silence. With her in his arms, clinging to his neck, he had walked for hours, four, five, in the darkness. The woman's tiny body was a weightless feather, a dry leaf. He finds a house. He knocks at the door. He lies. Everything at the same time. All of it without letting her escape the space of his arms. "My wife is ill. She will die." On the dawn bed, he spreads her legs and, fitting his body between them, penetrates her sex again and again, hastily, angrily. The drops of fevered sweat that soak Alberta's short hair are all real. They taste like mud, like salt. Joaquín does not stop.

"I am not going to miss you," he repeats again and again, in the voice of a man struggling against himself. On the steamship that takes him back to Mexico he repeats no other phrase. He can remember no other words.

Matilda is now holding the lamp above Joaquín's thighs, his ankles. He has a shoelace in one hand, the needle in the other. The insertion is perfect, a painless spear-thrust to the heart. As the liquid flows in, the wrinkles on Joaquín's face loosen. He is young once more, a boy of twenty-eight. He is running

No One Will See Me Cry

down the stairs in the house in Santa María, taking the steps two at a time. It is eight o'clock in the morning, April. His father is waiting for him in the entry hall.

"Did you know a woman named Alberta Mascardelli?"

A string from the pith of a mandarin orange on his lips, his breathing suddenly stops. *Did you know.* There is an open telegram, a white envelope, and a smile of triumph illuminating the face of the doctor, the legend.

"Yes."

"Then this is for you. It came three days ago."

I am not going to miss you. *Don't you find, Matilda, that the more you tell yourself that you will forget, the more you remember? A reflex of logic, I suppose. Automatic.* He takes the telegram out of the open envelope.

"Alberta Mascardelli died yesterday. I curse you and curse your entire family."

Joaquín smiles. An old family tradition, no doubt: curses. Then he opens the letter. A photograph. The palm of Alberta's right hand on a sheet, and in the center, an old scar. Underneath, the legend: "This burn I owe to you." It is her handwriting. The black and white image is blurry, out of focus. Instead of perfect contrast, everything is an uncomfortable, uncertain gray. In Joaquín's head there are only three phrases: "Graflex. Silver bromide. Mediocre work."

"Will the day never come when you find a woman that is worthy of you, Joaquín, and not these madwomen?" It is the voice of his mother.

A sentimental drama in 1908.

In the United States, Henry Ford has just introduced his Model T, and in Paris, Claude Debussy includes "Golliwog's Cake Walk" in his *Children's Corner.* Echoes of New Orleans jazz. Ludwig Wittgenstein has enrolled in the University of

206

Manchester. Joaquín walks down the streets of Mexico City with the haste of a man going nowhere. *What I want at those moments, Matilda, is to breathe again. I want the world to have the smooth surface of a motionless lake again. I want things to stop spinning all around me. Everything should have an order, and I want that order. 1, 2, 3, 4, 5, 6—ad infinitum. Like the night I found her lying on the muddy bank of the river, I want to pick up her name and carry it in my arms like a feather, a dry leaf. Alcohol makes one's head spin, alcohol is social and it always makes one talk, and that is why, instead, I look for the key that will allow me to lock the door behind which I have laid her name. Morphine is sweet, morphine is solitary. Everything is once again in its place. Peace.*

The lamplight falls directly on his face. Inside, at the bottom of his open eyes, the flame of a lighted match never goes out. The flame of time. The only burn.

"That's all? There have always been men who abandoned women, Joaquín, and there always will be. It's not the end of the world," she tells him.

Two months later, the second letter arrives. Another photograph. Alberta's face is framed by two creases in a pillow and, on top of her, cutting off her nose, a shoulder crops out all the rest of the image. The woman's eyes are half open, the expression on her face one of pleasure or pain. "Are you missing me yet?" Pleasure. Joaquín has no time to think. His hand goes to his fly and, with his closed hand, he tries to reproduce Alberta's moist vagina. The semen sprays onto the short hair, the forehead, the mouth, the back of the man who, deafened by the woman's moans, moving feverishly on top of her, does not realize that the camera button has been pushed. Unaware of the heavy breathing of the photographer who is hiding behind the curtains, the man continues. Three men have found pleasure at different times, in different places, but on the same skin. I am not going to miss you.

The envelopes arrive at irregular intervals over a period

of months. Each image surpasses the previous one in technique and audacity. Alberta's pubis. Alberta between the bodies of naked women. Male fingers inside Alberta's lips. Alberta squatting, her back against the wall with her skirt above her flexed knees, her sex totally exposed. Alberta with her hands pushed out of sight up between her own legs. Then Alberta's body is replaced by others. Her last name, then, begins to appear in the lower right corner of all the pictures. Mascardelli. *In those days, what I loved most about her was her intelligence, the cruelty of her intelligence. If she had sent love letters or pleas, I would have forgotten her in a couple of years, her memory diminished by the very intensity of her importunities. But what she sent me from Rome were my own eyes. My eyes seeing her, spying on the luminous corners of her life. My eyes looking at the impeccable technique of her triumph, the immense battlefield of my defeat. I love her pornography, its absolute lack of tenderness, the absence of mercy. Have pity on us, Alberta, by all you hold dear. All of her photographs wind up covered with semen and stuffed in paper bags in one corner of the brass trunk. Then, just when I have started expecting them, the letters stop coming. Without warning. And then, then, I begin to miss her. I hear her voice, I have conversations with her, I pursue her under Roman bridges in Mexico City, and when she tells me goodbye, holding up her hand and waving, there far away, the scar in the palm of her hand is like a blessing: "That burn will hurt you for the rest of your days, Alberta. God willing."*

Men who yearn for a woman consume more energy in that act than in anything else they do all day. Their faces look exhausted, the muscles that have to bear the weight of the ball and chain, the shackles on their ankles, are permanently tense. There is no rest, no rest at all; there is no peace. The muscle-cramps of need harass the hands and thighs. And the back ends up bowed by that steel ball that is anxiety. *"Yes, I'm missing you now. Are you happy? When will all this be over?" All of this will be over only in the parenthesis of morphine. There, in the stable and delimited context of an injection, I can face Alberta. I shout across to her on the other bank of the world and then, convinced that I am doing the right thing, I turn my back on her. I never return. No sentimental weakness will force me to carry her in my arms. She will triumph. She will always win. If women hide all the light in the world under their skirts, then it is preferable for the universe to remain dark, Matilda. I am convinced of that.*

Sunlight distracts them at the same time. It is a livid and noisy dawn. Under the covers, though still dressed, they lie on the floor and sleep in one another's arms. Without realizing it.

Eduardo Oligochea arrives one Saturday at three o'clock in the afternoon, bringing the medical certificate. His signature at the bottom of the document is small and spare, unadorned. Around his head, in the reflection of his gold glasses, is his own humiliation, in the humid light of July. Matilda and Joaquín have been waiting for him for weeks, and meanwhile they have prepared their welcome with great care. With the advances that Arturo Loayza sends them they have bought masks and makeup, crepe paper and a phonograph, copal. The rest they have spent on salt, soap, vegetables from the market, flowers. Their selection of goods is capricious, more the product of pleasure than of need or healthful habits. Unlike the dry days of spring when they entertain themselves by destroying things, getting rid of things, now they amuse themselves by creating a world in their own image, a place that fits them like a glove. All of Joaquín's photographs are pinned to the walls. Women and absences are distributed randomly in the salon and library, the kitchen and the bath. The images of Diamantina enlarge the piano. Alberta's pornography decorates the entry hall. To adorn the common rooms, Matilda has made strings of flowers out of crepe paper. Pieces of silk cover the lamps to change the tone and create "atmosphere." On the phonograph there are fox trots, Paderewski concertos recorded in England. When they see their first guest arrive, Matilda runs to Joaquín's old room and puts on his black suit. A white blouse covers her flaccid breasts and her hair is hidden under a felt hat. The parody of Santa, the première.

"We were expecting you." Joaquín's greeting has a touch of innocence and another hint of perversion. Before fully opening the door, he asks for the medical certificate. Then, once the document is in his hands, he allows the doctor to enter the house.

Matilda is straddling a chair, with the back between her legs. From her deep crimson lips there dangles a pipe. While Joaquín disappears for a moment, Matilda offers Eduardo the only drink in the house. Whiskey. He accepts.

"These women, we always have to wait for them, don't we, doctor?"

Before allowing him to reply, Matilda begins to complain about the violence of the Revolution, the danger of being ruled by a government of atheists, and the quality of the water in the Grijalva River. A wry smile appears on Eduardo's face, a recognition, the impossibility of reacting to her mockery. When Joaquín appears dressed in an organza tunic that shows his skinny legs and the sex hanging between his legs, Eduardo Oligochea jumps, startled.

"We are quite mad, doctor," says Matilda, cranking the phonograph and extending her arms to begin dancing with Joaquín. Their steps are grotesque, as is the way they kiss.

"Aren't you going to take notes, Eduardo?" the photographer asks him. "We are quite a case."

Instead of standing up and indignantly leaving the house, Eduardo sips at his drink and, with a slight smile, watches them as they dance.

"I've seen worse," he says dryly.

"But never participated in it, I'll bet," says Matilda. "In fact, I'll bet three kisses."

"I'll double that," says Joaquín quickly, nodding exaggeratedly, his chin moving up and down, as he walks around the doctor's chair. Eduardo's only response is to turn his eyes to the photographs that surround the piano.

"Very moving, Joaquín. An anarchist pianist. 1896 or 1901? Sometime after that, perhaps?" When he sees the suddenly fallen faces of the two motionless transvestites, he adds: "I did my job. I didn't find anything on you, Matilda. It is also more difficult, you'll surely agree, to investigate the life of a woman. In the end, a woman is not so important. She falls in love and lets herself die, and that's the end of it. But you, Joaquín, everyone has talked about you."

The photographer looks at him without much enthusiasm, half intrigued and half drowsy.

"Me? People talking about me?" he asks.

"You have no idea how many remember the evening when you met the Vicario woman," Eduardo says firmly, playfully. "And no idea how many remember the promise of your talent, and your fall."

His voice is lighter than air, surer than a dart hitting the bull's eye. The masked ball has become a funeral. As he speaks, Eduardo approaches the piano and takes his wallet out of the back pocket of his cashmere pants. Then he places a photograph among the others on the instrument. It is a panoramic view, somewhat out of focus, of a mound of half-naked corpses. A red circle has been drawn around the bloody head of a woman.

"This is not Río Blanco in January, 1907. It is the municipal morgue in December, 1906. Diamantina Vicario never managed to leave the city. No one can get the better of reason, Joaquín Buitrago. Not even the first woman."

Matilda picks up the image and touches it as though her fingers could detect the truth. "You have to talk to me, Joaquín." The crucifixion of hope, the always-punctual mockery of hope. Joaquín falls back onto the piano keys and, as the discordant clangor that no one pays any attention to fades away, does no more than look into Eduardo Oligochea's eyes.

"It hurts that much to take my money, then, Eduardo?"

"That much and more, Joaquín. Much more." He is silent for a few moments and then turns to look at them. "I'm waiting for my six kisses."

There are things about Matilda that he likes. Her nervousness above all. The sound of her skirt when she passes close by. The way her eyes glaze over because of things he knows nothing about. What is it that she is seeing? How does she see? With the passing of the days, he grows accustomed to her changes of mood, the sudden plunges of her energy: the days when she is gay, excited, filled with light, immediately followed by days of sadness. There are hours when Matilda is incapable of remaining seated, of doing nothing. Seized by feverish activity, she cleans the floors, mends curtains, or rehearses dance steps created by her imagination. She talks incessantly and her words spill over one another to escape her lips. She bursts into loud laughter. And then, without warning and for no apparent reason, there are whole days when she does not move or change position. Joaquín feeds her, washes her clothes from time to time, and heats water for tea or coffee. He is the only one who goes out into the city. Little by little, in the silence of the house without furniture, he is becoming the husband of the vanilla.

"You don't go to heaven with a broom in your hands," she says. "Wise up."

Most of the things she says disconcert him. He has the sense of having heard them and almost instantaneously forgotten them. All in the past. At this moment. Always. When he closes his eyes and tries to fix her image on his eyelids, there is always something that doesn't quite fit. A wink. The ragged fingernails. The laughter. The grimace of seriousness. Matilda, not uniform. Matilda is hard to remember. Then he opens his eyes and looks for her in all the rooms of the empty house, as though the woman might have managed to escape. Then she greets him with the news that her favorite day is Thursday and three o'clock in the afternoon is the hour she most detests. None of this is followed by any explanation.

When Arturo Loayza unexpectedly shows up at the door, they are both in a state of lethargy. Pacing carefully down the catwalk in the garden, and then through the hallways inside, the attorney wanders through the house in restrained silence. He likes the dapples of light that illuminate the walls and floors, and the smell of bleach that suggests cleanliness, neatness, care. In his poetic daydreams, he lives in a similar place, a place without furniture, without people, a place designed for the solitary task of thought. Creation. More than drawing his attention, the photographs that cover the walls wound his eyes. He had imagined them different, or not imagined them at all. The naked women in suggestive poses that he has seen in other portraits are really quite different. These women are out of fashion, and they also look real. It is not hard to see sadness or rancor in their open pupils, need. Then come the photographs of objects around which humanity is simply an absence. The human traces are dissimilar yet easy enough to recognize. Who has not gone daydreaming at the vision of a china cup with the imprint of a woman's lip, in lipstick, tattooed on the rim? Arturo Loayza has, many times. In parks, the swings recently abandoned but still in motion have also seduced his imagination. The photographs produce a fearful excitement, the foreshadowing of a revelation. Is this what can be caused by passion for a woman? The world that Joaquín exhibits in these black and white images has been wiped away time after time by the fierce, swift angel of progress, by groups of men who, like him, act knowing that they are doing the right thing, yet still cannot stop remembering. Was there once a different world? In Joaquín's images, all the objects of progress are small. The screws, shoes, microscopes, pins, plates, cigarette butts, stethoscopes, fences, buttons, and buttonholes that make up his universe seem removed from their surroundings, in unpredictable settings. The objects are timeless, but they make no sense.

"Don't look for beauty in them, because you won't find it, counselor." Joaquín's voice startles him. The photographer is coming out of the library where he has been sleeping with Matilda under the desk. The attorney's apology is just a stammer. A child caught in the act.

"Want to hear something interesting?" He does not wait for the answer. "To you, being sick is being healthy; not for you those stories that in distant childhood amused mere mortals, for your odor is sweeter than the fragrance of enchanted gardens of dream..."

"López Velarde?" Both men's smiles are cordial.

"Call me Arturo, please, Mr. Buitrago. After all, our families have known each other for many years."

"My name is Joaquín, Arturo, don't forget it," the photographer answers with amiability unusual in him. The two men look at each other with a delicacy that is almost feminine, a carefulness that they are accustomed to employing only with women.

"Are these all of your photographs?" Arturo asks, trying to interrupt or disguise the minute examination they are making of each other. His eyes turn avidly yet melancholically to the walls covered with black and white images.

"No, Arturo. I've made many more."

"Where are they?"

"Where they should be," replies Joaquín. "Lost."

Arturo Loayza does not believe him, and he pats him a couple of times on the right shoulder.

"If I had done this work I'm sure I would already be

famous," he murmurs as he crosses the room and carefully examines some of the other images.

"If you had done this work, Arturo, I'm sure you would be as damned as I am," says Joaquín, and then, without pause, without giving time for comments or gestures, he adds: "Would you like a cup of good strong black coffee?" Arturo, still moved and astonished, only nods.

When Matilda Burgos joins them in the parlor, the photographer introduces her as his wife. His two inter-locutors' surprise does not make him hesitate or try to correct himself. Matilda's almost lifeless eyes and yellow skin indicate that this is one of her despondent days. Before the one man's inquisitive, the other's loving eyes, Matilda wishes more than ever that she lived in a universe without eyes, a place where the only thing important would be the stories told at night. Silence. Men's eyes have pursued her her entire life. With desire or meticulousness, filled with lust or scientific curiosity, men's eyes have seen, measured, and evaluated her body first, and then her mind, ad nauseam. Literally. In the humid light of July, the only thing she wants is to become invisible. Her dream is to go unnoticed. Which is why she does not say aloud what she is thinking: "I'm not anybody's wife, Joaquín."

Around the table, while the men read documents, discuss numbers, and come to an agreement about the amount of the monthly income, Matilda goes off somewhere else. She is at the edge of the desert, where she has gone to be alone. Alone beside Paul Kamàck. His figure interrupts the horizon with firm but slow steps, a straw hat on his head; the air ruffles his hair. And silence. No eyes follow them, no cry frightens them, no ambition keeps them awake. These are the happiest years of her life, the peaceful years when she does not have to answer anyone. Pablo is still dreaming of bridges and mines, undecided whether to look at the world from up above or down below. Meanwhile, she is content with the warmth of his skin, his presence, the vertical shadow of his body, which, looked at out of the corner of her eye, is the arrow on the compass that guides her through the desert. Matilda is still snuggled in his eyes, the same color inside and out: sky blue. The images of her pleasure are many. Pablo approaching the adobe room with his binoculars around his neck. Pablo emerging from the bowels of the earth with his hair dusty and his eyes filled with wonders. Pablo lying on the ground, looking up at the night sky, counting stars. Pablo describing in detail the life of George H. Corliss, whose workshop in Providence produced 481 steam engines between 1847 and 1862. Pablo counting the exact number of thorns on a nopal leaf. Pablo drawing with a stick in the sand. Pablo letting her bandage his arm with pieces of old cloth after his only accident. Pablo, exultant, chewing words with peyote. Pablo's naked body lying beside her with all its scars visible. A love story. Above all things, the imperturbable sky. Drought. *Leave her there, let her untie the knots of the last afternoon and live in the air without consequences; give her time to put away his name, space to try to breathe again. "Did I ever tell you, Pablo, that I'm happy?"* An explosion. Everything ends with the echoes of the explosion. Afterward, there are only the ether-induced dreams in the streets of the city not her own, her vacant eyes as she stands before the marquee of the Fábregas Theater, the music of the Bonesi opera through the walls, a group of idlers following her footsteps. The thunderclaps of a summer storm bring her back to the city. There are two men with her, babbling numbers like thieves or businessmen and, through the window, a leaden sky casting a purple glow on the humid skin of a four o'clock afternoon. Sultry weather precedes the departure of Arturo Loayza, and then only the two of them are left, watching the first solitary drops run down the surface of the windows. Then, a hailstorm prevents them from hearing what each other is saying.

"I will protect you from the world. I will help you escape."

"What?"

"I will care for you every day. I..."

"I am nobody's wife, Joaquín."

"And you, counselor, what do you think about pain?"

Arturo Loayza returns at regular intervals to the house in Santa María la Ribera. If someone were to ask him why, he would no doubt answer that it is because of a family debt, his wish to help the weakest member of a family that was always close to his father. But no one asks, no one knows that when he leaves the office on Wednesday at four o'clock it is to arrive on time for his appointment with a failed photographer. Why? He has asked himself that many times as he crosses the city in his black Ford, but he has yet to find the answer.

There are mornings when Matilda breakfasts on her own fingernails as she watches her reflection in the windows. Haste drives her. She lives with the sense that there will not be enough time. How many years will it take her to erase thirty-six years of life? The stories never end, there are loose ends everywhere, digressions that become infinite. "Did I tell you about when...? Did you know that...?" "Once upon a time. Long, long ago." "Do you still want to know how a woman goes crazy, Joaquín?"

If only she could rest, if only she could stop talking. Words bubble out on her excited days. She can neither control them nor dissuade them, and they all come at once; she stutters. Some sentences are left unfinished forever, interrupted by the waves of others, much the same. At night the soliloquy is truly mad, demented. Talking, however, helps her to cleanse herself, to erase the traces of chalk left on the green slate-board of the world. Soon there will be nothing left. Soon she will be able to return to her refuge, to that place without doors that Eduardo Oligochea calls madness. A mental illness. Silence. There, in the house in Santa María that she dares not leave, she begins to dream about those other years, the remaining ones, all the years before she dies. They should be peaceful and silent; they should follow one another without any event of note whatsoever, without identity; they should be odorless and have the taste of water. Matilda is constructing her paradise. There, there are no visitors and no one cares about her past, her future; there, she alone can protect herself. No one else. There are no eyes.

On fall afternoons the haste, the hurry increases. There are fewer and fewer things to say. There are still many details, but there is no plot at all to guide them or stop them or give them meaning. The ether, the facade of a theater, three stars crowning the waning quarter of the moon, the smile of a stranger, fragments of broken dolls. Nothing has significance. The beginnings and endings have been left behind. Nothing has consequences. A wristwatch is a wristwatch. A silk tunic is a silk tunic. The desert is just the desert. Tautology is the queen of her heart.

"I don't feel like talking anymore, Joaquín," she tells him.

"That's how a person goes crazy, isn't it?"

"Maybe. Each person finds their own way."

Joaquín's eyes know it before his head: Matilda will leave. Around her body there is a transparent distance that he will never, ever be able to cross. The separation is not made of fear but of pride, strength. Like the time he photographed her in the asylum the first time. Matilda is still in her place, planting black flags along the borders of her territory, opening and closing doors in full awareness, full consciousness, and without resignation. Joaquín's attraction and rejection are simultaneous. Humiliation and relief, as well. The madwoman looks at him like an inquisitor, without kindness. What was Joaquín thinking? What did he think would happen? A wife. A woman saved from her own fall by the force of company. A sterile love, without bodies, that would last a hundred years. Gratitude, above all. Yes. The early smile of her gratitude for being able to enjoy the world of reason in a house filled with light. "I am nobody's wife, Joaquín." The abrupt movement of a sunflower. The decision had been made many years earlier, and not even a cataclysm would change it.

In December, when Matilda decides to leave the house in Santa María for the first time, there are little strips of paper stuck to walls downtown. "Life is a method without doors that rains from time to time." *Did you know that, Joaquín?* The advertisements for Buen Tono cigarettes have discarded forever the drawings of Frenchified women, and they now have the figure of an Indian with feathers and necklaces savoring a thick cigarette with his eyes closed. "The smoke from this tobacco tells you they're Buen Tono. The Aztecs enjoyed the taste of exquisite Mexican tobacco, which is the same tobacco used today by Buen Tono for its famous cigarettes." Matilda's features and the color of her skin are in vogue now. The Minister of Public Education is now thinking of the cosmic race. Joaquín Buitrago meets with strangers in the Nobody's Café, the best metaphor for a country.

Leave me alone. Just leave me in peace.

"You are not the husband of vanilla," she tells him. "No one can protect me; no one can watch over my sleep. I will find a way to escape by myself, Joaquín. No one will save me. Don't you know that?"

Matilda's words glide along the catwalks of his mind, pulled by gravity. Gravity. She is leaving him absolutely alone with his photographs. A lens, a room full of chemicals, the process of developing the film. What he needs to be happy. She tells him so:

"This is what you need to be happy." Her voice points to all the things that surround him.

Pride prevents him from crying. The absurd nakedness of a sentimental man embarrasses him. The sound of cars reminds him that he is in the city.

"You should know that I have loved you, Matilda."

In the woman's eyes there is only stubborn will.

"I know." The words like rocks.

The world is changing at dizzying speed on the other side of the windows. The speed makes his head spin, makes him nauseated, yet gives him hope at the same time. The Twentieth Century.

"I know," she murmurs. "You wanted a crazy woman in your house so that the house would be different."

Her self-possession is driving him mad; the arrogance of knowing what he was searching for, what he wanted. It would be better for her to allow him to feel grief or remorse, anger, uneasiness, any familiar emotion, but Matilda's words produce only confusion in him, the certainty of not knowing. Why did she force him to stare into the veiled images of her life? Why did she docilely follow him to the house in Santa María? The words were going to join them forever, the stories were going to reveal all the secret codes. Then there would be only trust, permanence. Union. Perhaps even happiness.

"I came to your house to find out whether I had been wrong; to find out whether things might have been different," she says, looking into his eyes.

An experiment. The last one.

"Let me rest. I want to rest. That's all."

Her stubborn will.

Now, after her departure, Joaquín Buitrago has furniture brought in and the curtains removed. "To be happy." He wants light and air, the images of a normal life. He wants another chance, the opportunity to find another place in the world. A new era. As he looks at the formless web that covers the ceiling, Joaquín knows that he will survive. At that moment, a sudden tingle runs down his spine and makes him get up. It is haste. The recognition of that makes him smile. There is still nothing to be done with happiness.

"Let me be quiet. Let me not say anything."

"Let me live in the desert, near Paul Kamàck's weariness."

To live in the real life of the world

We must praise, employing every strident note in our propagandistic scale, the present-day beauty that is in machines, the supple, athletic bridges recently stretched across pillars of muscular steel, the smoke of factories, the Cubist emotions of the great trans-atlantic steamers with their proud red and black chimneys, anchored horoscopically (Ruiz Huidobro) alongside effervescent, crowded piers, the industri-alist turn of our large, throbbing cities, the blue shirts of explosive laborers at this emotional, moving hour—all the beauty of this century...
Manuel Maples Arce
Actual, *No. 1,* Hoja de Vanguardia
December, 1921

Altagracia Flores de Elizalde thinks that a pistol costs thirty thousand pesos and a hacienda fifty. *Eccentric imagination.* Housewife, Aguascalientes.

Esperanza Garduño thinks that it all started when her husband left her and there was a family conspiracy, but she is also convinced that the loss of her reason and half of her palate is because of witchcraft and socialism.

Pedro Santa Ana writes letters to Plutarco Elías Calles, the president of the Republic, to criticize the governmental anarchy that rules the nation. Between each letter he also writes poems to the devil and to God.

Each time Cresencia Gómez has a visitor she is terrified by the evil spirits standing before her.

Everardo Ponce lost his will in the looms of a factory in the Belén prison.

Cirila Esquivel converses for hours on end with invisible beings whom she recognizes by their voices. She is preoccupied by the idea of reconciling everything so that once there is peace, she can reign with tranquility. Every Tuesday, she distributes to the other inmates the talismans she fabricates out of pieces of her blue housedress.

Rafael Mexica, aka "El Loco," killed his best friend in front of the Forget Me Not pulquería. He recalls none of it, because unfortunately, when he gets drunk he loses consciousness, awareness of what he is doing.

Teresa Olivares has an ill temper, and a certain proclivity for degenerate pleasures. In addition, she walks the streets alone and has no respect for anyone. Two lovers.

Guadalupe Quintana writes passionate love letters.

Juan Nepomuceno Acosta injects fifty grams of heroin a day. Law student.

Margarita Vázquez demonstrates an excessive love for another female inmate. Together they are a clear case of madness-of-two.

Carmelo Buendía lives in the center of a cosmos that smells of turpentine. He is a star.

Cándida Barajas' body was broken when she was thirteen. Since then, she has worked with acrobats and tumblers in a traveling circus. She repeats poetry by Amado Nervo.

Eros Alessi is the color blue in a palette of watercolors.

Cástulo Rodríguez thinks that the world will someday be different. He pulls pieces of red cloth out of unpredictable places and talks constantly about the day the bombs will go off. January first. The dawn of the Revolution.

Matilda Burgos sees them die, one after another, during the twenty-eight years she is an inmate in La Castañeda Insane Asylum. She says that it all began one night in July when a group of soldiers cut her off in the street as she was walking home. She had just left her job at the Fábregas Theater and still in a fog of ether she refused them her sexual favors. The soldiers sent her to jail and there a doctor diagnosed mental instability. Then she says no more. In twenty-eight years nothing has perturbed her and nothing has made her cry. With the passing of years, she has learned to laugh at everything.

Department of Rebozos and Serapes
  Psychopathological study of patient Matilda Burgos, non-violent ward, first section.
  Patient demonstrates good conduct. Likes to work; is dedicated and good-humored. Talks a great deal; that is the symptom of patient's excitation.
  Mixcoac, D.F. General Insane Asylum. June 30, 1935.
  Magdalena O. viuda de Alvarez, professor

With the passing of years she has started to write and has then stopped writing.

Mixcoac. August 30, 1932. Diplomatic dispatches.
Congress of Deputies.
With all due judicial respect in general—and for foreign judicial matters and also diplomatic matters such as naval wars and corresponding wars on land—As we already know the diplomats who come to install their governments and their nations—those who already have knowledge of warships and other naval vessels as well as some armed forces camps in Veracruz—with respect to suspicious people—evil promoters of world wars—I offer judicial diplomatic knowledge—I—Matilda Burgos—of meetings of foreign companies and colonies. While for all these industrious healthy thinking persons to be able with their healthy intelligent power to carry out a campaign against the evil Mexican people—thieves on the right—left—and pernicious—of evil origins—for the foreign and Mexican military and all the rest—sane healthy and supreme. Because in this insane asylum

non-violent first class on the first floor there are some
very suspicious doctors—thieves—promoters of
assassinations of presidents of the Republic—true
anarchist marquises for governments of the crown—
empire—and also for other governments—because there
are ugly people—evil Mexican citizens of the Republic—
very thieving very tiresome—very abusive of their
rights—very talkative lying thieves.

Mixcoac. September 26, 1932. Diplomatic dispatches.
Chamber of Deputies.
With all due respect putting before you for your
information what is happening in the La Castañeda
Insane Asylum with some female patients—insane but
also with suspicious diseases from being prostitutes—
wanting to smell the wet parts of other female patients—
and then carry off lovers with their beds and bed
covers—and they cannot stand Presidente Portes Gil or
don Adolfo de la Huerta, another one of our presidents—
or any doctor in the La Castañeda Insane Asylum—I—
Matilda Burgos—replying and giving judicial witness in
general—that if they can strongly effect some dangerous
assassination attempt on the other patients—the more
serious ones—and not well educated to judge by the way
they live in the real life of the world—and be thinking
beings so they can avoid punishment by the court's
justice—I reply, I a most loving and humble servant—my
name appearing after five other not very dangerous
patients. Your refined friend MB
P.S. The dangerous ones—in non-violent first floor—are
Josefa Santillán & Isabel Alemán de Servín (widowed).

Mixcoac. October 2, 1932.
Diplomatic dispatches and dispatches of war and navy, both foreign and mexican.

With all due respect—setting before you for your information—that in this place—La Castañeda Insane Asylum in Mixcoac—there are those ready to rise up in arms on the Mexican border and in police and army stations and to come to an agreement with the foreign navy diplomatically—because among bad—thieving cynical people—so-called red—with happiness—with respect to the revolution and the foreign gunpowder—no president of any republic in the world has any guarantee for any army or navy base. Or for company in general or for Bolivia or for you or for any region of Chaco or any parliament or any interim good—correct because it is the votes of the parties that have gotten disgusted with the abuses of trust—that there is among the good—this document—because they have been writing about the thieving chicken disgusting pig kidnaping anarchist people with real red hands like sickening disgusting vile little criminal animals that when you look at their faces—they have faces like balls of smoke—they inspire fear and terror and repugnance—like devils with tails too long and pointed for all the present good. Those annoying thieving people are the promoters of so many revolutions and world wars, so they are not goody-goodies by any means. Not goody-goody or really bad, you might say, because the good in them is all show and the bad is lies. So, Señor President of the Republic Señor Abelardo L. Rodríguez—putting before you for your information all this—because it is the duty of your very loving servant—Matilda Burgos—because I know everything—what I ask in return is my release—Señor Abelardo Rodríguez—and ask the current administrator-director-supervisor of the La Castañeda Insane Asylum—and since my affairs are somewhat

diplomatic for many serious reasons—these documents
be sent to all in general.
—Your servant MB

Mixcoac. February 1, 1933. Diplomatic dispatches.

 With all due respect setting before you for your
judicial information—that I—Matilda Burgos—having been
in this Castañeda Insane Asylum from 1920 until today
in the non-violent ward, first floor—have been
persecuted by evil people—true anarchists—since 1900—
These evil people, very hard to please, volatile
bloodsuckers of all and by all—are the promoters of
world wars and revolutions. I also plan when I get out
to say about my written affairs that they are blocked by
the diplomatic dispatches—by the thieving, lying people
of the La Castañeda Insane Asylum.—And I also put this
before you for your information because the clandestine
underground commits great abuse in everything—and by
everything—and it is full of upset people—don't take
away what you didn't give—Politics is politics and
anarchism is anarchism—red hands in this miserable
insane asylum—worse than the anarchist that did that
stupid thing with the death of the archdukes. First some
bad Mexicans steal and then some bad doctors in the
asylum have all this garbage with the presidencies—
reigns—and empires—and so forth—because of gangs of
supreme powers—and then come the world wars—
because that is the way it goes with me—with
some people that are incompetent concerning what
people call political principles and I mean that word
political. Which is why I—Matilda Burgos—ask the
diplomatic dispatches for judicial and corresponding
investigations. I beg—Mr. President—that you excuse my
writing but I know what I know. Can you Mr. President
conference with the foreign diplomats that already have

knowledge of all these papers—these bad, chiseling, pernicious doctors that mistreat people and walk around being perverted with things in general. And so—don Pascual Ortiz Rubio—I beg very cordially both you and the diplomats to forgive me for the bad writing but I write because I have had elemental geology and politics.

—Your very affectionate servant—I Matilda Burgos.

"I told you you'd be hearing from me again, you remember, Matilda?" are the first words that Cástulo speaks when he sees her walk through the door. The eighteen-year-old lover. He cannot sit still. His eyes blink constantly. The singular beauty of his face inflamed with passion is still the same.

"Everything is going to be different," he says. "Worse, but different."

The two laugh softly under the swaying branches of the chestnut trees. Then they fall silent; they have nothing else to say. Silence is the perfect mockery of reason.

"I miss Diamantina," she says, her gaze strangely motionless, filled with sadness.

"So do I."

Air.

Nothing else.

This is the only conversation that enters Matilda's memory before she falls. Barely a second. A luminous puncture of light. Then nothing. Cerebral hemorrhage. September 7, 1958. How does a woman go crazy?

Beside her, there is no one to lament what she has been, what she is.

Death certificate.
Matilda Burgos.
Papantla, Veracruz, 1885.
Female. 73 y/o. Single.
Mexican. No religion.
Asylum general population.
September 7, 1958, 4:00 P.M.
Non-traumatic cerebral hemorrhage. 10 days.
Essential hypertension 5 yrs.
Schizophrenia 38 yrs.
[signed]   Rosa María Puente Prieto
Lic. 24677 SSN 11098
No. 96 Bonampak, Vertiz Narvarte 23-81-68
Mexico, D.F. 7/9/58
Gustavo Abascal 6353 General Hospital for
the Insane

Let me rest in peace.

CRISTINA RIVERA-GARZA was born on the northeastern border of Mexico and, after a nomadic life spent mostly, but not only, in central Mexico and the United States, she now resides in San Diego/Tijuana. Author of transgeneric (fiction, poetry, essay) and interdisciplinary (literature and history) works written in her mother tongue (Spanish) and her stepmother tongue (English), she has published *Nadie me vera llorar* (2000), *La más mía* (1998), *La Guerra no importa* (1991), *Hombres frágiles*—books with which she has won six of the most respected literary awards in Mexico and Latin America. Some of her academic articles are included in the *Hispanic American Historical Review* and *The Journal of the History of Medicine*, among others. She is currently associate professor of Mexican history at San Diego State University and head of the Creative Writing (narrative) Program at the Centro Cultural Tijuana.

CURBSTONE PRESS, INC.

is a non-profit publishing house dedicated to literature that reflects a commitment to social change, with an emphasis on contemporary writing from Latino, Latin American and Vietnamese cultures. Curbstone presents writers who give voice to the unheard in a language that goes beyond denunciation to celebrate, honor and teach. Curbstone builds bridges between its writers and the public – from inner-city to rural areas, colleges to community centers, children to adults. Curbstone seeks out the highest aesthetic expression of the dedication to human rights and intercultural understanding: poetry, testimonies, novels, stories, and children's books.

This mission requires more than just producing books. It requires ensuring that as many people as possible learn about these books and read them. To achieve this, a large portion of Curbstone's schedule is dedicated to arranging tours and programs for its authors, working with public school and university teachers to enrich curricula, reaching out to underserved audiences by donating books and conducting readings and community programs, and promoting discussion in the media. It is only through these combined efforts that literature can truly make a difference.

Curbstone Press, like all non-profit presses, depends on the support of individuals, foundations, and government agencies to bring you, the reader, works of literary merit and social significance which might not find a place in profit-driven publishing channels, and to bring the authors and their books into communities across the country. Our sincere thanks to the many individuals, foundations, and government agencies who support this endeavor: J. Walton Bissell Foundation, Connecticut Commission on the Arts, Connecticut Humanities Council, Daphne Seybolt Culpeper Foundation, Fisher Foundation, Greater Hartford Arts Council, Hartford Courant Foundation, J. M. Kaplan Fund, Eric Mathieu King Fund, Lannan Foundation, John D. and Catherine T. MacArthur Foundation, National Endowment for the Arts, Open Society Institute, Puffin Foundation, and the Woodrow Wilson National Fellowship Foundation.

Please help to support Curbstone's efforts to present the diverse voices and views that make our culture richer. Tax-deductible donations can be made by check or credit card to:
Curbstone Press, 321 Jackson Street, Willimantic, CT 06226
phone: (860) 423-5110   fax: (860) 423-9242
www.curbstone.org

IF YOU WOULD LIKE TO BE A MAJOR SPONSOR OF A
CURBSTONE BOOK, PLEASE CONTACT US.